FOREVER FIERCE

FOREVER LOVED BOOK FIVE A PARANORMAL SHIFTER ROMANCE

L. J. HAWKE

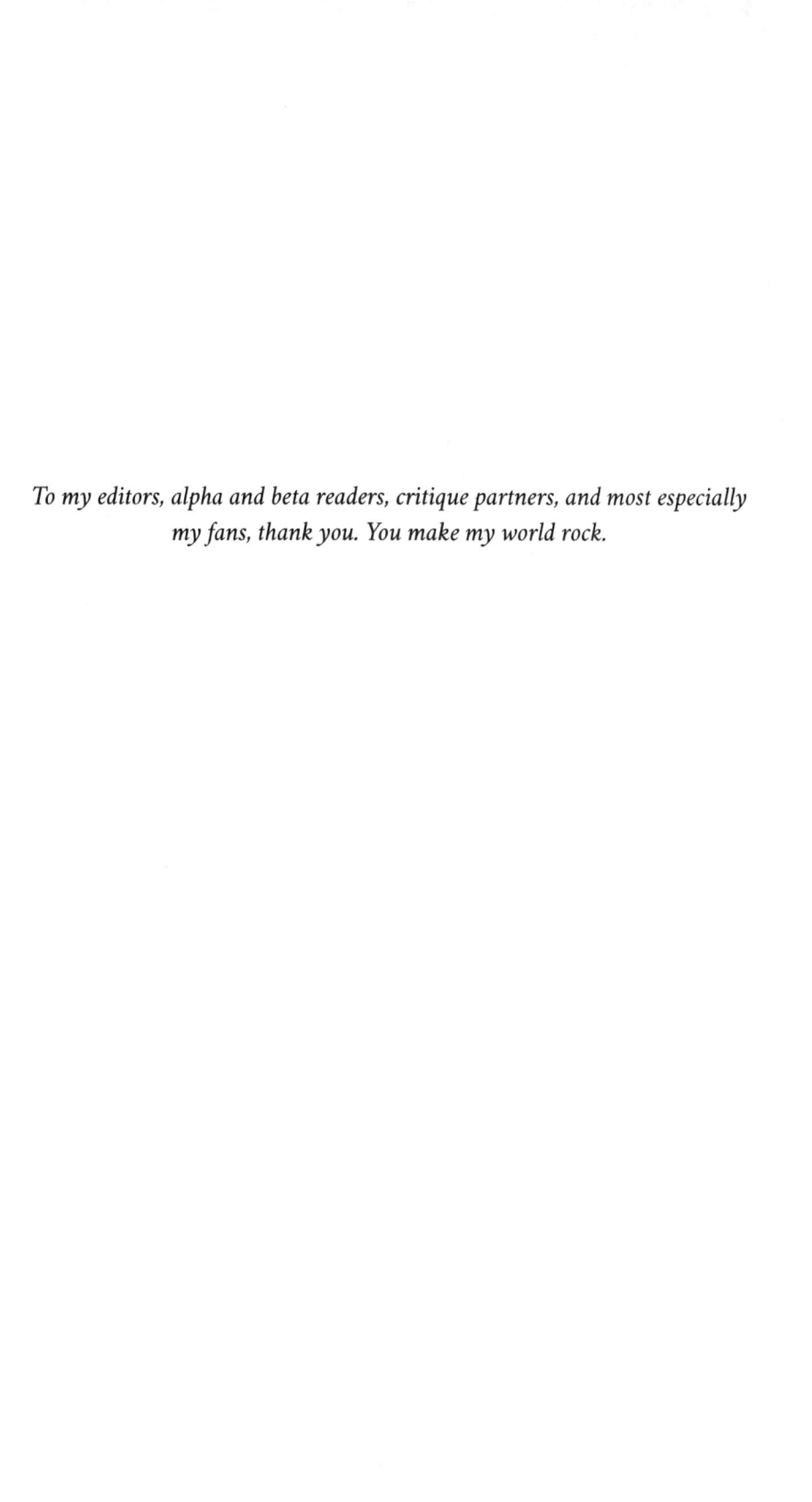

To my editors, alpha and beta readers, critique partners, and most especially my fans, thank you. You make my world rock.

WINTERGREEN

"We need another tray." Mary Beth Joy, the Girl With Three First Names pointed at the double chocolate mint fudge bark in the glass case. Sure enough, it was about two-thirds gone. Mary Beth had a sweetheart face, a gentle smile, and caramel-colored hair in a braid halfway down her back. "Next in line!"

Libby Camber, owner of the Sweet Thoughts Bakery, grinned. "Of course we do." She turned and went to the ovens, separated from behind the counter by both a half-wall and a huge pane of glass. People liked to watch her make her sweet treats. She took out the sweetened condensed milk, poured it into the top of the double boiler, turned on the heat, then took out the dark chocolate melting chips. She carefully measured the chips and put them in the top of the boiler.

Libby grabbed the sack of peppermint candies, already shorn of their plastic, and carefully checked them. Melted plastic was no one's friend. She beat the candies with her rolling pin, which brought kids to the counter to watch. Then she turned, carefully stirred the chocolate, and added the salt. She brought out her pan, lined it with foil, carefully poured the chocolate into the pan, and then added the crushed candy. She then melted white chocolate, added the salt, and poured it on top of the candy. She put the tray in the refrigerator, then took out a tray of already-chilled and cut peppermint fudge from the refrigerator, carefully peeled off the foil, washed and flattened the foil for reuse, and brought out the fudge. The smell of peppermint and chocolate did the trick; it brought people walking by into the shop.

Libby saw the full house and grinned. She left Mary Beth on the cashier station and bagged in waxed paper S'mores on a Stick, two fat marshmallows dipped in chocolate and rolled in regular, chocolate, or cinnamon graham crackers, the best seller with the after-school crowd. The apples were also selling well, drenched in caramel and rolled in pecans, peanuts, or strawberry cookies. Libby had no idea why the strawberry ones sold so well, but she carried what the customers wanted.

Mary Beth sold the entire tray of bark and one of brittle, and Libby had to rush back for more. Libby had to run back for more gluten-free balls as well, made from honey, coconut flour, and fruit, or with cacao-infused almond powder, almonds, and cherries or stuffed with peanut butter. The lemon ones usually sold out by early afternoon. They were in a separate case from everything else. There was a third case for no-peanut gluten-free items. Libby made the nut butter-stuffed ones in her home kitchen and sold them sealed, or had Vern deliver them. Community college student Vern had a little scooter, and delivered for half the businesses on Main Street.

The after-high-school rush calmed down, and Libby hurried to refill the cases before the hungry middle schoolers arrived while Mary Beth took a short break. Libby took her own fast break; time for a cup of coffee. Libby put the cup down the minute the first group of giggling girls came in. She sold out of the lemon poppy seed mini muffins, but she did have some lemon bars ready to replace them. The middle school boys came in and decimated the S'mores on a Stick, every flavor. Libby replaced all the trays while Mary Jane cleaned up. Libby took a deep breath before the elementary kids came in, dragging their moms, which meant selling a lot of coffee.

Libby made hazelnut mocha for the frazzled Missy Simms, mom to John, Jasper, and Jeff, seven-year-old triplets with dark hair, ruddy cheeks, and growls and grimaces towards each other. Libby divided the caramel-pecan apples into wedges so the triplets could eat them easily, and added little cups of chocolate almond milk. She handed the covered cups to each boy, and they ran to sit down. Missy took the plates over with napkins, then came back for her caramel apple muffin and her coffee.

"Thank you kindly, ladies." Missy stared at the muffin and coffee with undying love in her eyes.

"We love having you!" Libby smiled at the mother, who turned away towards her boys.

Mary Jane put on a bright smile for the next in line, Farrah Jones. Farrah had a face like she had been sucking lemons. Her dyed brassy blonde hair was sprayed within an inch of its life. She stood in front of Mary Jane, her arms crossed.

"And what is this child doing working here?" brayed Farrah Jones. "She's fourteen!"

"Are you ordering anything, ma'am?" Mary Jane smiled like an angel. Libby taught her counter help how to smile at anything.

"Libby, what are you doing hiring underage people?" Farrah demanded.

"If you have a problem with who I hire, please call the Labor board." Libby kept her voice bright and cheerful so as not to scare the children. "If you want to order something, please do that now, or step out of line."

Farrah glared at Libby. "I want my questions answered!"

"Next in line." Mary Jane got a little girl an apple, which Libby cut, and a soymilk.

"You can't ignore me!" Farrah's face turned a dark red.

"If you're not a paying customer, yes, I can." Libby kept her voice bouncy and cheerful. She selected two banana nut mini muffins and plated them for the little girl's mother. She made the mother a soy milk chai, and handed it over.

"I'm calling the police!" Farrah whipped out her cell phone. Libby completely ignored her, and plated some of her special wintergreen bark and a cappuccino for a frazzled father of two boys. The gigantic black espresso machine sounded like a hissing train, so Libby didn't hear Farrah's call.

Ten minutes later, Deputy Nat Sandawan showed up. Nat had short brown hair streaked with blonde peeking out under a police cap, and wore a freshly pressed uniform and shiny black cop shoes with aplomb. Luckily, they'd gotten through the elementary-student rush with everything plated and out to everyone, even the coffees. The line was gone, so Libby filled up the trays.

Farrah finally agreed to have Nat interview her outside the store. Nat's flinty brown-green hazel eyes stopped many would-be criminals from perpetrating anything. Libby let Mary Jane take another short break, while Libby restocked the plates and forks, took the dirties back to the sink, washed her hands, and came back out and wiped everything down.

Nat came in, and said, "Sorry about that. I'd like a lemon bar, one of those dark pecan clusters, and a double-shot mocha." He handed over both a credit card and a multi-visit stamp card. Part of the reason they had a full house was that every tenth item was free. The other reason was high-quality food at reasonable prices that kids and parents loved to eat, with some delicious health-conscious items.

Libby rang Nat up and moved to fill the order. "Need to talk to me?"

Nat nodded, and held up a tablet computer. "Filled out her form, and started on yours. Got your business address and everything."

"Okay." Libby made a chai tea for herself, and when Mary Jane came back, Libby cleaned off a two-top, washed her hands, and sat down with Nat. She knew Mary Jane would clean and restock during the lull.

"I know we've talked about this before, but this is an apprentice-ship and Mary Jane is fifteen?" Nat began.

"They normally start at sixteen, but Mary Jane is home-schooled, so it's kind of work-study too. She's doing both chemistry and life skills homework using her job here." Libby grinned. "Four hours a day five days a week, so part-time, and paid for every minute. And I have letters from her mom, the school board, and the apprenticeship program, with Mary Jane's case a hardship exception." Libby emailed the relevant documents to Nat, who grunted.

Nat read through all the documents, and attached them to the file. "How's her mom doing?"

"The new meds are working, and removing the stress has been good for Vernice." Libby swallowed a mouthful of the much-needed spicy tea. "She's already halfway through her emergency teaching certificate." Vernice had worked as a truck owner/operator and had loaded and unloaded trucks all over the county. A Parkinson's diagnosis meant Vernice had to give up her trucking career. Vernice had been awarded a special scholarship to get her emergency teaching certificate.

Nat nodded. "Farrah delights in making trouble. I cited her for causing a disturbance, and she turned beet-red and stalked off."

"You didn't!" Libby sipped from her cup, hiding a smile.

"I most certainly did. I got two moms and a dad on their way out to describe her behavior, and sign on the dotted line, too. I'll need your camera footage to make it stick." Nat gave a slow grin.

Libby grinned back and pulled her dark brown ponytail back up as she had to wash her hands after her break anyway. Nat asked a few more paperwork questions while Libby called up the footage on her cell phone and sent it to Nat. It included sound, and Nat had to turn down the yelling while watching the footage.

They finished their drinks, and Nat stood, plate empty. "Delicious as usual. And, thanks for this. Farrah will keep disrupting peoples' businesses until she has consequences that stick."

Libby gave a little laugh. "She needs a personality transplant."

Nat snorted. "Too bad that doesn't exist. I know some other people who need one."

Libby put the empty cups and Nat's plate on a tray. "Thank you for your professionalism."

Nat smiled slowly, like the sun coming out. "That's exactly what I want to project. One of my core beliefs. See you later." They both stood. Libby waved, and Nat left.

Libby cleaned off the tables, saying goodbye to parents and kids as they left. To her shock, the triplets were unusually clean, weren't fighting with one another now that they had been fed, and had bussed their own table. Libby went back to fill up the dishwasher, washed her hands, and came back out to see if they needed anything else before Mary Jane left for the day. She brought out the last of the muffins, hoping they would sell before closing.

"I'm sorry that woman caused trouble for you." Mary Jane spoke softly as she washed her hands, then dried them.

"No trouble. Lots of things are on record now. First, you're in the clear under the apprenticeship program, once and for all, and Farah got fined for causing a disturbance."

Mary Jane's face lit up. "Bet that'll chap her nether regions." Libby laughed so hard she startled the last mama, her baby dozing in her lap while having her tea and buttery almond scone. "It will. Now, you like doing setup, so go in the back and get everything ready for tomorrow."

"On it." Mary Jane enjoyed measuring out everything for the baking, putting dry ingredients in labeled plastic containers so Libby saved a lot of work in the morning. Libby made a few coffee and scone sales to dads, moms, and passing businesspeople.

The shop was empty when Jeb came in to read the paper off his tablet and eat a scone with his orange tea. He always came in after the pitter-patter of little feet had ebbed. He was a sixty-two-year-old middle-school-grade horror book author. He wrote in the afternoons, took a break, and then wrote half the night.

"How's it going?" Libby made his tea, the scent of oranges and spice wafting up into the air.

Jeb smiled. "Robert has another monster."

Mary Jane came out, minus her apron. Libby had a small stackable washer and dryer in the employee bathroom; she washed all the rags and aprons herself. "Bye Libby, Jeb!"

"Bye!" Libby made up Jeb's tray with a butter knife and napkin.

"See you, darlin'." Jeb grinned. "Great catch, hiring that one."

"Don't I know it. I take it Robert hasn't figured out how to stop dreaming monsters into existence." Libby plated Jeb's scone, then heated it in the microwave. She put two pats of butter on the tray.

"No, he's still flummoxed." Jeb loved talking about the character in his book series.

"Well, if he figures it out, you'll have to write a new series."

Jeb snorted as he paid, then took his tray. "Either that, or he dreams up other problems that become real." He sat down with his tray at a small table on the left-hand side of the shop.

Libby cleaned off every table except Jeb's, swept, mopped, sold the last of the muffins to two hungry teenaged girls who took them to go, bundled that day's deposit into its locked money bag in the safe in her office, and began taking empty trays out of the denuded cases. She piled the empties up, then brought them back to the kitchen.

Libby heard the ringer, walked back out, and saw Jeb with his hands up. The woman with the sawed-off shotgun had a pasty face dotted with pimples. She wore blue jeans and a black hoodie, and she had a manic look in her bloodshot pale blue eyes. "Gimme the money!"

Libby said nothing, just opened the register and started filling up a bakery bag. Jeb sat frozen rock-solid, the last of his tea getting cold.

Libby handed over the bag. The thief opened the bag and peered in. "This ain't all ya money. Lift up the tray."

Libby lifted it up; the big bills were already gone. "Where is it?" screamed the woman.

Libby shrugged. "That's what I have."

"Safe!" the woman screamed.

Libby slowly shook her head. "Timed. I can only open it four times a day. The next time is in half an hour."

A gun cocked behind the woman. Nat pointed a police-issue nine-millimeter at the woman's head. "This is how it's going to go. You will lower your weapon, and I will arrest you. If you do anything else, I will drop you."

The woman swore once, twice, three times, each one a worse curse than the first. But, she lowered the shotgun. Nat passed the shotgun to Jeb, who broke it. Jeb stood by while Nat arrested the robber and read her rights to her. Deputy Amir Cazalos came running in, and Jeb wordlessly handed the shotgun to the sweating deputy. Leland took the weapon and spoke in law enforcement codes into his radio. The deputies took the gun and the woman and left the restaurant.

"Are you good, Jeb?" Libby moved toward her patron, surprised her knees were holding her up.

"Alive." Jeb put his elbows on the table and put his head in his hands. "How the hell..."

Libby put a hand on his shoulder, gave him a little pat, then dropped her hand. "A hidden button on the cash register calls the police. I pressed it at the same time I opened the drawer." Libby took a deep breath, then another. "Until they come back, I'm emptying the dishwasher so I can fill it again. Can I get you some hot water for your tea? I have one scone left, too."

"Sure. We'll probably be here a while, huh?"

"I expect so." Libby flipped the sign in the window to closed, gave Jeb his hot water and a new scone, took everything out of the dishwasher as quickly as she could, washed her hands, took out the trash, then washed up again. She was putting the last trays in the dishwasher when the front door opened. "One minute!" Libby turned on the dishwasher and came out front. Nat sat in front of Jeb, so Libby handed the deputy a bottle of water then ran back to clean and disinfect the back room. She washed up, came back out, and made herself a chocolate mint cocoa. "Nat, I can leave the front alone until tomorrow."

"I'd prefer that. It's a crime scene."

Libby sat, and told Nat the story as Jeb finished his tea with shaking hands, nodded at the deputy and Libby, then left.

Nat made copious notes. "That secret button's perfect. The outside button to turn off the door chime is smart, too. I'll turn it back on when I leave." A crime scene tech showed up, dusted the outside door, and left when Libby assured her that the robber didn't touch anything else. The tech also bagged, tagged, and took the money with her, less than two hundred dollars.

Libby put the cups on the side counter where the now-empty cold water pitcher was located rather than walking on the pristine floor in the back. Libby's cell phone went off. She rushed back to her safe, hidden in her tiny office. She came out with her bank bag full of that day's cash. "Safe's on a timer."

Nat nodded and went through what happened one more time as Libby counted the money, filled out the bank slip, locked the bag, and logged the amount on her pad. "I'll walk you to the bank." Nat stood and waved towards the door.

"Okay." They went out the front, Libby locked up, and Nat walked with Libby to the bank. The spring flowers in their bright tones of pink, purple, red, blue, and white in their half-barrel sidewalk planters hurt Libby's eyes at first. How had a robbery turned her world black and white?

Nat sighed. "I am so sorry this happened to you."

"Meth addict?"

"Second generation."

Libby sighed. "That sucks. But, she could have shot Jeb. He may write horror, but he wouldn't hurt a fly." Libby felt a sick melange of rage and terror. She wondered where those emotions had been located; she had only felt shock and an overwhelming sense of determination to live and to protect Jeb while it was happening.

"Just so you know, Jeb regrets not being able to help. I told him he made the right call, that any 'helping' would have gotten your head blown off." They arrived at Valley Days Savings and Loan. "You think of anything, have any questions, you call me." Nat gave Libby a little salute.

"Will do." Libby smiled rather shakily at Nat, then went into the bank.

Libby made the deposit quickly because June Wilder, the business account specialist, had a short line. "Thought some fool woman stole this." June was like boiled leather, brown and smooth, tough to ruffle. Her keen hazel eyes sized Libby up for buckshot or bullet holes.

"Timed safe." Libby always took out big bills throughout the day at set times; it kept her from having too much in the drawer. She was afraid of sticky-fingered teens, though, not armed robbers in a town as safe as hers.

"You all right." It wasn't a question.

"Am, mostly." The shakes would come later as the adrenaline dumped into her system wore off. Libby looked down, and her right finger twitched. "Shakes are starting."

June handed over the receipt. "Get your ass home, then, before your brothers come and try to cart you off to the hospital." She looked up. "Too late."

Libby sighed and turned to see Vic, whom his coworkers called by their last name, Camber, standing in the doorway, backlit by the sun. He had Libby's brown hair, dark brown eyes, and caramel skin, so his uniform shirt looked blindingly white next to his skin and hair. He was an EMT, so word about the aborted robbery would have reached him from his cop friends. He had the bright blue strap of his duffel strapped across his front like a bandolier.

Libby walked towards her brother and said, "Adrenaline dump, but I'm okay."

Vic held her close right in front of the savings and loan employees and customers and the people passing by on the sidewalk. "I'll walk you home." His voice was rough with his own adrenaline. "Are you still going to the cookout?"

Libby held him close, then dragged him out into the sunshine. The door whooshed shut behind her. "Yes, because if I don't, no kid goodness. But, I'm going to get an earful." He walked Libby across the street and two doors down back to her shop. They walked down the alley to the back of the bakery, and Libby jogged up the circular metal stairs, her brother right behind her. She unlocked the door, kicked off her black running shoes, strode past her fat blue recliner couch, and headed towards her loft. The kitchen was under the loft, cabinets in bright white melamine, her pale blue breakfast bowl, spoon, and mug still in the dish drainer. "Be down in seven, unless you're still on-shift."

"Although I'm still in uniform, I got off twenty minutes ago." Vic closed the door with his freakishly large basketball-sized hands. He was rangy, long, and lean, and occasionally did Search and Rescue as well as driving an ambulance. He liked to save citizens' lives.

Libby headed up the narrow stairs to the loft while her brother shut the door, unslung his duffel, and dropped it onto the couch. She slid off her clothes and put them in the hamper. She put on her robe and walked back down, careful to hold onto the railing on the narrow stairs. She had a quick shower, put on some lotion, put her robe back on, and came out of the bathroom. "After you." Vic laughed.

Libby climbed slightly up the stairs and skirted her platform bed with his gel mattress. She sat down at her makeup table, dried her hair, and put on light makeup. She put on dark blue jeans, a blue and yellow college shirt, and soft socks, then she climbed back down. The nights were still a bit cool, so she grabbed her blue jacket and smiled at her brother. Vic now wore black jeans and a dark maroon top. His close-cut hair stood up a little, but his hair dried quickly. Libby put on her pink-and-purple trainers, stood, and led her brother out the door.

Libby locked the door, then they clanged their way down the circular staircase. "Feel like I'm going down playground stairs on the other end of the mesh tower in the park." Vic sighed when they reached the bottom.

Libby laughed. "Dad talked you into helping with the giant kiddie play set, didn't he?"

Vic laughed. "Yes. The thing will take up half the backyard."

Libby nodded. "I suppose you and Dad will bond building it?"

"Of course."

Libby snorted. "Let's go."

COOKOUT

They headed down the alley to the street behind. The building behind Libby's held a dry cleaner, Laundromat, convenience store, and an amazingly good Chinese/Thai restaurant. They ignored the delicious smells of lemongrass and pork buns, entered the convenience store to grab some drinks to fill up their carafes, then walked to the curve in the road that led to the library. Vic liked to park there in the morning because he drove an ambulance with Ripley Wallace, known as Rip. Rip was a compact gymnast, with arms and legs like strong cords. She lived behind the library and picked up the rig at the hospital four blocks away. Her roommate and sister Trace was one of the town's three librarians. Trace and Rip shared a bright blue house with white trim two blocks away.

Vic's truck was a four-wheel drive. They hopped in and Libby sipped her cherry cola. Vic set its navigation to slow, making sure not to run into the kids going to and from the library, daredevils on scooters and skateboards that seemed to enjoy leaping directly in front of Vic's tires.

They were on the road up the mountain when Vic stared at his sister. "So, tough day?"

Libby realized the hot shower had done her good, but her hands still shook. "It was great until Farrah showed up."

"Heard about that. She's whining to anyone that will listen to her, which at this point is the checkout person at the supermarket, that she's been unfairly targeted by the police." He said the anti-police comment with Farrah's angry clenched jaw and tight lips.

Libby snorted. "Farrah spouts nonsense, and Nat was great about it." Libby looked out the window. Sunlight dappled the leaves in thirty shades of green, the branches overhead nearly tunnel-like in some stretches of road.

Libby held out a hand. It wavered in the slanting sunlight coming through the windows. "Adrenaline is still dumping."

Vic stared out the window. "Glad Nat was there. That is one excellent deputy. Always moved well. Remember when Nat was Nathaniel?"

"Nathaniel became Nat during volleyball season."

Vic nodded. "That would be high school, freshman year. Nat grew into the name real good." Nat's short stature and lack of an Adam's apple had resulted in a DNA test that showed Nat was XXY. It had led to hazing that Nat ignored. The hazing continued until Coach Ma had Travis "Train" Wakowski booted off the football team and out of the school. That shut everyone up really quickly.

They stared out the window some more. Libby sighed. "I know you want me to talk about it. Staring at a woman pointing a sawed-off shotgun at me was not fun, I'll tell you that. I think my heart actually stopped. The air got heavy and fluid. I tried to focus. Flipping out and running around like a chicken would have gotten me and Jeb killed."

"I like Jeb's books. Kinda deep, actually, about creating then facing your own fears. Read 'em to Adam and Bobby."

Libby sighed. Their little brothers' bio dad had been an abusive monster; he had turned up missing after his ex-wife Jetta had left with their four kids. The girls were barely three, River and Bethany, the boys six years old. Jetta had married Charlie Camber, their dad, joining Charlie's other wives, Lynette and Jen. Their family was a little complicated. And large. "Adam is still wetting the bed?"

"Nope, the night terrors are gone."

Libby sighed. "Maybe the books did some good."

"They remember." Vic's voice was tight. "They remember their mom screaming and crying. They remember the night River and Bethany were born. Adam had to call the midwife because their dad was at the bar and couldn't be bothered coming home."

Libby held out her hand again, and it held steady. "Good to know that someone had a thousand-times tougher life than we did."

Vic sighed. "Len lost a brother and a dad." Libby closed her eyes against the pain. It was always there, like a sore tooth. Their brother Len's twin brother Jonah fell after climbing onto a roof when he was a little boy. On the way to the hospital, his dad and Jonah had been killed by a drunk driver. Then Len's mama Lynette had eventually married their dad.

Libby opened her eyes again, looked at her brother. "That's old, ugly pain. Why bring it up?"

"Because it coulda happened all over again."

"It didn't." Libby kept her voice even, her tone flat.

"I saw what almost happened." Vic referred to the recording Libby had of the incident.

Libby grunted, annoyed, but of course someone had shown the recording to Vic. Or he had access to her camera feed. Probably that one; their security was paid for via clan funds. "I do not like you all up in my business. But, I used my brain. I installed the call-the-police button as you asked me to, had an electronic entry rather than a tinkly bell so the police could turn off the ringer and enter silently as Nat did."

Vic blew out a long breath, inhaled, and let out another one. "We need to have a celebration tonight. We've still got a sister." He wiped a tear away.

"I made it out alive." Libby reached out, touched his shoulder. "Brothers want to protect their sisters, but I did everything right." She looked out the window again. "So did Jeb."

Vic cleared his throat. "Buying his books that help our brothers not pee their pants is not enough. I'll personally buy whatever he wants for a year."

"Tea and scones."

"He English? Never met the guy."

"Mother grew up there."

Vic nodded. "One year. Figure out the cost with taxes, divide it up into twelve months and bill me."

"Sure. If he comes back." Libby took a quick moment to try to get her stomach to stop falling. What if people quit coming because of the holdup? She could lose the business she spent years building up.

"That man has built a business on confronting fears. He'll be back."

Libby nodded. "Figured that." She willed her stomach to stop dropping. She was alive. She decided to concentrate on that.

Vic blew out another breath, and they lapsed into silence. Vic put on what Libby called "shitkicker country" music, and they sang about trucks and tequila until the curves in the road brought them to the turnoff to Touchstone Haven where Vic and his family lived. The commune rose up on the hillside, with its wide streets and huge lots. As a poly commune, the houses tended to be enormous because spouses wanted their own spaces. "Need to order some lavender honey." Libby pulled out her phone and ordered. Touchstone Haven had a beekeeper; the honey was astonishingly good. The honey went into special shortbread and her strawberry-apple tarts.

They pulled in front of the house. It had been carved into a hill, and nearly the entire back was glass. Libby stared out the window. "I was going to bring some apples, then we sold out. I would have made a few more trays."

Vic snorted. "Be taken care of. You are not the Maker of Things today." They got out of the truck, and Libby drew in a cleansing breath.

Bobby came flying up the hill to the four-truck parking lot. He attached himself to Vic's leg. "Unca!"

Vic laughed. "Dude, you have three uncles. Which one am I?" He picked up the boy, put him on his back, and headed down the hill. They were actually brothers, with the boys' mother Jetta married to Charlie, Vic and Libby's dad. But, they went by "uncles" and "aunts" because of the huge age difference. The neighbors in the poly commune would understand, but people in the outside world would probably become confused.

Libby followed the giggling, squealing boy, and ended up with her other nephew attached to her leg. "Hi." Adam grinned up at her.

Libby ruffled his dark brown hair. "Hi yourself."

"I'm glad you didn't get deaded."

Libby sucked in a breath. "I survived. The best you can do, some days."

"Like when you have the flu so bad you can't even watch TV."

"Yeah, like that, but a much shorter time frame." Libby kissed the boy's sweaty head. "Get off my foot so we can eat."

"You didn't bring stuff." Adam sighed. "That's okay. At least you didn't die."

Libby nodded. "At least that didn't happen." Bringer of Things was probably a very good name for her if the kids expected it, and only a near-death experience could get her out of it. She shuddered at the thought.

Adam nodded, got off her foot, and dragged her down the hill. Once the weather broke, the boys had "expeditions," pretending to climb mountains, courtesy of their uncle Len. Len could move like a snake, all sinuous and smooth. They had obviously been on one of those hikes, because they smelled like the woods, loam and pine.

At the bottom of the hill, Jetta took huge bowls from Lynette, her sister wife, and put them on the table. Jetta's black hair glistened in the light, her skin burnished into a rose gold from the summer sun. The woman who used to be brittle, nearly broken, now had a huge smile that reached her eyes as she put the bowls down, put serving spoons in, then walked back to the outdoor kitchen to get more. Jetta was a full-time mom of four. Lynette was taller, a bit more graceful. Lynette and Jen raised plants, goats, tiny houses on wheels ready for delivery, and children.

Davis, Libby's older brother and Vic's twin, on an off day after several long days as an orthopedic surgeon, had chicken sizzling and fish in pouches with herbs on the grill. He used his precise hands and long tongs to flip the food. Davis gave Libby a quick once-over with his eyes, using his professional-doctor mein, then turned back to the grill.

Kandace cored apples and Jen, Lynette's other sister wife, diced them, putting handfuls into a bowl. Kandace's enormous Maine coon cat, Sam, guarded the girls. Kandace worked with a team to map holes in the ground called hyperloops. Jetta's little girls, River and Bethany, were carefully carrying things that were light enough for them to the table, napkins in rings. They put one at each place at the huge table. They were elven-like beauties with sharp chins and wide eyes, dark hair held back in French braids.

"Go help your moms," Libby said to Adam, stepping up to do the same thing. "What do you need?" Libby asked Lynette as she stepped closer.

Lynette put the serving spoon into the honey mustard potato salad, turned, grabbed Libby, and crushed her daughter to her chest. Libby breathed, let her mother fuss for a minute. "If you die, I'll kill you," whispered Lynette into Libby's ear.

"Good to know," Libby whispered back.

"Mine now," said Jen, from just behind Libby. Libby let Lynette hold on as long as she needed, then gently extricated herself. Jen's hug was faster but no less emotional. "We need you."

"Need you back."

Lynette dried her eyes and stalked towards the boys, eager to get them working. Davis flipped the chicken, and Vic stood beside him and carefully pulled the corn off the grill with tongs.

Jetta jogged up, held Libby close, let her go, grabbed her upper arms, and looked into her eyes. "You're fine. Looks like the adrenaline wore off. Expect to collapse very soon with exhaustion. Mortal fear tends to do that to you."

Libby's eyes teared at the burst of understanding. "I can't say enough that I'm sorry I didn't know your ex-husband existed. I would have done something. How did you go through that on a daily basis?"

"I couldn't go to jail and not see my babies. I finally let thoughts of murder go. That's energy best spent on the kids. You pissed at the tweaker?"

Libby thought for a second, then slowly nodded. "She had a choice."

"She did." Jetta looked Libby up and down again. "You're fine. Get the knives and put them out. That's a bad chore for the little bits."

Libby nodded and headed into the house to get the sharp steak knives. She put them into a metal cup, and also brought out the bright blue meat dishes. Anything with meat was on a color-coded plate in case someone was vegetarian or was taking a no-meat day. This prevented the long "explanation" phase of going vegetarian in the valley where everyone else ate meat three meals a day.

By the time Libby came out, the boys had the forks on the table and Lynette took the blue plates to Vic and Davis. Libby headed to the table and dropped off the knives. Libby went back in for the kids' boosters and brought them out. The tables, all pushed together, were lovely, with a light blue plastic tablecloth, pots of fat hyacinths in pink and purple, and bright yellow, blue, and red stoneware plates.

Huge crimson plastic tumblers were on the table. Libby realized there were no sippy cups, so she went back in to fill them up with apple juice. Libby came back out and put them in the corners where the girls sat across from each other. If they couldn't see each other, they got nervous. Libby went back in to get the pies. She found apple, chocolate silk, and peach pies sitting out on the counter. She cut them into bites, then in the refrigerator she found "gummy dirt" cups, dark chocolate cherry pudding with crushed chocolate cookies and gummy worms poking out of the cookie "dirt." She took out small blue plastic kiddie spoons, slid one into each cup, and leaned them against each other so they wouldn't fall down.

Libby grabbed the condiments in their squeeze bottle cardboard trays, then carried out two trays. She put one on either end of the table and went back for sriracha sauce. She found the bottle and a tray of cruets of homemade honey mustard, balsamic vinegar, and ranch dressings, and brought them out to the table.

She had just emptied her hands when Davis held her close. "Glad I didn't see you on my table."

"Didn't happen." Libby clung, let him go.

"Good." Davis let her go then smiled at her.

Lynette came out with a huge pitcher in each hand, one of cherry lemonade, the other of limeade, and put one on either end of the table. Kandace brought over a bowl of raw spinach with nuts and mushrooms, and a rainbow of bell peppers in a little bowl. The boys hated red or yellow bell peppers, but they would eat stuffed green peppers.

Kandace grinned at Libby. "Bet you're tired of all the hugs." She held up her arms, and the bright blue flame tattooed on her stomach, a symbol of her sobriety, peeked out. Libby laughed and they bumped fists.

The boys complained loudly as Jen forced them to go to the outside sink and wash up. Kandace laughed. "A little required cleanliness and they're acting like they're being tortured by velociraptors."

Libby laughed, letting the nervousness bleed out of her. "Adam told me that velociraptors equal distance raptors over time raptors. It took me a minute to remember my high school physics. That kid is smart."

Jetta came up, a girl under each arm. Vic took one, and the girls slid into their high seats with no problem. " 'Course he is," said Jetta. "Got his Uncle Davis to help him with his math homework, didn't he?"

Libby nodded. "I can see how that would happen."

Len glided over, all calmness in moss-green yoga pants and a gray shirt. He was short and a tad stocky, his arms and legs ropy from all the yoga he taught when he wasn't being a physical therapist. He hugged Libby and smiled up at her.

They got the boys in their seats, held hands, and sang. They sat down, and passed around the green salad, pasta salad, tabbouleh salad with fresh mint and tomatoes, potato salad with dill and mustard, corn on the cob, falafel, Jamaican jerk chicken, and lemon fish stuffed with crabmeat. Libby took some of nearly everything, suddenly ravenously hungry. She listened to the conversation ebb and flow, the boys indignant that a teacher had told them to sit down, despite it being a "moving story." The adults all laughed, the play of words going over the children's heads.

Meri rushed down the hill, two bags in hand. She put the bags over on the counter near the outdoor grill, grabbed a basket and put the garlic bread in it, came to the table, sang, then sat next to Libby. Meri was a home chef and made a good living helping people with special dietary needs, creating delicious food no matter what the parameters. Her hair was longer than it had been, two braids meeting and merging into one. Her face was rounder than Libby's, despite the fact she made healthy food all day. "Sorry I'm late. I figured you wouldn't have time to bring anything, so I brought some stuff."

Libby nodded. "True."

Meri had just given herself some potato salad when Charlie drove up, the big truck rumbling. "Daddy!" said the boys. They had to be restrained from popping up by Lynette on one side, Jetta on the other.

Lynette held Adam in his seat by one leg. "Stay still. Your dad knows there's fish on the table."

Charlie moved his weight down the hill, light on his toes. He rushed to wash his hands, sang, kissed each boy's head, then sat at the end of the table with his daughters. Kandace sat on the other end. "Good to see you, Libby," said Charlie.

"In one piece," said Meri. Libby punched her in the arm. "Ow!"

Charlie grinned. "Gotta petition the city to give Nat a raise. Fast mover."

Vic nodded. "Volleyball."

Davis grinned. "Fast and fierce. Couldn't hold that officer back with a wall. Nat would just punch right through the thing."

"Gotta bake all the cops something." Libby decided on an assortment, then broke the no-electronics-at-mealtimes rule to make herself a reminder.

They ate until every plate and bowl was empty. Then Charlie and Vic cleared the table while Meri and Lynette brought out all the desserts. Meri had brought lavender honey cream for the desserts. The kids went completely crazy for the gummy dirt with a little bit of whipped cream. Then, Len washed all four of them and he and Davis chased them around making monster noises, making them scream. The remaining adults all moved closer together.

Charlie stood up and hugged Libby tight, then sat back down to eat his apple pie. Apple pie with lavender honey cream was serious business.

Jetta discussed the pink elephant in the yard. "Ain't none of us getting out of this life alive, but if you had died, Libby, what would you have left undone?"

Libby slowly let out a breath. "The shop is up and running, I work regular hours now because Daisy does the weekends with Bryant." Both were college students. One opened and the other closed the store. "The shop is only open six hours a day, everyone loves the menu, and even with the gluten and nut-free items, I don't have a single thing that isn't selling. Dropped all the poor sellers like a hot rock."

"That's your livelihood," Lynette said gently. "It's not your life."

Charlie nodded. "It's one of those moments where, you ask yourself, what would I want to have in ten years? Then you ask yourself, what if you only had a year? Six months?"

Libby looked poleaxed, then blurted out the first thing that came into her mind. "I want this."

Vic looked around. "Your apartment is kinda small."

Meri snorted. "That's not what she's talking about, doofus."

"I want to be married, and I want to have children." Libby pointed her chin at the yard, the kids running around. "I want to have to pick up dog turds off my front lawn, make sure the kids are pulling the weeds and not the flowers, and live near the library so I can read all those delicious books all the time."

"You do live near the library and read those delicious books all the time." Jen took more cream for her pie. "In fact, I doubt you can count all the books on your e-reader."

Charlie grinned at his daughter. "Anything else? Close your eyes and say it quickly."

"I want to go to the gym and work out. My job makes me put on weight, but then I'm not doing anywhere near enough to keep it off."

"Gym membership, check." Lynette pulled up a menu from her wrist comp and typed in the list.

"I want sex in the morning so waking up at five in the morning doesn't suck quite so much." That made Kandace and Meri snort.

"It's still going to suck, but now you've woken up someone else to have sex with them," said Vic. Kandace punched his shoulder.

"What you need is someone who gets up at the same ungodly hour." Meri nodded at her sister. "Someone who will go to the gym with you, help you become a gym rat. Someone who loves kids and dogs, and probably cats, cuz I know you love them too. Someone who likes chocolate and tea and scones."

"But not too much, or they'll eat your whole store," said Vic.

Kandace punched him in the arm again. "Can't take you anywhere, even our own backyard!"

"Anybody we know like that?" Kandace looked into everyone's eyes. "We're a big ass family. We know half the people in this town, plus people in the commune."

Vic grunted. "I do not have a big ass." Everybody laughed.

DAYLIGHT

*N*at sipped coffee like it was going out of style. Three drunks had been arrested and booked in two days, one of them armed with a baseball bat. That one had serious charges with real time behind them. Nat hoped Davy, a blond-haired, green-eyed, bad-boy heartthrob, would get sober this time. Since he was sixteen and hell-bent on taking out himself and anyone around him, that probably wouldn't happen anytime soon. The other drunks had already been arraigned and had gone home.

Nat put his coffee cup down and prepared the prisoners for transport. The prison transport van was outside, ready to pick up Davy and take him to juvie, and to pick up Ruby Vail, a high school dropout, former math whiz turned tweaker and armed robber. She was being carted off to the detox unit of the prison rather than have her heart stop due to withdrawal. Nat was exhausted from the opioid epidemic. It turned formerly reasonable, normal people into either shambling, zombified walking corpses of their former selves or violent psychopaths.

"That's the last of it." State Deputy Rhonda Meyota, a prison transfer specialist, had the flat face of her ancestors and the eyes of someone who had been on the job about a year and a half too long. She took her pad back, slipped it into a special pocket hidden in her jacket, and reached out for Davy. That's when things went haywire. Davy reached for Nat's stylus. Nat knocked his hand, then threw him up against the wall. Davy yowled. Ruby saw an opportunity and tried to bolt. Rhonda made a noise that meant, *Don't get anywhere*, grabbed Ruby's chains, and pulled upward. Ruby squealed as her feet and hands couldn't move. Nat grabbed Davy's chain and pulled upward like Rhonda. Davy grunted.

Deputy Amir Cazalos dashed forward, opened the door, reached back and grabbed Ruby by the front chains, and pulled. Ruby, pushed from the back and pulled from the front, stumbled to the prison van. When she saw the van she went insane, trying to kick and scream. Her fit failed, and she ended up in the van anyway. Rhonda got her into the cage and locked down, and Nat followed with Davy. Davy started a cursing contest with Ruby. Rhonda got Davy into his seat and locked down. All five of them were sweating. Amir got off the transport, then Nat. Rhonda shrugged, shut the door, and sat down next to the driver, Ed. Ed looked like the total opposite of Rhonda, thin, wiry, with reddish skin and a tiny nose. The only thing that he had in common with Rhonda was calm impassivity. He turned on the GPS, and the van made a loud beeping before reversing itself.

Nat and Amir got the hell out of the way and back into the building, out of the wind. "That was fun. Not," said Amir.

Nat shrugged. "Addiction is lovely and gorgeous."

Amir snorted. "Getting sober is also so much fun," he said in a singsong voice. They shared a satirical moment, then they both remembered exactly how much work they had to do. Their pads had enabled them to get rid of most of the actual paper, and 3D scanners scanned evidence and retained it virtually as well as physically. But cops always had work. They had to see anyone who had a complaint, and there may be a pile of them far longer than the hours in a shift. Then, there were meetings, training, making sure all the documents got where they were supposed to go and did not get lost in the usual inter-agency squabbles, speaking at schools and community organizations, practicing on the shooting range, and working out. And the list went on and on.

Nat sighed as his pad dinged, a complaint about a party during business hours. "Thanks, Amir, gotta go."

Amir nodded. "Have fun." He looked at his own pad; the next complaint would be his unless it was close to or in line with where Nat was. Nat got into his car and put the GPS from the complaint into it.

Nat sighed when the address was for a brand-new music school called G Clef. Students could study the piano and keyboard on the first floor, violin, cello, bass, viola, or guitar on the second one, woodwinds on the third floor, and the drums in the basement. Nat circled the building with a decibel meter program on his pad. He heard faint sounds, and a burst of sound as a door opened, then closed. The spike lasted less than ten seconds. So, the place had sufficient sound baffling.

Nat found the complainer in the antique store two doors down, Checkered Pasts. The owner, Ridley Oklil, was nicknamed Rid. People called him Rid Kill behind his back. Rid was portly, with almost no hair on his wrinkled head. Nat had no idea how he got through the aisles of his own store. He had tables piled up on other tables, cases stuffed with costume jewelry, and a disturbing taxidermy section. He wore chinos and a black short-sleeved shirt, making him look like someone about to play a depressing golf game. He wore his black hair down to his collar and had a squeaky voice despite a huge body.

Nat favored the man with a tight smile. "Hello, Mr. Oklil. I see from your complaint that you believe the business G Clef is making too much noise?"

"The music is making my head pound."

Nat stared at Rid. "I have used a decibel meter. The few sounds I have heard are well below regulation."

"So, you aren't going to help me?"

"Sir, unless you have proof of a decibel level above regulation, there is nothing I can do."

Rid sighed and made an angry gesture. "Go ahead. Take their side."

"I am on the side of science, sir. I have proof that the new business is not breaking the law. In fact, they spent a lot of money sound-proofing their business."

Rid sighed gustily through limpid lips. "Very well."

"Have a nice day, sir." Nat nodded, turned, and walked out. Nat slid down shades, the sunlight like a hammer after the dimness of the antique store, and pondered how people saw anything in Rid's store well enough to buy it. He decided to do a bit of a patrol walkabout and called it in.

Nat was happy that he had when he saw Mosman Sesun sitting on a bench in the square. Mos had a huge nose, dark, choppy hair, and kind brown eyes. Nat walked up to the bench. "Hello, Mos."

Mos grinned. "Nat!" He held out a hand, and they shook. He stood up, and said, "Shall we get some ice cream?"

Nat laughed. "Why not? You only live once."

Penny had bright red hair, dancing green eyes, and a wonderful ice cream shop called Flavory right next to Libby's Sweet Thoughts Bakery. People would bring cups of things from each shop and mix them together. She had a little window in front of passersby who didn't want to go in. The shop was empty, so Penny was at the window. "Hey, Nat, Mos. Cardinal Sin?"

"But of course," said Mos. The dessert was butter brickle ice cream with cherries and chocolate chunks.

Nat held up two fingers. They paid for their sweets and took their cones back to the bench. They sat in the sun. "How's it going, Mos?"

"We fill the strangest orders. I was sitting here thinking I should write a book about it."

"Blog. Or vlog."

"Hmm. I printed a 3D plastic dog yesterday, an exact replica of a dearly departed."

"Better to go to the pound in Sunset and get the exact same breed of dog again. Or, hell, surprise yourself." Nat breathed through brain freeze.

Mos grinned. "I agree. How is Spook?"

"She climbs that cat tree like it is her own private Matterhorn."

Mos nodded. "My Citrus is the same." Citrus was a fluffy orange tabby with golden eyes. Spook was Siamese and, therefore, talkative. Another gorgeous cat, but with very specific opinions about her life.

Nat thought a bit. "Aren't you doing well making the plastic food in the display and menu cases of restaurants?"

"I make enough for my loft, so I am content." The town had the brilliant idea to sell one of its oldest properties to Charlie Camber. Charlie had used his tiny-house skills and hired an architect to divide up a former button factory into a mix of apartments and lofts, with businesses on the first floor. Mos' 3D printer business took up half the bottom floor; he and his apprentices printed everything from farm parts to, apparently, sculptures of deceased dogs. Mos also had a loft on the top floor of the same building, with an elevator ride his entire commute.

Nat ate the chocolate-filled bottom of his cone, then dusted off his hands. "That makes your life a thousand times better than two of them I saw today."

"That's the key to life, contentment."

"Word." Nat's pad dinged. "I have to go." There was a car accident near the high school. Nat took off at a jog for the police vehicle.

Luckily, the car accident was actually a teen on a skateboard who bailed before the skateboard hit the car. The electronics of the car tried to swerve, and one wheel was up on the sidewalk. Autumn Reynolds, the thirteen-year-old skater, had been wearing a helmet and pads but, unfortunately, not gloves. Her gangly form shook as she held out her bleeding, gravel-embedded hands.

Lydia Yu, a petite woman in a black suit, shook as she leaned against her car. The car had been the one to call the police. Nat filled out a form on his pad based on the car's recording of the accident. Lydia said, "Autumn, what happened? Street here, sidewalk there!"

Autumn pointed to a stick on the sidewalk. "Stick there, air here, fall over there!"

Nat raised his eyebrows. "Why is no one talking in complete sentences? So, Autumn, you hit a stick and went airborne?"

"Yep. You gonna call my mom?"

"Have to." Nat checked Autumn's hands. "Road rash. You forgot your gloves."

Vic and Rip's rig pulled up. Rip got out first, case in hand, and jogged over. "Road rash, mild case. Five minutes and you can go home, Autumn. Sorry, we gotta get permission to treat."

"On it." Nat instructed the pad to call Autumn's mother, Rhia. Nat used the bodycam to show Rhia the stick, the car, the somewhat damaged skateboard, and Autumn's hands. "Do we have permission to treat?"

"Do it," said Rhia. "I take it your feet work?"

Autumn flexed first one foot, then the other as Rip sprayed Autumn's hands with a numbing agent, then removed the gravel with tweezers. "Feet are fine. Knees very slightly bruised."

"I'll check it out." Vic came up behind Rip.

"No, check out Lydia there." Rip pointed with her chin.

Lydia waved her hands. "I can't engage the car without the seat mesh. So, just adrenaline."

Vic grinned. "I think you should go somewhere you can relax that will give you food and drink."

Rhia sighed. "I think he's referring to a restaurant. Autumn, come to my office. You can do your homework in the meeting room. I know it's stupid…"

"But you have to physically see I'm fine." Autumn hissed as Rip dug a large piece of gravel out of Autumn's right hand. Rip sprayed more numbing spray.

"She does." Vic knelt to check out Autumn's knees. He carefully pulled down each pad and made sure nothing was damaged. "Minor bruising." He sprayed her knees, then put the pads back on.

"Told you." Autumn grimaced. Vic took out his own tweezers, sprayed Autumn's left hand, and was fast and precise getting the gravel out.

Rhia's voice held a world of concern. "Layla, your car didn't kill my daughter, and I am grateful. Go to Benson's and eat on me."

Layla nodded. "Thanks." Rhia hung up. "Can I go?"

Nat shook his head. "A few more questions. I've got the footage from inside and outside the car. Now, did you hit your body on anything in the car?"

Vid nodded. "Good question."

"No, I've been using the mesh." The mesh was a seatbelt that went over the entire torso. It enabled people to lean back and sleep if they wanted to during long trips.

"I'll check it out." Vic completed the hand and left Rip to spray SkinOnFast and wrap the hands.

Rip wrapped Autumn's palms and slid on a special mesh palm bandage that left the fingers free. "Way cool." Autumn looked at her hands and wiggled her fingers.

Vic took off Lydia's blue silk shirt; she had on a matching tank top with a shelf bra underneath. Her skin had faint mesh marks, but she was fine. He checked her collarbone and arms and had Lydia put her shirt back on.

Lydia glared at him. "Now that I've stripped in the street, can I go?"

"Yes, but you have to leave the car here. The company should come by in about an hour." Nat read from the pad.

"How am I supposed to get to my meeting?" Lydia complained.

Nat pointed at Autumn. "Girl, bleeding hands. No one died. Be happy."

Lydia narrowed her eyes. "If this project goes through, I'll be hiring five people."

"Fine. You are not injured. Did Autumn leap in front of the car deliberately?"

"Hey!" Autumn glared at Nat.

Vic glared at Autumn. "Shush. Nat has to ask."

Layla shook her head. "No, she was windmilling."

"Did you just shush me?" Autumn asked Vic.

"So, this is an accident." Nat poked on his pad.

Autumn threw up her newly-wrapped hands. "I've been telling you that!" Vic narrowed his eyes at her, and she quieted.

"Yes." Lydia drummed her fingers on her elbows, arms crossed.

Nat nodded. "Got everything. Go." Lydia took off at a light jog down the street, not waiting to call another car.

Rip whistled. "Impressive. Hope she doesn't trip in those heels."

Vic grinned. "The sidewalk wouldn't dare." They both snorted.

Autumn rounded on Nat. "I. Didn't. Try. To. Kill. Myself."

Nat nodded. "I know. Have to ask. It's on the report when people nearly hit other people with vehicles." He showed the report to Autumn.

"Well, that's…"

"A good question." Vic made sure all the supplies were logged and put away. "Not all mentally ill people realize they are in trouble until something like this happens." He gestured to Autumn's hands.

"I'm going to walk six blocks that way." Autumn pointed down the tree-lined street. "I take it my board is toast?"

Nat nodded. "The insurance guys will call, and I'll retrieve it then."

Vic pointed at the ambulance. "You can ride in the rig with us. We're going in that direction."

Nat shook his head. "No she can't, it's against regs. You're going to be followed, though. Don't worry. I'm not a stalker."

Autumn snorted. "Fine. I'm getting hangry. I'm walking now."

Nat walked with Autumn and asked the teen a few more questions. Autumn stopped at the health food convenience store, River Notes, to buy peanut butter balls and almond milk. The rig followed them. Nat left Autumn at her mother's law office. The rig drove away, and Nat turned and walked back to the slightly damaged car.

The car company rep came in a smooth ride, a shiny silvery-blue single-person electric vehicle. The inspector was a female in a blue tunic with a Mandarin collar and black sacks. She had blonde hair in an uber-tight braid and sharp blue eyes. "Investigator Decca Bradson. You're Deputy Nat Sandawan?"

"I am." Nat was silent as the investigator investigated. Inspector Bradson already had all of Nat's reports, the crash data, and the car's video. "Kid okay?"

"Gravel in the hands, no serious damage."

"Good." Investigator Bradson took 3D pictures and data of the skateboard, the stick, and the blood on the ground. "This wasn't the car's fault, but the girl who was nearly hit shall get a payment, as will the rider."

"Okay. Not my purview, but good."

"In fact, this is great data." The inspector crouched to take a closer picture of the skateboard. "The skateboard is mostly intact, the car has a scratch, and the girl was never hit, from the data I have and my own eyes."

"I would say all three are true." Nat finished the last form.

"Good then. I have my own repair kit. The car will be repaired and sent outside...Lydia Yu's office?"

"She's at a meeting. I don't have her GPS. You'll have to link to her."

"Okay." The investigator went to her car for her kit and pulled up the side door. She closed the door, a white box in hand, and pointed at the skateboard. "I can give repair funds, but I have no idea how or who to..."

Nat held up a finger. "Three minutes."

While the inspector was waving some sort of wand over the front bumper, Skeet Koston zipped up on his electric skateboard. He had a long beard, shaggy amber hair below his shoulders, and piercing blue eyes. "Heard about Autumn. Major goodness that she wasn't killed." He knelt and checked out Autumn's skateboard. "Be an afternoon."

Nat nodded. "Ask the lady inspector to fund you, and deliver it back to Autumn." Decca Bradson linked with the skateboarder and shot some funds at him. "Thanks, investigators. Going to work!" Skeet heaved up the skateboard, walked to the sidewalk, and took off on his own skateboard.

Nat nodded. "I'm going."

"Thank you, Deputy." Decca Bradson turned to the car again.

Nat had forty-five minutes left in the shift, so he jogged back to the vehicle, drove to the office, then did a mound of work, including rechecking evidence from cold cases. As every new test or technique came out, it was used on cold cases to close them. They were a tiny town, but they had shifters.

Nat had been read in on the first day. At first, he thought his boss, Sheriff Taylor, was insane. He'd seen that college student change on the news from years back, but some debunkers said that video wasn't real. Taylor took Nat out to the woods, took away his weaponry, and made him watch a young man turn into a wolf. "We've got shifters. Bears, wolves, coyotes, eagles even."

Nat had felt like life was suddenly an episode of some dark-themed scifi show. Nat nodded at the wolf shifter, who had been a skinny, pimply teen with knobby knees and elbows in a ratty black and yellow Imagine Dragons t-shirt and bright blue running shorts a few minutes before. Nat slowly turned to Sheriff Taylor, a wiry man with a bristly mustache and a long, slow walk. The deputy suspected that, as an ex-track star, that he could hustle if he so desired.

Nat took two deep breaths, then turned to his boss. "Okay. What problems does this cause? What can shifters do that we can't, and how can we use those things to our advantage?"

Sheriff Taylor raised his eyebrows. "Now you're thinking. They police themselves. We're lucky because it's apparently difficult for them to get drunk or high. They have to go skydiving or some shit to get an adrenaline jump. Go on, Sparky, see you later." Sparky gave a little *aroo*, picked up his clothes that he'd put in a bag with his teeth, and took off at a lope.

"Good to know." Taylor gave back Nat's gun, backup gun, Taser, and heavy flashlight. Nat hid shaking hands while putting the weaponry back on and tried to keep breathing. Nat's breath wanted to hitch, and thoughts went so fast through his brain they made smears in his mind.

Taylor hooked his thumbs through his belt loops. "I haven't thought about how we can use them to our advantage. That's your new job."

Nat gave a sharp nod. "Okay."

So, Nat had ways to find perpetrators other people didn't. Sniffers, trackers. People who could smell blood, body fluids, even fear. They didn't often find evidence, but they could point Nat in the right direction. So far, they'd found Bo Valchi, the rapist who had circulated due to his sales work, and Quentin Batch, the man who had killed his wife and thought they wouldn't find the body buried on the corner of the property, plus missing hikers and kids found who might have died when temperatures plunged at night. Nat had an edge and planned to use it.

PUSH

*M*eri went over her fact sheet as the cargo van took her to the next job. Denise Corsica had been hiking when a friend thought it was funny to push her off the trail. Denise slipped on the leaves and slammed into a tree, which broke her right arm in two places, hairline fractured her leg, and cracked three ribs. The so-called "friend" was on the hook for assault and battery charges, and had to pay every single bill Denise had while she was recovering.

Denise was staying in a rented cottage, the same one Meri's sister-and-law Kandace had recovered from a climbing accident when she first arrived in town. Now Kandace was married to Meri's brothers Len, Davis, and Vic, and the man who had assaulted her was long dead. The cabin was rented out to hikers, cross-country skiers, bird-watchers, nature lovers, and writers seeking quiet. Now, it had been pressed into service to another recovering person.

Meri saw her brother's car and laughed. *History repeats itself*, Meri thought. Len was a home health nurse and a licensed physical thera-pist, as well as being a yoga instructor. He had met Kandace while helping her recover. Meri got out the double cooler and walked around back to the kitchen door, stopping for a moment to stare at the gorgeous outdoor couch, fire pit, and grill. She'd have to grill something when Denise felt better.

Meri whistled first, then knocked on the back door. "Who is it?"

"Ya sista."

Len laughed and opened the back door for her. Meri washed her hands in the galley sink and went to work unloading the coolers. She stepped out of the kitchen and saw Denise for the first time in the black recliner, half-reclined. Denise had her wiry black hair in two clips, the right side of her body in casts, and one of her brown blood-shot eyes ringed in black and purple. Meri stopped, stunned. "Omigod! I thought you didn't get a head injury!" It had been several weeks since the incident, and Denise shouldn't have a black eye.

Denise shook her head, then thought better of it. "Nurse. She was changing my IV and hit me in the face with her elbow."

"How do you even…" Meri blew out a breath. "The point is, can you chew well? I did bring carrots. I can bake them…"

Denise held up a delicate right hand. Her hand and the crook of her elbow looked like pincushions, dark with bruises. "Don't worry. I can eat just fine. Just one-handed."

Meri smiled. "Let me introduce myself. I'm Meri Camber."

"Camber, like Len here?"

"My brother."

"She looks down on me," said Len, referring to Meri's greater height. Denise laughed. Len checked her finger strength, as the cast left Denise's fingers free. He handed her an egg-shaped gel hand exerciser. "Squeeze this."

Denise grimaced, her very white teeth showing. "Ow."

"Not so hard. Build up to it."

Meri held up a hand. "Okay, Denise, to distract you from the pain, let me tell you what's in the refrigerator. Snacks in the yellow boxes are in the form of red bell pepper hummus, carrot, cucumber, and red and yellow bell pepper sticks, whole wheat pitas, seedless grapes, and cherries. I already took out the cherry pits. Today for breakfast we can go egg, cheese, and bacon sandwich, a chicken Caesar salad wrap, or butter chicken with garlic naan bread."

"Butter chicken. Caesar salad thing for dinner, with some cherries. Hummus thing for a snack with some grapes and pita, and the bacon thing for breakfast." Denise grimaced as she squeezed the gel egg again.

"Coming right up." Meri reheated the butter chicken and garlic naan, cut the naan into rectangular pieces easy to wrap, and included a towel. Meri draped the towel over Denise in case she dripped, and Denise got the hang of one-handed dipping. Meri poured some cherry water in a water bottle with a built-in straw and put it on Denise's table.

Denise ate like she hadn't had food in months. "So much better than hospital food. Meri, you're a genius. I knew this would be a better option than the rehab facility! It's not like I can take whirlpool baths anyway."

Len knelt on the ground and checked Denise's feet under the light cranberry-colored blanket. "Your feet are fine. We'll get Jaclyn in here to give you a mani-pedi and Verna to do your hair."

"Bless you." Denise narrowed her eyes. "Be sure to charge it to Trina."

"Why did your friend push you off the trail?" Meri made sure there were a fork and a napkin. She had already cut up the food.

"She says it was a joke, but I've been hearing from friends that she thought I was on the tumbling team by mistake. She wanted a friend of hers to get chosen instead at tryouts."

Meri stared at Denise. "That's why no head injury. You knew how to roll."

Denise held up her ragged nails. "I also clawed like hell to keep the impact minimal." She waved at her right side. "Wish I'd taken Trina down with me."

Len took away the gel egg. "Let the rage go. She's been charged. Take it out on the poor, defenseless squeeze ball. But not today. Ten seconds, building to one minute, each hand. You're a tumbler, so you'll try to push yourself too hard."

Meri had just washed the containers and put them away when there was a knock at the door. Verna came in pushing a cart with a basin. The woman was dressed in black pants and a sparkly shirt with Hills Day Spa in black glittery lettering, her hair platinum to match her shirt. "Hey Len, Meri. Denise, I am so sorry this horrible thing happened to you. I'm Verna. I'm going to wash your hair. If you want to keep it long, we'll braid it in some way where it won't get in your way."

Denise sighed. "Slash it. Washing your hair one-handed sucks as it is."

"Are you sure, honey?" Verna put on a silver apron.

"Go for it. It's just hair. It will grow out."

Verna nodded, hard. "On it."

Meri grinned. "That's my cue to leave. Verna, give Denise the stuff in the yellow containers when Trina's done with her. It doesn't have to be reheated. That's her snack. I'll be back for lunch."

Verna put a bright pink clip in Verna's hair. "Will do."

Denise waved. "Thank you."

Meri grinned, waved, and went out the door. She drove to Ravel's house next. The backwoods woman had suffered a back injury, and definitely needed her neighbor Garrett's help. Unfortunately for his friend's health, Garrett brought over unhealthy food that Ravel couldn't eat for dinner like pies and sweets, nothing savory.

Ravel was on her front porch in an Adirondack chair that took the pressure off her spine, with pillows for her back and feet. She wore faded jeans that were too big for her tiny frame and an ancient blue sweatshirt. Her face was a mass of wrinkles, her normally sharp blue eyes clouded with pain. "Hey, there, Meri."

"Hey. Y'all want some stew? I've got cornbread to go with it and honey butter."

Ravel grinned. "You know I do."

Meri brought over her hot box and brought out the still-steaming stew. "Pork and cider!"

Meri gave Ravel a soup spoon and butter knife, and Ravel buttered her cornbread. "Slow cooker. Made my place smell heavenly."

"You bring me more?"

"Enough for about six meals." Garrett was good at reheating things for Ravel once Meri had spoken to him sternly for harming Ravel with his non-protein food. There was no microwave; all reheating was done on the stove. "Plus a whole dish of jalapeno cornbread, and an entire container of honey butter."

"You know I love my cornbread." Meri filled up Ravel's ancient white refrigerator with the stew and cornbread. She went back out and brought in foil packets. "What's those?"

"Trout with lemon and dill. Also, you've got some catfish and hush puppies made with the last of the cornmeal. I order that by the ton, working around here."

"Damn, woman!" Ravel gestured with her butter knife. "I'll eat good tonight!"

Meri made one more trip with more wrapped things. "These are biscuits with cooked bacon in sandwiches with a little cheese baked in. They'll be breakfast." Meri filled up the refrigerator, wrote the reheating instructions on a little card, and used magnets to put the cards on the refrigerator door. She came back out and was unsurprised to find that Ravel was done. "Got some good green beans with the fish for tonight, if you'd like that."

"Good."

Meri took the containers and went to the car. She put them in the to-be-cleaned bin and came back. "Let me help you to the girl's room."

Ravel laughed. "Naw, girl, Garrett be coming' here real soon."

"He's sweet on you."

Ravel laughed, which sounded like the stream behind her house. "Naw, he ain't. You get on, girl."

Meri smiled. "See you in two days."

Meri decided to get her own lunch. Odette had a small sandwich place just inside the holler. The benches and tables were hewn wood. There were only six sandwiches–Ruben, pulled pork, grilled cheese with mustard and bacon, cherry tomato and mushroom with goat cheese, hot browns with turkey and bacon, and fried chicken. The food was all from local farmers. Meri ordered the grilled cheese with wedge potatoes and lime water and a second sandwich to go. She ate her food in the dappled sunlight under giant trees over a hundred years old and put the tomato sandwich wrapped in waxed paper with a little container of potato salad made with wide dill pickles in a little sack in her cold box. She waved to Odette, the stick figure woman who made such amazing sandwiches, and Meri pulled out.

Meri went home to unload empties and wash them, then filled the van with more food. She swung back by Denise's cabin and fed her lunch, made sure a friend named Ainsley would feed Denise dinner, then she had three more clients before she could relax.

Roger was eighty-six and still did all his own gardening. He was slowly going blind and had enough tremors in his hands that cooking was ill-advised. Meri pulled up to his little white house, an American flag flying in front. Roger was digging in the dirt, pulling weeds, a soft fishing cap on his head, his tools in a tray. Meri took out her cooler and walked up to the porch. It took her two trips, then she got it all to the door. Roger finally made it to the door and opened it for her. The man was as slow as molasses. "Thank you."

Meri walked the coolers to the kitchen, went back and shut the door, and smiled as Roger's ancient basset hound Trixie followed her into the kitchen. Meri knelt, petted the dog, and gave her a bone treat. Trixie smiled around her bone, then went back to her bed to rest.

Meri washed her hands, then filled up the refrigerator with turkey chili, Manhattan clam chowder, chicken tortilla, split pea, and traditional chicken soups. She lined up the sandwiches like soldiers, turkey and cranberry, sun-dried tomato and chicken, and basil pesto chicken. She also put in containers of tortellini with mushrooms, pork tenderloin with cherry sauce and asparagus, salmon baked in foil with asparagus, and Roman chicken with green olives and red bell peppers. Roger was on a fixed income, and the food would last a week. Meri put the reheating instructions in extra-large print on the refrigerator. Len worked with Roger as well since his stroke and could help with meals.

Meri carried her empty coolers out to the vehicle. "Bye, Roger." He waved. He had spoken to her maybe ten times in the two years she had been delivering food to him. He ate every bite, however. Meri suspected Roger was sharing his food with his next-door neighbor and best friend, Bernie, also on a fixed income. Hence the soups and sandwiches, easy to reheat and share.

Next, Reiko had two children and two jobs, one as a book designer and a second as an illustrator. Being in a wheelchair didn't slow her down; her busy schedule and kids in soccer that also needed to hit up the library made it hard to cook. Meri was unsurprised to find Neko the tabby cat sleeping in the window, the only one home. She filled up the refrigerator with bento box lunches for the kids, taco rollups, cheese and crackers, almond butter and jelly, and fruit all cut out into fun shapes. Reiko also got the soups and main meals she'd made for Roger, and adult bento boxes of stuffed pitas, sushi, strawberry salad, chicken salad, and hummus and vegetables.

Meri filled up her coolers with all the used bento boxes and containers. She carried them back out and sat in her car. She ate her second sandwich and washed it down with the last of her water. She stretched, wiped her hands with a wipe, and went to the last house.

Meri pulled up to the Ferris Heeder's gray house on a lonely road. Heavy blackout curtains blanked the windows. The house was small, only two bedrooms. Ferris used one as a bedroom and the other as a place to do his coding. There was a helpful ramp to the front door because Ferris' dad Kevin was in a wheelchair after being shot in the back by a hunter while he was in his own yard. Meri left the food in her vehicle; she wanted to talk to Ferris first because he was agoraphobic. Meri was genuinely concerned that Ferris would become depressed over the lack of face-to-face humans in his life, except his dad. Ferris had numerous online friends and was even "dating" another agoraphobic whom he had never seen in person.

Meri knocked; there was no twitch of the curtains. She knocked again, called out, and heard nothing. She used her code on the door and entered. "Ferris! It's Meri!" Meri had entered before when Ferris was working on his app in his office or on a call. He seemed to fluidly switch between coding and gaming. But there were no steady voices calling out directions, no sounds of aliens dying by the dozen onscreen. The living room had only a couch and a huge TV. The floor was bamboo so his dad could roll around with his wheelchair.

Meri stepped forward and shut the door. She checked the kitchen; the empties from Meri's food were in the case. Meri stepped into the hallway and called out. No answer. "Ferris! It's Meri Camber. Are you hungry?" She walked to the half-open office door. Meri saw feet and stepped into the room. "Ferris!" Meri knelt, and touched the ankle. No pulse. The brown eyes were staring into space and already filmed over, brown hair falling over his brow, the face slack and gray.

Meri stumbled backward and called the emergency line. She then called Kevin, and said, "Get someone to help you, and get over here."

"It's my boy, isn't it." Kevin's voice was heavy and sad.

"I don't know what happened, but he's gone." Meri stayed on the line as Kevin started to cry. The line went dead.

Five minutes later, Vic came in and stood next to Meri. "Go to the van, sis. You can't help him, and we're going to be with him until the coroner gets here."

Meri nodded and passed Rip calling the coroner's van. She stumbled out onto the wide porch Kevin hadn't really enjoyed, gulping fresh air. She hadn't smelled anything yet, so she doubted he'd been dead long. She knelt, hoping her stomach would stay put. She felt like she'd been punched in the gut.

Meri levered herself up when she saw Nat's deputy vehicle. He was careful to park on the street to give the coroner room. He strode over in his long legged, birdlike gait, and looked at Meri. "I'm sorry you found him like that. Can you walk me through exactly what happened?"

"I came to drop off the food. I went in because he'd given me permission to come in when he didn't answer. I had the code."

"Walk me through exactly what you did, what you touched."

"I opened the front door with my code and the door to his office with the heel of my hand. I also touched his foot to see if there was a pulse."

"Okay. Walk me through, moment by moment."

"Two minutes. The whole thing took two minutes." After she'd discussed it twice, Nat went in. Meri went boneless and sat on the porch. She held on, managed not to cry.

The coroner's van showed up, and Doctor Nicholas Justain got out with his black bag. His medical assistant and sometimes investigator, Sage Richardson, got out on the other side. She ran around back to get the gurney.

Doctor Justain walked up to the porch and looked down at Meri. "Are you all right?"

Meri shook her head. "No. I found him."

"Very well." The coroner opened the door wider with his cane, which Vic and Rip had left open, and entered.

Sage pushed the gurney up the slope, and it evened out on the porch. "Meri, are you going to hurl?"

"Nope. No smell yet." Sage nodded, and entered the house, pushing the gurney.

Kevin drove up. His buddy Frankie got out, her long braid of blonde hair streaked with gray swinging as she ran around the car, opened the special elevator, and waited until Kevin was completely out to run the elevator back up. Meri stood and staggered down the ramp. She knelt at Kevin's wheelchair; he had the special black one that he could drive with a gaming stick he could control with a finger. Ferris had bought it for his dad two years ago and had bought the van last year. Kevin was just forty-two; the death of his son aged him ten years in twenty minutes. His dark hair stood straight up, and his normally ruddy face was gray. "I am so sorry." Meri tried not to cry.

Kevin reached out, patted her hand. "You literally fed my son."

Meri nodded. "He had to set timers to remember. I know, because I set them for him. Drinks, snacks, meals."

"You treated my boy right." Kevin patted her hand again.

Meri stepped out of the way and let Kevin go talk to Nat. Nat came outside and gestured to the porch. Kevin zipped up there using the ramp. Frankie followed him, her braid swinging back and forth like a metronome. Frankie had tanned skin, green eyes, and corded muscles from helping her friend get around. Nat knelt and spoke to Kevin in a gentle voice.

With that, Meri lost it. She made it to the van before she burst into tears. She got in and let them flow.

TAILSPIN

*L*ibby stayed after work to make extra trays; sales of caramel apples were through the roof. She heated the separate double boilers of caramel and chocolate slowly and added the salt. She turned off the heat, then took out the top of the double boiler and put it on a trivet on her granite candy making table. She stabbed the apples with popsicle sticks, dipped each one in the caramel, then rolled them in the pecans. She drizzled some with chocolate. Then, she dipped strawberries in chocolate and then poured the last of the caramel and chocolate over peanut brittle. She broke up the brittle while the apples cooled, then slid the trays into the refrigerator.

Her link whistled, and Libby said, "Answer link."

Meri's voice came on, shaky with tears. "I lost a client."

"That sucks. Don't worry. You'll advertise, get another."

"Libby, no! Ferris, he's dead!" Her voice broke.

"Oh, my stars. Tell your vehicle to come to me. I'm at the shop. I'll lock up and we'll get... something."

"On my way." The link went silent.

Libby put away the cooling candy, cleaned the pots, made sure everything was turned off, cleaned the counters, and sanitized the floors. She'd already cleaned the front an hour ago. She washed her hands and stepped out into the sunset.

Meri tumbled out of her van and crashed into Libby's arms. "Upstairs." Libby pointed. "I smell."

"Like chocolate." Meri turned and stumbled up the stairs. Libby followed, put in her code, shut the door behind Meri, then ran to get her shower in.

When Libby came back out in jeans and a scarlet shirt, she dragged Meri up. "We need to get drunk."

"With you on that." Libby put on low black boots, grabbed a jacket, and got Meri back down the stairs. They took Meri's van to Stollenback Tavern. The air was warm inside, the pool tables full, the music a two-step. Several people were line dancing on the floor to the left.

Meri took one of the only remaining two-tops, and Libby went to get the drinks. Ash Stollenback was behind the bar, her black hair shading to blue in twists, her eyes sad. "Heard about Ferris. You need Johnny." She poured from the red bottle.

Libby nodded. "Hit my account. My sister needs to get drunk. Add a dollar fifty to each drink for yourself."

Ash nodded. "Will do."

Libby brought the drinks to Meri. They stood, then downed them together. They sat back down. "Talk." Libby pointed at her sister with her glass.

"I went in to deliver the food. He was dead on the floor. Vic and Rip showed up, but his eyes were open. Nat showed up and asked questions. His dad showed up…" Meri let the tears flow down her face, then blotted them away with a bar napkin. "His dad did his best, and Ferris did his best for him."

Libby patted her sister's arm. "What caused his agoraphobia?"

Meri sighed. "He saw his mother die." Meri caught Ash's eye, and Ash nodded.

"What? I thought she was hit by a car."

"Helen was changing a tire. Her son was in the car. He was twelve."

"Oh, shit. But I remember something about his attending school."

"He did, but he had to be heavily medicated. His dad realized that wasn't working, and homeschooled the kid. Ferris left the house to move into his own place when he earned enough from coding; he said their house reminded him too much of his mom."

"Kid couldn't get a break."

Meri waggled her hand. "Yes and no. He won the parent lottery. His dad is great. Ferris did well enough that he only worked six hours a day, and then he played video games with people all over the world."

Tau, the server, came over in her sports jersey and jeans. Her black hair was pulled back into a high ponytail and her normally sparkling dark eyes were sad. She'd gone to school with Ferris. "Two Johnnie Walker Black." She deposited the drinks on the table and took the empties.

"Thanks." Libby swiped some money, added a good tip.

They sipped their drinks. Libby pointed at her sister with her glass. "So, you're saying even though he didn't go outside, he had a good life."

Meri shrugged. "I couldn't do it. My job has me moving around, and I love it. Not in the rain or snow, but I love the sun."

"Not the sleet. Or sneet."

"What's sneet?" Nat stood just to the right of their booth, eyes sad. He was dressed in a cobalt shirt and jeans, uniform long gone. "Oh, snow mixed with sleet."

"Yes. You questioned my traumatized sister."

"I did. To be realistic, most of the people I talk to during the day are traumatized."

Meri gave her sister a narrow-eyed stare. "I know. Not upset. Or, not upset with you."

"I am so sorry." Nat waved at Ash, who nodded.

"Does Doc Justin…" Meri waved her hand around.

"The scan says he had a massive brain bleed."

"Are you asking if my sister…" Libby pointed her glass at Ned.

"No. We talked to her van. She was across town when it happened."

"He had a stroke." Meri's voice was flat.

"He did. I doubt they'll find much difference from the initial scans."

"Sorry."

"She gets protective when she gets drunk." Meri poked at Libby's arm.

"And sober," admitted Libby.

"I'll get wings. And potato skins?" Nat gestured towards the menus.

Libby glared. "I haven't forgiven you yet, so mozzarella sticks too."

"Done." Nat walked over to the bar to put in the order.

Meri stared at Libby. "Libs, I know we didn't run with Nat when he was younger. Then he went away to get a criminal justice degree."

"We all pretty much split up," Libby had to agree. "Plus, we're different." She made a claw with her hand, and Meri snorted.

Nat came back with a dark bottle. "What's that?" asked Meri.

"Spiced apple cider, sans alcohol. Can't drink. Might be called into duty."

Meri nodded. "I hit my limit. Financially, too. Sis, Johnnie Walker is expensive."

"On me. Horrible day for you."

Meri nodded. "I see people damaged, and my food literally helps get them better. I didn't see this coming. I fed him as best as I could, making food fun for him, but he ate bags of Doritos while gaming and consumed sodas by the two-liter."

Libby said, "Lots of people do that. They don't die from a stroke at twenty-three years old."

Meri sighed. "That's what gets me."

Nat took a pull of cider. "Your time is your time. Had an actual car accident yesterday."

Libby and Meri swiveled their eyes to the deputy. "Really?" asked Meri.

Libby nodded. "Autumn and her mom Rhia came in yesterday and today. Autumn was wearing some sort of palm glove over bandages. Wanted brickle to put under their ice cream from next door."

Meri nodded. "Sounds like she fell onto her palms on a road. And she's a skateboarder, keeps to the sidewalks. Never had to dodge her. Did she leap out in front of a vehicle?"

Nat shook his head. "It'll be in the Country Journal tomorrow. Becky Sue does love the police blotter. Anyhoo, Layla Yu was on her way to an appointment, and Autumn hit a stick on the sidewalk and went airborne into the street. The skateboard slightly scratched the vehicle."

"And poor Autumn hit the ground, palms first," Libby guessed. "I'd feed my kid brickle and ice cream for two days in a row, too."

The food came, and Libby and Nat ate like wolves, while Meri managed to get down three mozzarella sticks and two loaded nacho chips. They talked about high school sports; football had good tryouts that year, and this year's girls' volleyball team looked great.

Nat shrugged. "I help out where I can, but my schedule has too much for me to do. The town hates overtime. Saves it up for all-hands-on-deck situations."

Meri nodded. "We can't play volleyball. We need our hands for our jobs."

Libby nodded. "I lift sacks of flour and heavy trays, and Meri lifts coolers and some warmer boxes. I would like to get in shape."

Nat gave Libby the once-over. "Your arms are good, but you're lacking all three fundamentals, which are strength, endurance, and flexibility. If you have all three, you can handle most of what life throws at you."

Meri loaded another nacho chip. "I take it you go to the gym."

"Yes, I go to Body Tech. Cops use it because the kickboxing gym uses a different door from the machines and classes. And ten percent off for law enforcement."

Meri nodded. "I'll join. I'll even pay you to teach me."

Nat shook his head. "I'm not a licensed personal trainer."

"You started training young," Meri countered. "I bet you've made every mistake there is."

Nat snorted. "I have."

Libby tilted her head to the side. "And why is that a good thing?"

Meri dipped her mozzarella stick in marinara sauce. "Ruling out what doesn't work."

Nat grinned. "Efficiency."

Libby shook her head. "I get up at five in the morning and start making candy by six."

"Why? You don't open until eleven on most days." Nat gestured for more spiced apple juice, and Meri held up two fingers.

"What I've been saying!" Meri ate a cheese stick.

Libby narrowed her eyes at Meri. "You get up early, too."

"I cook in huge batches, and have my daily people, twice weekly, and weekly. I do have ways to keep up with it, doing the prep work the day before cooking."

Libby glared at her sister. "Are you saying I'm fat?"

Meri pressed her fingers into her eyes. "No, love, I'm telling you that we both can work out in the mornings, find what we like to do. Maybe salsa dancing is your thing, I don't know. But we both have put work first, and now our businesses are doing well. We need some me-time. Also, I'm getting sick of yoga with Len. I keep falling over." She finished off the last of the alcohol, handed over her empty glass to Tau, and said, "I'll have what Nat's having." Tau came right back, and Meri sipped the spiced non-alcoholic apple cider. "Whoa! That has a kick!"

Libby grinned. "One for me. I'll need it to get home."

Meri shrugged. "Why go home? I'm depressed, not you. Mostly just sad and shocky, actually. Dancing would be good."

"I hate drunken farmers. I may be bi, but I hate it when they start making cow eyes at me."

Meri sighed. "Alex Weaver turned her off dating for the last six—no, seven months."

Libby pointed at Meri. "You've atrophied. Jazz was eighteen months ago."

Nat nodded slowly. "Almost two years." Two heads swiveled to stare at the deputy. "Her name was Quallie. Weird name, extraordinary woman. She moved to Denver. I got my degree in criminal justice, and I'd been studying and training, so the police academy wasn't so bad. Had some dustups there. Some dumbass released my medical records into the wild."

Meri pointed with her bottle of apple cider. "Nastiness. Keep kicking its ass, and it keeps coming back."

"Word," said Libby. They clinked bottles and drank. "So, they found out about the Klinefelter's."

"Good old XXY genes. My mom thought I wasn't masculine enough, had since I was little. My uncle tortured me because he thought I was gay. But, that wasn't the reason I don't like pronouns. Just never gave a shit about gender. It's a checkbox on a form to me. People are just people."

Meri grimaced. "Your mom is an idiot."

"How 'bout them Tigers?" Nat pointed to the screen where the high school practice game was showing. They all watched Dakota, their quarterback, make a touchdown again. The crowd in the bar cheered again, even though they'd seen a nearly identical practice last week.

They ended up line dancing, and even Meri found herself laughing. They had fun, stomping and clapping, and ended up sweating and drinking a lot of apple juice.

Nat walked them out to their vehicle. "If either one or both of you are serious, meet me at the gym at six in the ay em tomorrow."

Libby threw up her hands. "Omigod."

"It's not that late." Meri was right, it was nearly eleven. "I'll be there."

"Fine." Nat grinned and waved goodbye.

The next morning, Libby was glad she'd made extra trays the night before. She felt exhausted from grief. Not for Ferris; she hadn't really known him, but for Meri. Her sister was a mess. They had showered, then Meri had slept in the loft with Libby, something they hadn't done in years.

Meri was downstairs filling up bottles with lime water and a pinch of pink Himalayan sea salt when Libby stumbled down the stairs. "You stole my yoga pants and my Evil Bunny shirt." Libby looked dow. She was wearing the same thing, except that her shirt had an alien on it that said, "Leader. Now."

"Let's go. Shoes. Chop chop."

"You are an evil, controlling cow." Libby stumbled to the bathroom, came out with her hair up in a high ponytail, then aimed herself towards her shoes. Meri had a gym bag with more of Libby's borrowed clothes in it next to the door.

They made it to the gym on time. They bought day passes, and at that hour there weren't many people. Nat led them to the heavy mats for stretches and had them do thirty seconds each of lunges, toe touches, high marches, and so on. "One foot on the ground at all times. No use damaging your feet, ankles, or knees on the first day. Libby, land on the balls of your feet, loosely, knees soft. Good."

Then, they started with the half-kilo hand weights. "This is way too light," Libby groused.

Nat shook his head. "First, form over weight. I hated starting light, too. But, after you do the 'humblers,' you'll thank me."

"Humblers?" asked Libby.

Meri snorted. "I remember from gym class. Arm circles."

They sweated through a classic hand weight set, including some kettlebell exercises that were ridiculously easy with such light weights. Nat showed them how to do the exercises. "Don't overextend, and don't raise your arms above your shoulders until you build up your strength."

Libby narrowed her eyes. "What's harder?"

Nat raised one eyebrow. "Okay, floor exercises. Put the little weights on either side of you." They went through stretches and lifts, including weird ones like laying down, holding the weight in between the ankles, and lifting the feet. By the time they were done, they were sweating profusely. They drank water, then Nat put on some music, since they were alone in that part of the gym, and taught them some basic jump rope moves.

"Stop," begged Libby. "I've got to open up, Meri has breakfast to drop off, and we haven't eaten yet."

"Fine, go shower." Nat pointed at the locker room. They stumbled off, groaning.

They got themselves washed, lotioned, hair braided, and dressed. Nat wore the deputy uniform and tipped an imaginary hat to them. "Have a good day." Nat took a long-legged stride to the front door.

Libby stood up straight, groaned. "What just happened?"

Meri snorted. "At least Nat didn't call us ma'am." They both laughed.

They stumbled out of the gym, and they rode back in silence. The sun was out, golden, like warm maple syrup. They called ahead and stopped in front of Desi's. Desi ran out with packets of warm egg and maple bacon sandwiches. They walked over to Libby's place, walked up the stairs, and finished the sandwiches and drank orange juice in Libby's kitchen.

Meri threw her trash away. "I'm off. Only three breakfasts and one of my clients tends to sleep in." They hugged, and Meri slipped out the door.

Libby changed into her work clothes, khakis and a light blue Sweet Thoughts Bakery shirt. She jogged downstairs, let herself in the back, put on her apron, cleaned the cases inside and out, then filled them up. She dipped more bananas in chocolate and baked lots of banana nut, lemon poppyseed, and chocolate fudge brownie mini muffins. The locals started staring in the window, attracted by the smells wafting down the street. She made pots of both regular and decaf coffee, put the chairs down, washed her hands, and opened for business.

Libby had a line for nearly half an hour of people grabbing coffee and muffins, with the occasional sale of dipped bananas or strawberries or brickle. By the time Mary Beth arrived there was a line again. There was talk of Autumn's mini-accident and Ferris' sudden, inexplicable death, but not in front of the children. A few mothers came in with little ones, enjoying coffee or tea and a treat while their babies slept or babbled and played with plastic keys. Once there was a single baby or child in the restaurant, no one talked about anything disturbing. Everyone knew little children had big ears. Libby had avoided talking about the holdup that way. She sometimes found her fingers hovering by the call-police button when she wasn't paying attention.

Some authors came in. Luis Tortola wrote travel books and was determined to visit every single Spanish-speaking country in the world. He had worked his way down to Nicaragua on his last vacation. He was a slight man, with a carefully trimmed beard and pressed pants. Yesira Allegheny wrote romance novels about a newly turned vampire with big appetites. She had wavy chocolate hair and big brown eyes, a hatchet nose, and a braying laugh. Luis liked espresso and banana muffins, and Yesira black tea and dark chocolate pecan apples. Luis wrote on a military-grade tough laptop, and Yesira had a top-of-the-line tablet with a tiny, thin keyboard. They both enjoyed writing outside their homes. They moved on about every hour and a half, hitting up diners, coffee shops, the creamery, and the library, or just walking around to clear their minds and get new ideas. They sat in opposite corners, her sun to his moon.

They were so busy that Libby remembered lunch for Mary Beth, but forgot about it for herself. She had to bake and dip more apples twice. She ate one of the apples as the muffins baked and the chocolate melted. She washed up and filled up the glass cases again. They even sold out of all their gluten-free treats.

Libby sent Mary Beth home, shocked it was that time. She went through two more lines. Finally, the shop was nearly empty.

Libby wiped down the counter, made a money deposit into the safe, and wiped down the cafe tables.

Jeb came in with a gentle smile. "I'm so happy you came back," Libby blurted.

"I'm just sorry I couldn't do anything to stop it." Jeb's voice was soft and a little shaky.

"Nat did the work we couldn't do." Libby patted Jeb's hand, then took his order of a scone and tea. She slipped his scone in the microwave and started on the tea.

"I was never happier to see a deputy in my life."

"Amen." Jeb tried to pay, but Lydia wouldn't take his money. "My brother will pay for your scones and tea for the next year. He said your calmness saved both our lives."

Jeb turned aside, tears welling in his eyes. "Your brother... I take it you're talking about Vic Camber? He left the nicest review. He said your young nephews are doing better because of my little books."

Libby put his warm scone on a plate and added some clotted cream. "Your little books make kids happy. Keep writing them."

Jeb smiled. "I think I'll do that right now."

By the time she turned the open sign to closed and did the last spray and scrub, Libby was ready to drop. She was also ravenous. She crossed the street and walked down under the leafy trees. She waved to a few people, but she didn't feel like talking to anyone. She was getting hungry.

Her feet led her to The Red Lion Tavern. She stepped in and ordered a grilled fish sandwich, a side salad, and cherry water. She ate quietly, interested in shoveling in the food.

Vic plopped down in front of her. "No fries?"

"I guessed I would see you, and deliberately didn't order food you would steal."

Vic looked sheepish. "Fine, I'll order my own." He ordered fish and chips, and a side of honey mustard sauce. He was not a fan of vinegar on his chips. "How are you holding up?"

Libby pointed her fork at him. "You've been sent by the family to make sure I'm good."

Vic shrugged. "Better than sending Dad. He'd give you a lecture about finding a nice person to settle down with."

"Or more."

"Or more." Vic's soda came and he drank half of it.

"Surprised you found Kandace."

"Stunned that she wanted all three of us. We're not polygamous because of religion. We just like sharing."

Libby laughed. "I actually just want…" She stared at the last few olives at the bottom of her bowl.

"Love." Vic dunked his fry. "So did we. Just open up and relax. We were looking for other bears when we found Kandace."

Libby sighed. "I tried that. All the way to Idaho. Wen wanted to live in thigh-deep snow all the time. Zane wanted to herd cattle in Wyoming. They had great lives, just not anywhere near here. Finding a shifter is hard enough. They tend to date in their teens and marry in their twenties. By the time I'd built my business, they were taken."

Vic nodded. "We found every crazy shifter woman first."

Libby laughed. "Luckily, mine were just…entrenched. I want to live near our family. Wouldn't have opened a business here otherwise."

"Getting little brothers and sisters a few years ago probably helped that decision." Because they were so much older than Libby's kids, they called themselves "uncles" and "aunts," although they had no genetic relationship with them. Family was family.

"Did." Libby stole one of Vic's fries. "They're so cute that it's criminal."

Nat came in and ordered something in a brown bottle. "What's that, beer?" Vic asked, pointing in Nat's direction.

Libby shook her head. "Not beer, spiced apple cider. Non-alcoholic."

"Ah, on duty," Vic called him over. "Hey, Nat. Take off your jacket and stay awhile."

Nat grinned. "Sure." Nat slid into the booth next to Libby. "Your sisters are coming along nicely."

"What?"

Libby grinned. "He's our trainer."

Vic stared, nonplussed. "That's... never happened."

Nat's salmon salad came, and he dug in.

"Busy day?" asked Libby.

Nat swallowed. "First chance to eat."

Libby laughed. "Me, too." She ordered the Apple Brown Betty made with fresh apples, knowing her brother would eat most of it. She snagged another fry and he growled at her. Bears were territorial about their food.

Nat's loaded nachos arrived. "Just complaints, follow-ups. We found out who's been going after mailboxes with a baseball bat."

Vic's mouth dropped open. "What? Who?"

Libby held up a finger. "Coach Carlson's son." Coach Darlene Carlson coached the field hockey teams. Her son, Morgan, was trying out for football this year...but probably not anymore, with a charge of criminal mischief. "Or so Patty Francis said today."

Nat sighed. "No secrets in a small town."

Vic' shook his head. "I hope he straightens out."

Nat's eyes went flat. "He will. He's losing out on what he values most because his friend Tim decided to get him drunk and take him out doing the stupid when they were supposedly studying."

Libby sighed. "Some friendship."

Nat gestured with his cider bottle. "Exactly."

They chatted about the school dance coming up. Nat would be on duty. Vic would be busy too, on ambulance duty. "I think you'd make a good chaperone."

Libby snorted. "I wasn't the one doing Tim and Morgan stunts with baseball bats, but I wasn't much better of a human being in high school."

Nat rippled with laughter. "I was into sports. Do you think I was a paragon of responsibility?"

Libby snorted. "Jocks and bakers didn't mix. Sorry about that."

Nat laughed. "I was a gym rat. Still am."

"Now I'm becoming a gym rat." Libby finished her dessert.

Vic stared at his sister with mock horror. "Universe forfend." Libby kicked him under the table and stole another fry.

THE BIG GAME

*L*ibby unloaded the blue three-shelf cart, expanded it, locked it in place, then loaded the cart up with boxes. Meri did the exact same thing at the back of her vehicle. Meri had the tables; they slipped into place on the side of the cart. Meri closed the hatch and grunted as she pushed the cart with the folded tables up the sidewalk. Libby followed, parked her cart, set the brake with her foot, then helped Meri open the tables, pull down the feet, and tilt them upright. Libby opened the blue pack on her back and pulled out two bright blue tablecloths and tape. They taped the bottoms of the table-cloth to the table legs.

Meri put the tape away. "Unload while I reload the cart. You have a better eye and you can arrange them beautifully."

Libby smiled. "On it." Once Meri walked away, Libby groaned. She'd been doing planks every day. Her arms and shoulders were sore, and Meri tended to overstuff her coldboxes with Tetris-like fervor. Still, the stackable cases had wheels.

Libby looked up and saw someone in a referee's bright yellow shirt and black shorts coming towards her. She was stunned to realize it was Nat. "What are you doing here dressed as a ref?"

"There are at least two, usually three refs, so if I get called away, we're covered." He tilted his head. "Do you need help?"

Libby pointed to the two cases, both a dark blue. "These on the ground, please. They're stackable."

"Shoulders hurt, do they?" Nat lifted one and lowered it to the ground. "Are these the snacks?"

"Waters and food in refillable containers, no more disposable water bottles. Trash laws. I brought the snacks. Robbie Fuller and Denise Johnson are both allergic to peanuts, and Robbie is gluten free, so…"

Nat lifted the heavy cooler on top and put it on the ground, muscles bulging in his legs and arms.

Libby raised an eyebrow. "Nice legs. Cardio?"

Nat laughed. "Absolutely not. Squats. Lots of them. Muscle burns fat throughout the day."

Meri rolled by with her own boxes and tables. "Hey, Nat. Didn't know you were a ref." Meri grinned, the breeze making her razor-cut hair sway.

"I help where I can." Nat began unloading Libby's boxes with quick hands. Meri set out the reusable boxes of power pieces, as the kids called them. Libby nodded approvingly, and pulled the labels out of her backpack, which specified lemon blackberry, cherry, chocolate coconut, and apricot mango protein snacks formed into balls. The waters were plain, lemon lime, or blackberry, and color-coded clear, lime green, or purple. Libby fished out the water labels and put them in front of each row of color-coded water bottles. "You have a lot here," Nat observed.

Libby laughed. "The moms pay us to set up the tables, provide the snacks, then haul back the empties." She grinned. "Now I have to repeat over there." She pointed to the other side of the soccer field.

Nat grinned. "I guess that makes me the stacker. I'll go help your sister." Meri and Nat went to set up Meri's tables. Libby took a moment of indulgence to watch Nat's muscles jump and release. She let go of the thought; the family would be arriving soon.

Nat caught an errant table as it began to sway and Meri dashed over to help. They got the tables set up with the tablecloths, signs, snacks, and liquids.

Meri stretched until her back popped. "Thanks, Nat."

Nat grinned. "No problem. I'll say goodby to Libby, then I've got to ref." They fist-bumped, and Nat headed back across the field to see Libby.

Nat reached the other table just before a wall of kids crashed into Libby's legs. Nat grinned. "I think I know who these people are."

Adam disassociated himself from Libby's legs and strode over to Nat. Nat got on one knee to look the little boy in the eyes. "I'm Adam. You ref'd at some other games, but not ours, I think."

"You're right. I usually don't arrive this early, but I went to check in. Then, I saw that your aunts needed help."

"That's good." Adam stared up at Nat. "Are you my aunts' friend?"

"Nat sure is." Libby disentangled herself from a very clingy Bobby. "And our fitness instructor, teaching us how to move."

Adam puffed out his chest. "That's easy. I can teach you."

Libby let out a bright peal of laughter. "I'm sure you can." She looked down. "This other one is Bobby."

Nat grinned. "Nice to meet you both. I think I see your coach and I've got to go get my cards and flags. You have fun out there!" Adam nodded seriously. Bobby just shrugged. Nat rose and jogged over to the refs in the far corner of the field.

Charlie came up, Bethany giggling madly on his shoulders, River with her feet on his. Libby caught her breath. "They are just gorgeous."

"They're girls," said Bobby, dismissively.

Adam poked his brother. "Hey. We're sheepdogs, remember?"

Libby looked down at her little brother, confused. "What?"

Bobby sighed. "Some people are sheep. Some are wolves that hunt sheep. Some are sheepdogs, protecting the sheep. But we're not! We're bears!"

Libby knelt. "You know you can't go around saying that, don't you?"

"Why not?" Bobby said, his lower lip stuck out defiantly. "Normies can say who they are."

Libby knelt, then caught his shoulders. "We're special, Bobby. We protect others. We can't help them as well if they know who we are."

Adam came over to stand next to his brother. "Remain hidden, because if they don't know you, don't know where you are, they'll be surprised when you find them."

"Someone's been listening to Dad," said Libby, with a smile.

Bobby sighed. "We're not in a war."

Libby shook her head. "Yes, we are. We're much safer here, because there are other specials here, but you wouldn't say that if you lived somewhere else. We made agreements, and we have to stick to them."

Bobby sighed. "I'm tired of talking about this."

Libby stood. "Have a good game, and have fun!" she said brightly. Bobby and Adam jogged to their coach.

Charlie walked up to stand in front of Libby. "Do you know that there is a child on your head?" asked Libby.

Bethany giggled. "It's me! Auntie Wibby!" She dived off of Charlie's shoulders. Libby stepped to the side and caught her. She put the giggling girl on her own back. Bethany attached herself like a limpet.

"Hey, River," said Libby.

"Hey."

Libby knelt to look River in the eyes. "One of us has to stay here, and the others over there with Meri." She pointed at the other side of the soccer field. "I'm sure we have enough chairs." Libby noted the brace of folding camp chairs Charlie had slung onto his back. "Do you want to be here or there?"

River shoved her sharp chin into her father's stomach and looked up at him. "Daddy, where you gonna stay?"

Charlie pointed to the ground. "If we go over there, it'll look like we're cheering for the other team. So, I'm staying on this side."

Bethany said, "I don't care! I'm goin' wif Auntie Wibby to see Aunt Meri!"

Libby laughed. "Okay, one chair for each of you. Yellow or blue?"

"Boo."

"Okay." Libby took the blue chair and a red one for Meri, and hauled the girl and chairs back across the field.

"I think I'll sit here. If we get a mite thirsty, we have water and food in our own pack." Libby opened up Bethany's chair then her own camp chair and sat down next to her table. "You should take the table next to the tribe."

Meri groaned. "You know they'll be all worried about me."

Libby grinned unapologetically. "My turn last time. Your turn to get grilled and fussed over."

Meri glared at her sister. "You are so mean. Fine. Bethany, are you coming with me or staying here?"

Bethany grinned. "Here."

Meri ran across the field before getting run over by the soccer teams, grabbed a camp chair, and flopped down.

Lynette hiked over to Meri's table. "I take it we're setting up here?"

Charlie grinned. "I want to be here, but I suggest we sit a bit back from Meri's table. Be liable to be run over by little bits at halftime."

Lynette laughed. "True." She made herself busy setting up chairs, a camp table, and a bright red cooler stuffed with cherry waters, limeade, and similar snacks to Meri and Libby's, having long ago stolen their recipes.

"How are you?" Charlie asked Meri.

Meri grinned. "Good. Sore, a little, from learning to do new things with my arms and legs. I'm strong, but strong isn't flexible. I am pretty good with endurance."

Charlie nodded. "Comes with the territory." He dropped his last three camp chairs. Meri took out and unfolded her father's and River's chairs, and hung the sleeves they had come in on the back of the chairs. River squealed when she saw her mother, Jetta, and took off running.

Meri laughed. "Here one minute, gone the next."

Charlie laughed with her. "She does attach to me, though."

"That's good," said Meri, softly. They had been just babies when Jetta had escaped from her abusive husband with all four little kids. Their dad, a bear shifter, hadn't had a brother to knock some sense into him, because his brother had died in a bar fight. Bear shifter law was quite strict on the penalties for abuse; they were severe and permanent. Meri guessed that Jetta's ex-husband was long dead.

"I was worried about it. But loving on them as babies did something for them. They feel love for me, and I for them." Charlie growled very faintly under his breath. "If anyone ever hurts them…"

"Stand in line, behind Jetta, Lynette, and Jen. Moms and cubs, you know." Meri looked around. "Where's Jen?"

"Working on a house." Among other things, Charlie made tiny houses and Jen did excellent woodwork. "Client wants one on wheels, which is great because we can work on it at home. You know how your mom is with those little touches. She can fit more little spaces in a kitchen, like you can with your cases of food."

Jetta came up, huffing and puffing loudly, River giggling in her arms. "This. Child. Is. So. Heavy."

"Am not!" River sprung out of her mother's arms. Charlie lowered himself and River climbed on his back. "Horsey!" Charlie made horse noises and galloped off.

"That girl's going to be the death of me." Jetta stopped and touched Meri's shoulder. "Sorry, I…"

Meri grimaced, sighed, and hugged Jetta. "Sorry, moms, just getting irritated by everyone trying to guess how I am. I'm fine, but pretty tired. We hired Nat, the ref who's the deputy, over there, to train us." She pointed.

Jetta looked, let Meri go, then laughed. "Heard about that from Len. He's pissed as hell that you didn't want to learn acro yoga."

Meri snorted and sat down in her chair. Jetta sat down next to her, and Lynette passed over iced limeades. Meri pulled down her shades; the sun was striking the field, lighting up little kids in red and blue uniforms, determined to run after a black and white ball. "I don't want to make other people fly with my feet. You know me. I'm not that touchy-feely. I spent most of my time in beginner yoga falling over."

Lynette snorted. "That's why you and Libby never went into business together. Libby would hug everyone that came into her shop if it didn't break health regulations."

"She's got the human touch, that one." Jetta nodded her head. "Game's starting," They watched the kids run up and down, cheering for Adam and Bobby. They were cheerful and positive, never critical. There were strict rules against what they could and couldn't say. Coach Marguerita de Santos, known as Maggie, was small, short, and fierce in her devotion to soccer and her players. She wouldn't hesitate to cut parents out of games if they misbehaved. Coach de Santos had her caramel hair braided down her back, wild locks escaping as she ran up and down the field. She wasn't much taller than her tallest players, middle school girls who played later in the day.

Charlie left several times, once to exchange twin girls, and the other time to help Jetta take said girls to the bathroom. He cheered both teams equally because some of the kids from the polygamist community were on the other team, the one in blue. Charlie came back to help with Bethany on his shoulders during halftime, so Lynette went over to help Libby. They passed out water, saving the snacks for the end.

The game started again. Meri found herself noticing Nat running up and down the field, strides sure, ready with flags. She hadn't noticed Nat in school. Meri had stuck close to her sister and her family, and she just wasn't into track, soccer, basketball, hockey, volleyball, or football. Running bored Meri to no end.

Hiking, now that was fantastic. Hiking in the woods, turning into bears and running free. They stuck close to the clan's property during hunting season. The laws against poaching were quite severe in their hills. People tended to get more than fined; there was real jail time behind killing bears, wolves, or coyotes.

Charlie, Meri, Lynette, and now Jetta pooled their funds, and everything beyond running the farm and providing for four very active young kids went into buying land. They either left it undeveloped or gave it to the county in exchange for making it a crime to do anything on the land except provide hiking trails and camping areas with ceramic fire pits so the surrounding woods didn't catch on fire. Meri's brothers Len, Vic, and Davis and their wife Kandace were doing the same with land that abutted theirs and surrounded the commune. The polygamists thought that having bears and wolves around was interesting, especially since they never invaded backyards, attacked household pets, or rooted through garbage because most of them were actually shifters.

The game ended and the crush began. Lynette broke down their "camp," Jetta corralled the girls, Lynette helped Libby and Charlie helped Meri dispense food and drink and make sure empty containers ended up back in the coolers, and they all helped break down and fold tables and lug the tables and coolers with the empties back to Meri and Libby's vehicles. "Home," Charlie said to Meri and Libby. It wasn't a suggestion.

Libby and Meri grinned as they saw parents coming in for the next games lugging heavy coolers from their vehicles. "We'll end up being here longer next week," predicted Meri.

Libby groaned. "Don't wanna. I've been crazy busy all week. I want to put my feet up."

"Whiner," teased Meri. Libby pretended to punch her sister. Meri danced away, laughing.

They met back at the house and the boys seemed to have more energy, not less, after the game. They stood at the fence line and watched the boys run up and down the new bendable metal "hills" made for the goats. The goats joined in on the game, of course. Meri stood there with her mouth open. "That's just...wrong."

Libby laughed. "They're like wind-up toys. They've got three moms giving them chores just to get them worn out."

"Wibby!" Bethany yelled.

River slammed into Meri's legs. Meri *oofed*. "And the games begin." Libby and Meri took turns hauling the girls around like packhorses. They weren't allowed in the kitchen because both of them cooked for a living.

Lunch was blue corn soup with crabmeat, hot fresh herbed bread, and a salad with spinach, egg, and bacon. Dessert was little brownie bites with caramel Libby had brought from her shop. The boys ate, put their plates in the sink, washed up, then Jen led the boys off like a pied piper.

Charlie rinsed the dishes and filled up the dishwasher. "They're getting good at using sandpaper. Jen found gloves with Velcro attached, and she attaches the sandpaper to the gloves. She also has them varnishing and sealing the wood with polyurethane. They wear kid-sized masks that make them look like bugs. They love it."

"Any thoughts about bringing in another wife, maybe another set of kids?" Meri put the dishwasher soap in, closed it, and turned it on.

Charlie shook his head. "Not a one."

Lynette came up behind Charlie, and kissed him. "Right answer. Even if Jetta hates you tomorrow, she's ours. Not going anywhere."

Jetta came back down from upstairs. "They say they hate naps as their eyes close. Who's not going anywhere?"

Lynette laughed. "You. We've got ya, we're keepin' ya."

Jetta grinned. "Well, of course."

Meri glared when everyone stared at her. "Hey, I'm sad a young guy I knew died. His dad is devastated. The only good thing to come out of it is that Kevin Heeder realized he was in love with Frankie. They've moved in together."

Lynette grunted. "About time. I think Kevin was so busy concentrating on his son Ferris that he didn't notice Frankie was always there."

"Horrible way to find love, though," said Libby.

Charlie grinned. "I caught your sister eyeing Nat."

"Dad!" Meri glared at her father.

Lynette filled up the coffee pot, took down the tea. "Too blunt, love."

Jetta filled up a tea ball with lavender chamomile tea, her special blend, and turned on the electric kettle. "Way too blunt. Did you know that Nat was…"

Meri fished out another tea ball and filled it with a mint blend. "A jock? Yes." She pointed to the tea, and Libby nodded.

Libby handed Meri two fat black mugs. "Neither one of us are."

Lynette wiped down the table and counters. "Besides, those two were looking for bear shifters in other states."

Libby snorted. "We all know how that turned out."

Meri poured hot water over all three of their teas. "Hey, mine were great. Just very invested in where they lived."

"As are the both of you," Lynette pointed out.

"I always thought…" said Meri.

Libby sighed. "That we'd fall in love with another shifter. So did Len, Davis, and Vic."

Meri grimaced. "We live in a small town. Dating is so…public."

Lynette poured her coffee, doctored it with milk and lavender honey. "Who says you have to date anybody? You said you never really hung around Nat. You don't know Nat, his wants, dreams, if Nat is even looking to date."

Jetta sat with her tea at the breakfast bar. "Think of Nat as being behind a veil of light. You'll have to look past the light to see inside." Everyone stared at Jetta. "What?"

Charlie poured himself a cup of coffee. "Deep, honey." He reached over, took her hand and kissed it.

Libby sighed. "I want what you have. Closeness."

Meri snorted. "I want someone who gives me my 'me time.' Lots of it."

Libby laughed. "I think even if you had a sister wife, you'd take extra time for yourself."

Meri cut her eyes at Libby. "Who said anything about a sister wife?" Libby shrugged her shoulders. "No, just no. I like my own space, my own time."

Libby shrugged again. "You said it, I didn't."

"No. Just. No." Meri gave her sister a slitty-eyed glare.

Libby held up her hands. "Okay. Whatever you want."

"I've gotta go." Meri finished her tea, took her cup to the sink, then headed out the door.

Jetta stared, wide-eyed, at Meri's retreating back. "Way to drive her away."

"No, it'll take time. A seed was planted." Lynette looked over at Libby. "That was calculated, even for you. How long have you been considering this?"

Libby smiled. "About a year."

"Do you like Nat?" Charlie asked, stunned.

Libby smiled slowly. "I do. I like the way Nat touches me when showing me how to lift, snorts when I do something stupid. The problem is, Nat is understandably guarded. I don't know how to read that deputy."

Lynette nodded slowly. "Not yet."

Libby grinned. "Not yet."

CRAB SHACK

*D*elia was late; but Nat wasn't worried. Delia was always late. Nat had arrived less than five minutes ago, a full fifteen minutes after Delia demanded to meet. Nat perused the menu. Delia entered, braids woven through with gold and silver beads, scarlet nails covered with lines of gold. She strode in like she owned the place. Delia rarely came to the valley anymore; she lived nearly an hour and a half away in Columbia.

"Hey." Nat stood up.

"Hey." Delia gave Nat a brief hug, then daintily sat down in the chair. She waved over a server. "I'll have sparkling water with lime. Nat will probably have that spiced apple juice."

"And what would you like to eat?" Hayley took Delia's menu, a very fake smile on her face. She'd waited on Delia before; this was the only restaurant where Delia would meet Nat.

"I'll have the oysters on the half shell, and the cheese grits with shrimp."

Nat handed back his menu. "Crab cake sandwich, wedge fries." Hayley nodded and spun off.

Nat stared at his sister. "So, how's the party and wedding planning going?"

"The usual, professor meet-and-greets, engagement parties, weddings."

Nat wondered why Delia hadn't moved to either St. Louis or Kansas City, but apparently there was enough business in the sleepy college town where she lived in the middle of the state. "That sounds....interesting."

Delia laughed. "You would find it so boring that you'd kill yourself."

Nat nodded slowly, agreeing. "I might."

"Heard you had a murder." Hayley came back with the drinks. Delia wrinkled her nose when Nat took a pull from the bottle, not using a glass.

"Last death was natural."

Delia waved her hand. "Six months ago. Serial killer."

Nat nodded. "Painstaking police work. Took us months to put it together, get enough evidence so a conviction was a slam-dunk. Got him off the street on another charge while we built an airtight case." Nat did not mention that a wolf shifter had tracked a scent into the woods and they had caught the guy trying to burn evidence there. They had initially arrested the killer for starting an illegal fire.

Delia waved a hand, dismissing an investigation of a serial killer as unimportant. "So, you're good."

Nat sighed. "Yes, I'm good." Delia had been trained to poke at Nat from their mother. Nat decided to stop beating around the bush. "So, why did you want to hang out, Delia?"

Delia waved a taloned hand. "Can't I just want to spend time with my sibling?"

Nat gave Delia a flat stare. "A cliche? Really?" The server brought their plates, vanished.

Delia sighed. "It's Toni. She and I are kind of..." Delia ate some grits and shrimp with her spoon, careful not to damage her perfect manicure.

Nat shrugged. "Dated her nearly three years ago, she moved to join the fire department what...twenty minutes from you? And I live here, nowhere near you. Also, I dated one...no, two people since then."

"Who were they?"

"Does it matter?"

It was Delia's turn to shrug. "Not really." The waiter brought their food, and they dug in.

"Now that we've established that we don't care who the other person is dating, why are you really here?"

"Toni said I had to get your permission. So it wouldn't be weird."

Nat ate more of the seafood sandwich and grinned. "So, this isn't weird?"

Delia glared. "You know what I mean."

"Nice person, she moved away. A three-hour round-trip commute to see my girlfriend sucked too much for me to do it. The fact that I wasn't willing to do it made it clear we were in something that wasn't love."

"Lust? Sexual healing?"

Nat thought a minute. "A friendship with benefits, mostly. The sexual healing thing was kind of what we were doing. You know about Claire?"

Delia nodded. "Lied, cheated on her, lied some more."

"Nutcase of a woman. I'm not talking about someone with an actual mental illness. Claire enjoys chaos. That's something different."

"Yeah. So, you were her rebound person?"

"I had just broken up with Tricia, who moved to Canada. Loved her, slamming body, but her mom got sick. So, yeah, for both of us."

Delia sighed. "I forgot how blunt you are."

Nat shrugged. "No point beating around the bush. I've dated some excellent people. The point is, I give my blessing. I want you to be happy. I want her to be happy, with or without you. I hope you two make it."

"But you doubt it." Delia tapped a manicured nail on her glass.

"Wow, who's being blunt now? Your personalities are entirely different, and you're the ex-cheerleader and she's the working-class person who's going to be gone three to four days a week, and could be on call anytime. Dating a firefighter is never easy." Delia was usually into females with money, but Toni had investments and was smoking hot besides. Nat doubted it would last, but if both of them had fun, more power to them.

Delia grinned. "I'm busy with my new business, too." Delia had just gotten her real estate license when she realized catering didn't give her the life she wanted to become accustomed to. Nat suspected catering would end up being a side business in the future and eventually dropped, some poor sucker conned into buying Delia's catering business for too much money.

"I bet you are. Selling condos?"

"Like hotcakes. New subdivisions, plus a few classy old ones. Singles, new families."

"That's wonderful."

"You really mean that." Delia's eyes widened in surprise.

"I mean that. Haven't you figured out yet that Mom did the whole 'special child' thing with you to drive us apart? I've always been different. Never pretended to be something I'm not. That drove her crazy. So, any bad blood between us was artificial."

"And because we're totally different."

"Totally. But different isn't bad. It's just like, you know how people think country means you're stupid?"

"Is that a dig because I worked so hard to not order sweet tea and use doilies?"

Nat laughed. "No. I am proud of my love of sweet tea, and that I'm from a holler. I get that you are doing business every day, and that there are ignorant people who do think that country is stupid. So, no, be who and what you want to be. The past doesn't need to define you unless you want it to."

Delia snorted. "Too much introspection for me."

"Okay, no deep thoughts. What was the last home you sold?"

"This darling little two-bedroom townhome, actually, with a view of the cutest artificial lake with ducks…"

Nat smiled and listened to Delia prattle, keeping an eye on the room. Nat always sat facing the door to see who came in.

Delia had just paid when she said, "Nathaniel…"

"Call me by my name, or I won't answer."

Delia sighed. "Fine. Nat. Are you lonely?"

Nat thought for a minute. "Sometimes. People I care about move away. There aren't that many jobs. People tend to get something better and move on, even if they grew up there. Sometimes, especially if they grew up here. Living in a small town is like living in a fishbowl. I'm a jock. I like lifting weights. I also have a job where I can easily work a 12-hour shift if all the stuff doesn't get done, and I have to put in a double if anyone else is sick. Plus, I can get called out at any moment. Not someone a lot of people want to date."

Delia nodded. "Living in a larger town would be…better."

"Define better. Sunshine, mountain trails, lots of wildlife up in the hills. Mountain lions, bears, wolves. I can hear wolves howling at night sometimes. A million stars in the sky. No traffic, unless you count when a slow-moving tractor gets on the road. There's kindness in the people here. A slower pace of life I'm drawn to."

Delia signed the pad, added a hefty tip, and handed it back to the server. Nat didn't argue. Besides, Delia made nearly double Nat's salary with her new career. "What about love?"

"I gotta believe that if the Universe wants me to stay here, then I will find love. Or, the universe says no." Nat shrugged.

Delia stood. "You're so weird."

Nat grinned. "Yes, I am."

~

*N*at spent the rest of the day going out on call after call. Wilma Tain decided to walk her dog in the middle of the street. Nat established that Wilma was drunk, cited her for reckless endangerment twice, first for herself and second for her little pug Giggles. Nat arrested Wilma, put her in the back to curse up a storm, gave the dog some water from his own water bottle, and put the dog in the special soft dog carrier and enclosed the carrier in the mesh seat belt for pooches.

Nat called Bonnie, Wilma's sister. "Damn." Bonnie groaned. "She had been sober for two months. Would it be legal for me to take the dog?"

"I arrested her for being drunk with the dog in the middle of the road, traffic whizzing by. Don't see how a police officer like myself can cite you for stealing. Be protecting the animal. I seriously considered calling animal control, but sweet dogs with stupid names should not be in the drunk tank or in a pound."

"Can you bring the dog to me?"

"Don't see why not." By the time Nat dropped the dog off, Wilma was sleeping. Nat filled out the forms in the car, and woke up Wilma when they parked.

Deputy Carol Anne "House" Howser collected a stumbling Wilma. "When she comes to, tell her she won't be getting her dog back without a six-month sober chip," Nat told House.

House raised her eyebrows. "Can we do that?"

"Since she just recklessly endangered an animal on video, and I suspect her sister Wilma won't be giving the pooch back anytime soon, I reckon it's a true statement." House nodded.

Nat went back to the vehicle to do the computer work in a quiet place. His stomach sank when the call went out about a missing boy, Travis Yule. Travis had never made it home from soccer practice. A parent had taken video of the practice, and there were only hot, sweaty boys and girls, the coach, and a few parents, no one strange hanging around.

His mom, Barb, a bank teller, had returned home twenty minutes late when Mrs. Kavinsky wanted to open a new account five minutes before closing time. Barb had entered her home and found no son in the shower or at the kitchen table doing his homework. She'd immediately called his friends Augie and Dayton, but both boys were home and didn't know where Travis was.

Nat had an idea, and went to the place where hot post-practice tweens liked to cool off, the ice cream shop. His stomach lurched downwards when Travis wasn't there. Nat walked into Libby's bakery, and his stomach stopped its free fall. From the detritus on the table,

Travis had gone next door to the ice cream shop, ordered a double, came into Libby's shop, demolished a piece of brickle with his spoon, and dumped the mess onto his ice cream. Nat tapped his HUD by tapping his sunglasses, told the rest of the force to stand down, and called Barb. "Barb, your son is directly in front of me. He just got hungry."

"Oh thank God oh thank God." Barb's voice was teary with worry and relief.

"I'll get him home safe." Nat dropped the link.

Libby looked from Nat's face to Travis, who had looked back and spied Nat. "Oh, no." She walked right up to Travis. "Did you forget to tell your mom you weren't coming straight home after soccer?"

Travis' face was bright red, but that could have been from an entire afternoon of soccer. "I, um..."

Libby nodded. "So, here's what's going to happen. You're going to tell your mama where you're going every single time you come here before you come, you hear?" Travis nodded like a bobblehead. Libby looked up at Nat. "Do you have to bring him in, Officer?"

Nat made his voice gravelly. "That's a real serious offense in this town. What I think we need is an apology to a mom. What does your mom like to eat here?"

Travis pointed a shaking finger to the wall between the ice cream shop and the candy shop. "Kinda...not this. Green forest ice cream. The kind with mint, nuts, and malted milk balls?"

"Sure. That's coming out of your allowance. You're also making a contract between yourself and your mom to tell her where you are if you don't go home right away."

Travis nodded again. "Yes, officer."

"Now, clean up, so Miss Libby here doesn't have to. Then we need to buy ice cream for your mom."

"Yes, sir." Travis got up, cleaned off the toffee detritus by swiping a napkin over his table, and put the bowl and spoon in the bin to be washed.

Libby smiled. "See you soon. And, Deputy, please come back for your fudge and coffee."

Nat raised an eyebrow. "What for?"

"Saving boys from their mamas murdering them."

Travis gulped. "You won't let my mama murder me, will ya?"

"That's what the ice cream's for." Nat winked at Libby over Travis' head. "Mamas find it hard to kill their offspring while eating hardpack ice cream with a spoon. Too much trouble."

Nat walked Travis next door, helped the boy order the ice cream, then took Travis for a ride. Nat put Travis in a special protective seat. "Never been in a cop car."

"Don't make a habit of it, unless you have my job someday."

"I'll stay out of the back." Travis stared goggle-eyed at the bullet-proof screen behind Nat.

"You do that. Now, I suggest you write up a contract that you will tell your mama where you're going to be." Travis sighed and went to work. Nat parked, looked it over while they were around the corner from the house, approved it, then told the car to move again. They pulled in the driveway and got out.

Barb came out, and saw the ice cream bag in her boy's hand. "Don't think that makes this right." She hugged her boy hard, then said, "You've got half my chores for two weeks."

Travis nodded. "Yes, ma'am." He started to go into the house.

"Give me the bag." Barb took the ice cream. After the door slammed, she fervently said, "I thank you, Deputy."

Nat nodded. "Don't kill him. I promised you couldn't kill him while trying to eat hardpack ice cream with a spoon." Barb laughed, then the tears came. Nat held Barb around the shoulders until she pulled herself together.

"Nat, thank you." Barb wiped away her tears.

Nat nodded. "Anytime. Seriously, you needed help, you called. You did the right thing."

Barb nodded and wiped her tears. "I've gotta not kill my boy."

"He wrote out a contract." Nat sent Barb the link. "He says he won't let it happen again."

Barb nodded. "I didn't think of that." She held up her ice cream. "Melting. Thanks."

"Anytime." Nat trudged back to the car, and had the report nearly complete by the time the car pulled up to his next call. "Really?" Nat asked the Universe. Sure enough, Mrs. Mack's cat Bopp was in the tree right over Nat's head. Nat pulled off his low black cop boots, climbed on top of the car, and got the recalcitrant kitty to jump into outstretched arms.

Mrs. Mack came out of her tiny white shotgun house in a fuschia housedress such a bright orange-pink that Nat could find her from across the state line in the dark. "Bopp! Bad kitty!" Mrs. Mack yelled. Nat's sympathy was with the cat; the woman had a grating voice. Nat got a badly scraped arm when Bopp leapt away and ran around the back of the house. Nat sighed, climbed down, and put the boots back on.

"Can't keep that dadburned thing inside, howls like the dickens."

Nat ignored his scratched arms. "In the future, please call the non-emergency line."

Mrs. Mack snorted, and crinkled her enormous nose. "Who has time to look it up?"

"You do. If you call 911 for anything that isn't an emergency again, ma'am, I'll cite you."

"Idiot." Mrs. Mack went into her house, and slammed the door.

"You're welcome." Nat put on his boots, got back into the vehicle, and completed his report while the car took him, surprisingly, to the cop shop. Nat got out and walked into the small white brick building. Deputy Howser was at the front desk. "Hey. Sorry about the cat, glad the kid was okay."

"Hey, me too." Nat smiled at the scent of coffee. "You stole from the chief's stash." House put her finger to her lips, and Nat did too. Nat poured a cup of delicious coffee and grinned upon realizing it was a dark roast. He took the cup back to a battered metal desk with a chair that no longer reclined, and trudged through the backlog of electronic work–reports, file requests, requests for work on cold cases. The most interesting report was the robberies from cars and even of a motorcycle a few years back. Nat suspected a high school student because the robberies had abruptly stopped in late August four years before. Nat figured the student might come back from college, and may begin stealing again in order to finance student debt.

Finally, shift over, Nat stood to go, washed a coffee cup in the sink, and realized the cat scratches were still bleeding in three parallel lines. The deputy went to the first aid station and put antibiotic cream and a spray of SkinOnFast. Nat had gotten so caught up in busywork that the feline-related injury had been forgotten. He changed into jeans and a soft dark blue shirt in the locker room, signed out electronically, and headed to the door.

Nat walked out into the sunlight; the sun was low in the sky, so the lenses darkened. He took a single-person zip vehicle to the sweets shop.

Libby was there alone. "Where's Jeb?" asked Nat.

Libby looked up from cleaning a case. "Just missed him. I've got some toffee left, and a cappuccino?"

"Put some chocolate in the coffee." Nat paid for the sweets.

"Will do." Libby pointed to Nat's arm. "Let me guess. Mrs. Mack's cat treed himself again."

"Got it in one." Nat sat and smelled chocolate and coffee emanating from everywhere. Libby dropped off the food and drink and disappeared to clean up.

Libby came out and found the toffee and coffee both gone. "You must have been hungry."

"I am. I ate dessert first, but I've got to eat something. You seem to be about done here."

Libby smiled. "I am. Twenty minutes, and I'm out of here."

"Want to get something to eat together?"

Libby looked at Nat, and smiled. "I...I think I'd like that."

"I'll occupy myself. Front or back door?"

"Back. Make it thirty minutes. I have to change."

"See you soon." Nat waved goodbye.

Nat went to the vehicle and went home. It was time to feed Spook, a talkative Siamese rescue. Spook ate, kissed Nat's hand, then ignored

Nat in favor of climbing her cat house. Nat went back out and decided to walk back.

Libby was atin front of her door dressed in jeans, dark blue low boots, and a soft gold shirt when Nat arrived, smiling, at the base of Libby's circular staircase. "Hey, Nat." Libby clunked back down. "Where should we go?"

"I went to the crab shack today, but don't let that stop you. I could eat crab twelve meals a day."

Libby laughed. "You eat twelve meals a day?" She clanged down the stairs.

Nat walked with Libby out to the main street. "Six small ones. I travel all over town, so I bring stuff I don't have to heat in boxes."

"Good idea." They turned right onto the main street. "Garden Ristorante?"

"Sure."

There was an actual garden patio. The wind wasn't chilly yet, so Libby requested a table there. "Tapas?"

"Sounds good." They ordered bruschetta with olive tapenade, artichokes stuffed with sun-dried tomatoes and black olives, garlic shrimp, tiny potato omelets served in ramekins, and goat cheese served with peach alioli.

"How's the shop?" Nat grinned when the bread came first.

"I love serving the little darlings, until they deliberately spilled chocolate milk on my floor, then threw their plates on top of it."

"Cute. Love climbing on a car to get a cat, then get yelled at because the person didn't want to call the non-emergency line."

"Adorable. Oh, and the mom that thinks it's okay to let three–not one, but three–children run laps in my place."

"Mrs. Tiller. I've cited her several times." Nat sighed. "May I be blunt?"

Libby laughed. "You always are. Go ahead." The artichokes arrived, and they each took one.

"I thought it was undiagnosed depression. I tried to get her help. It turned out..."

"That she just doesn't give a shit. I know! I've tried talking to her until I'm blue in the face. I actually banned her."

"Really!"

"Absolutely. Her kids are eventually going to cause an accident she can't not-care her way out of."

Nat sighed. "Or get themselves killed. Or at least damaged."

"I wish I could call Child Protective Services, but she feeds them and doesn't beat them. They're growing up snotty and ruthless because she doesn't correct the things they do."

Nat ate a bite of artichoke. "This is amazing."

"Thought you'd like it. My last date took me here." She snorted. "Only date. He kept forgetting my name and talked over everything I said."

Nat snorted."Not from around here."

"Nope. Worked on tiny houses. My dad eventually fired him."

"Sounds like a peach." Nat grinned, then finished his artichoke. The potato omelet came. "This is even better. I don't usually eat fancy food."

"When would you have time? You're either working or at the gym. Or refereeing soccer for kids."

Nat laughed. "I also do go hiking and canoeing."

"Nice. You should hike on the trails behind my family's place."

"I might."

The shrimp came, and they dug in. They chatted about canoeing in the local rivers. Libby smiled. "Gotta dose yourself with sunblock and mosquito repellent once an hour, on the hour." They also agreed that the quarry swimming hole was the best on a boiling hot day. Spring didn't last long before summer's heat and humidity struck the town. "Gotta go when it's so hot you can cook an egg on the sidewalk, and the sun is so bright even your shades don't help."

"Absolutely. The water's like ice, but it's heaven on the hottest days."

They sampled the goat cheese. Nat groaned. "This is amazing."

Libby grinned. "The cheese comes from my family's farm."

"Ah."

Libby took a deep breath, then jumped in. "Why didn't we date in high school?"

Nat choked on his water. "Jocks and nerds didn't mix then."

"And half the people thought you were transgender."

Nat choked again. "What?"

"Sorry. I thought you knew. And that you, um, were."

Nat finally felt able to breathe. "Actually, I'm the wrong person. Jammy Newson is trans."

"The wrestler?"

"Yep, lives in Portland with her new husband."

It was Libby's time to choke. "What?"

Nat laughed. "I can't believe you didn't know."

Libby shrugged. "Learn something new every day."

"So, what is this? Two people who know each other from high school and around town? Possible friends?"

Libby grinned. "Wanna date me?"

Nat nodded. "I guessed that's where this was going."

Libby pushed away her plate. "How come tiny plates fill me up so much?"

"Don't know."

"So. Wanna date me?"

Nat laughed. "I heard you the first time." Nat ordered Italian blackberry soda. When the bill came, Nat split it with Libby.

Libby grinned. "Okay, so that's a no."

Nat smiled back. "I didn't say that."

"Would you rather date my sister? I can ask Meri."

"Actually, Meri's kind of cute." Nat grinned again.

Libby pretended to pout. "I'm excellent. But..."

Nat smiled gently. "I know that you come from a polygamist family."

"I do. Are you asking if I have polygamist leanings?"

"I know you're not religious."

"I'd consider it. I grew up with love and joy. I love my family. I wouldn't have it any other way."

Nat nodded. "You want marriage and children?"

Libby raised her eyebrows. "We got deep fast."

"No use dating someone if you don't know."

"As many as life gives me." Libby smiled softly. "I love kids, or I wouldn't do what I do."

Nat nodded. "Me too."

"Meri, too." Libby took a deep breath, plowed on. "I've been thinking about your dating both of us at the same time. This is a weird idea that's blowing my mind, and I have no idea if Meri's up for it. She's opposed now, but I suspect she's lying to herself."

"It could go horribly wrong," Nat agreed. "Also, I'm...let's just say we'd need extra help if I were to decide to be a baby daddy. My parts are smaller, and I'm sterile."

Libby blushed bright red, sipped soda. "What do you think of dating us?"

"Very simple. I get to date two people at the same time, and we can see if I'm compatible with either one or both of you." Nat finished the Italian soda.

"I'll send that balloon up, but it could turn lead-like real quick," Libby pointed out.

Nat shrugged. "It's just an idea. Nothing more. And the answer to your question is yes."

Libby smiled slowly. "Good."

"Why me? I'm a gym rat with a 24-hour job."

Libby grinned. "You're also hot."

Nat laughed. "So are you." Nat sighed. "I look like...well, a short man or a strong woman. I don't care. I am agendered. That means my own gender is not something I think about. I go by 'he,' by the way. Small town people generally don't want to use 'they' as a pronoun for a single person. In the big scheme of things, pronouns are less important than other stuff to me. Being what I am makes dating a bit more difficult."

Libby shrugged. "Actually, I find your compact body strong and attractive."

"I do try to keep in shape."

Libby grimaced. "Says the person going after my sister and I with calipers to measure our body fat."

Nat grimaced. "No numbers, then you can't see the change. Not weight, fat content of the body. We're changing from fat to muscle."

Libby held up her hands. "Okay." And that was that.

SHOCK

$\mathcal{M}$eri was on her way to her third food dropoff of the day when Libby called. "I had the weirdest time last night."

"Are you dead or maimed?" Meri asked.

"No. Why?"

"Unless either one is true, too busy. I have five breakfasts this morning, and I have to be done by ten."

"I'm talking as I'm dipping bananas. Lots of bananas. Then I have to roll them in cinnamon apricot granola."

"Yay. Not maimed, gotta go."

"Wait! Went out with Nat last night."

"Did you lift weights? No time." Meri dropped the link and grabbed the correct hot box. Mrs. Moulson was a stickler for on-time service. Meri entered the small but scrupulously clean home with a minute to spare. Mrs. Moulson had fallen and broken her hip last month, but was as sharp and feisty as ever. "I have your omelet."

Mrs. Moulson, a retired pharmacist, was dressed in a lilac long-sleeved top and purple sweatpants. The sweatpants annoyed her, but they were easier to get on and off. Her face was fading from a deep nut brown from all of her gardening to a far more chalky color. She still wore her patented pink lip gloss, and her nails were done in a pale gold. Her blue eyes in her narrow face were dulled from the meds and pain. "Hello, Meri."

"Good morning. I'll have your breakfast in just a minute." Meri plated the mushroom omelet, got the fruit salad she'd already brought out of the refrigerator, added the blueberry yogurt and some chia seeds, and brought the food out on a tray with a spoon, fork, and napkin. Meri made a little strawberry smoothie in the tiny blender and brought it to Mrs. Moulson.

Mrs. Moulson already had her meds lined up like little white, blue, and pink soldiers. She had also already consumed half her omelet. "Thank you, dear," she said in a scratchy voice tight with pain. She consumed her pills.

"What else can I get you?"

"Nothing. Jeppy will be by to work on me, and he'll clean up." Jeppy was a home health nurse who was also a licensed physical therapist, a huge ex-football player. The man knew pain, and was the most gentle person ever.

"I'm going to go, two more people to see. I'll see you for dinner." Jeppy would reheat Mrs. Moulson's lunch.

"Thank you, dear." Mrs. Moulson gave Meri a little wave.

Meri locked the door behind her. She tried not to run to the vehicle, but Bonkers and Richard were both on the other side of town. She got in and told the vehicle where to go. Meri did some accounting on the way. Mostly everything was online and her software was very good, but clients came and went. Her schedule was a color-coded mess. Meri had to make the food, get it where it needed to be, and run the business too.

Bonkers' real name was Yonkers Pugh. Bonkers had bright orange hair, a flat face, a beak of a nose, a ready half-smile, and a loopy way of looking at things. He'd been hunting for fallen branches when he fell and threw out his back because he was a whittler, sculptor, painter, and occasional photographer. The yard in front of his trailer had a giant metal bird in flight, a glassy round water feature that wasn't plugged in, and a man's head Bonkers had carved with a chainsaw that looked like a cross between Presidents Lincoln and Obama.

Meri hopped out as soon as the car stopped. Yonkers was on his front porch, whittling one-handed with the wood between his knees. "Hey, girl, what's up?"

"Got steak and eggs."

Bonkers grinned. "Now, that's how I like my morning." Meri brought out the hot case, and walked it up with the silverware wrapped in a napkin. She knew better than to get him a plate; he ate it right out of the little box inside the case. "Meri girl, is this a pepper steak?"

"With mushrooms and roasted bell peppers." Meri had sliced the steak and veggies thin, making the food easier to eat.

Meri opened a second container for him. "Hoo-ee! Home fries with jalapenos! Y'all sure are good to me!"

Meri laughed. "Your insurance company is good to me. I'll make you some fresh lemonade, and then I'm on my way."

"Naw! You can't sit a spell?"

"Sorry, no can do." Meri carefully closed the screen door so it didn't bang shut behind her. She'd done that her first day, Bonkers had started, and his subsequent groan had made her feel guilty for a week. She made some lemonade with a bag of fresh lemons she'd brought with her, and she macerated some fresh bing cherries and threw them in, too. She filled up a water bottle with the drink and brought it out to him, and he sipped it right away.

Meri checked and made sure Bonkers had sandwiches and cut-up fruit for lunch, and the carrot curls he loved to dunk in ranch dressing. He was low on ranch dressing, so she ran back to her vehicle to get another container out of her cooler. She put the dressing in the refrigerator, and ran back out to the porch. "Bye, Bonkers! Talk to ya when I can't see myself coming and going!"

"See ya, girl!" Bonkers waved to her with his fork.

Meri made it on time to see Richard, the retired electrical technician who lived in a Craftsman-style wooden home in a gorgeous glen. He had a mop of white hair that looked like spun cotton, a round face, wide nose, and huge hands. Meri went around to the backyard. Richard sat in an Adirondack chair he had made himself. He was a quiet, reserved man, more at home with his hands in wires or planing wood than talking to people. So, he'd turned to woodworking.

Richard smiled at Meri. "Hello, Meri."

"Hello. Excellent day, isn't it?"

"It is. Not hot yet, but it will be soon enough."

Meri unloaded her hot and cold packs. "Eggs, bacon, biscuits." Meri emptied the other pack. "Strawberry yogurt." Meri sprinkled muesli and chia seeds on top.

"Just like I like it." Richard liked to eat healthy. He had been a meaty man, with years post-high-school football of lifting weights. Then, his wife had died suddenly, and he'd alternated eating nothing and bingeing, making his weight yo-yo and giving his doctor fits. Richard's listlessness after his wife's death had made him uninterested in cooking, so his doctor, pharmacist, and psychiatrist all suggested using Meri's service.

Richard had begun feeling better while eating healthier food, and spent most of his time outdoors. When it rained that spring he began to learn advanced woodworking. His teacher, Old Man Ruiz, came twice a week to teach Richard how to make things like wooden boxes or lamp bases. Both men would silently work, Richard watching Ruiz like a hawk. Richard did fine milled work, nothing like Bonker's sculptures.

Meri checked the refrigerator, and walked out with the empties in a storage bin. Meri brought Richard more than enough for three days–whole wheat pasta with pesto, chicken enchiladas, Reuben sandwiches with small red baked potatoes, a chicken Caesar salad, and a red sweet pepper sausage bake.

Meri went back out to talk with Richard. "How are you?"

He gestured towards the Adirondack chair next to his. "Hear you found a dead body."

Meri sat down on the chair next to Richard. "My first. Actually surprising it hasn't happened before now, considering a lot of my clientele are recovering from major illnesses or injuries."

"Injury." Richard felt the word in his mouth. "Yes, losing Etta was an injury."

"Kinda felt like then when I saw Ferris. Like I'd been stabbed in the heart. He was a nice guy, you know?"

Richard nodded. "Etta was a really good person. Came from a farm west of here. Never minded my long hours, being called out in all kinds of weather to restore power, fix problems all over town. She never minded a thing, just kept on giving back in any way she could."

Meri nodded. "I know. She was concerned about others, you know? I'm hearing from people all over town how her passing has cut a hole in all sorts of organizations. The donated clothes closet, food pantry, after-school programs."

Richard huffed out a laugh. "She called herself a 'professional volunteer.' Ex-military, you know. Gotta be in the thick of things. She went out with the other ex-soldiers after catastrophes. Tornados, hurricanes, floods. The only thing she wouldn't do was gardening. Said she had a black thumb. She'd dig a hole for a tree, that sort of thing, but no working in the dirt."

Meri realized she needed to eat; her stomach was trying to gnaw a hole straight through her belly. She patted Richard's hand, got up, collected the plates, rinsed them and put them in the dishwasher, then made sure she had all the empties. Richard came in, washed his hands, and went out into the woods with his walking stick to the trail behind his house.

Meri put her empties in the vehicle and decided to head to the diner. She parked, went in, sat down, waved at Ruby, and ordered a chicken burger on whole wheat and fruit salad with a strawberry lemonade. Nat came in, saw her, smiled, and sat down across from Meri in the booth.

Ruby, her hair dyed so red that it hurt people's eyes, came up with a pot of coffee, snapping her gum. "Usual?"

Nat shook his head. "No, I like Meri's lunch. Bring me one of those, no onions, honey mustard, bacon wrapped instead of bun."

"Got it." Ruby snapped her gum, turned, and went to fill up everyone else's coffee.

"Why me?"

"Your scintillating conversation?"

Meri snorted. "My abs hurt and I had trouble washing my hair in the shower."

"So, you hate me?" Nat grinned.

"No, just deep dislike. You torture me."

"Hey, I told you low impact does not equal low intensity."

Meri glared at Nat. "You used torture devices."

Ruby dropped off the food and whirled away. Nat calmly ate a strawberry, then laughed. "You stood on an elastic band and lifted weights. Not so bad."

"The one around my thighs hurt!" Meri complained. "And I want to eat more. A lot more."

"Good. The harder you work, the more calories you burn. Remember what I said about the correct proportions of fats, carbs, and protein, and about consuming more protein at night. Have you found a protein powder you like?"

Meri grimaced. "They taste like chalky powder in almond milk."

Nat laughed. "They are chalky powder in almond milk. Some are too sweet, some will pucker your lips. You'll have to experiment. Some are white or clear powders that can be mixed with juice."

"Ugh."

"Did you have a chance to talk to Libby?"

"Too busy." Meri ate her last piece of cantaloupe. "I had five break-fasts to deliver this morning. I'm good for lunches; most of my clients have helpers, physical therapists, or home health aides who help them heat up my food. Plus, lots of the lunches are just sandwiches, salads, and/or soups."

"Alrighty then. What do you enjoy making the most?"

Meri tilted her head. "No one's ever asked me that question."

"Not even your sister?"

Meri shook her head. "She makes candy, scones, that sort of thing. I make regular food. I prefer...I think it's the entire process. I put soup in the slow cookers; I have two huge ones. Then, I make the things that need to bake, then start cutting up things for the sandwiches and one-pot dishes or stir fry. I put everything in the boxes when it's had time to cool, then do other things until the slow cookers ding at me. It all comes together at the end."

"Nice process." Nat grinned and ate the last bite of chicken burger.

"It all just...flows."

"I'd like to taste your cooking sometime."

Meri looked up. "Are you fishing for a date?"

"Not fishing, asking. Do you want to date me?"

Meri waved her hand. "Don't know."

Nat stood. "Think about it." Nat grinned, paid the bill, and left the flummoxed Meri to process what just happened.

~

*M*eri muttered to herself about her strange day as she went back home and picked up her afternoon food. Mrs. Moulson liked soup at night, and loved Thai chicken soup with fresh Thai basil. Richard was good, so Meri didn't have to worry about him, especially since he seemed to slowly crawl out of the sink-hole of grief every day. She made Bonkers his favorite, catfish and corn fritters, all baked. They tasted like they had far more calories than they actually did.

Charlene Oskamp was a runner and didn't eat after six at night, so she was right after Mrs. Moulson. Charlene also had twin tweens who were never home because Karli was heavily into track and field and Bobbi played drums in the marching band. Bobbi hated vegetables, and only ate them if they were "hidden" in her food. So, Meri made wraps for her with dipping sauces. Karli and her mother Charlene ate nearly all veggies, lean meats, and sushi. Meri was getting sick of making such boring food, but the clients were nearly always right.

She dreaded visiting the last family. Mrs. Tiller cared enough about her kids to make sure they ate properly, but couldn't be bothered to actually make anything for them. Denver was eight, a towhead with a motormouth, at least one limb always moving. Ricky was six, a serious boy with curly dark hair and huge brown eyes who got into trouble because of his brothers. Beau was five with blond hair and was absolutely fearless. Beau had no idea what would or would not get him killed, maimed, or yelled at.

Their mom, Josephine Tiller, never raised her voice at them. She didn't correct them at all, refusing to tell them to sit down, stop, be quiet, none of that. It wasn't that she was a so-called "free range" mother who let kids push the envelope to figure out what they could and couldn't do. No, Meri believed, and from talking to Libby, so did her sister, that the woman just didn't care. The walls were covered with crayon markings. Toys were everywhere and most of them were completely shattered. The furniture was sagging where the kids jumped on it. But, the kids wore clean clothes, and the kids ate because she paid Meri to make meals that even Beau could make.

There were no bugs in the house and the bathrooms and kitchen were clean, the floors mopped and vacuumed, because Mrs. Josephine Tiller paid Consuela Ochoa to come in five times a week to clean and do the laundry. Consuela had cleaned out the refrigerator and washed out all the empties.

Both Libby and Meri had dutifully reported their concerns to Nat. The deputy had explained that there is no law against outsourcing parenting. In fact, the boys were better off with professionals feeding and cleaning up after them.

Luckily, all three kids were in the backyard and not under Meri's feet. They ran around screaming like banshees, destroying the swingset. Mrs. Tiller sat in the backyard drinking her way through a six-pack of soda.

Meri heated the food and put it on the table, along with plates, silverware, and little sealed cups of almond milk. Chocolate for Denver, and strawberry for the other two. Beau hated beef, so that was out in the house, except for when Mrs. Tiller specifically requested a steak. Tonight it was turkey burgers, baked French fries with the requisite puddle of ketchup, except for Beau, who liked a puddle of mustard instead, and brown sugar baked carrots. Meri knew most of the carrots would end up in the trash, but she felt she had to try. She put the little ramekins of apple cobbler in the microwave oven to be reheated later; even Beau knew how to press the buttons.

Meri hauled the empties out to her vehicle, then went around to the backyard to call the kids in. Meri pointed towards the kitchen. "Food. Clean your hands." She made her voice clear and concise. "If you don't, I'm taking your dessert away." They ran, screaming, to the bottle of antibiotic hand gel just outside the door. They each slathered on the gel, wiped it off onto their grimy jeans, then ran inside.

Meri turned towards the woman on a lawn chair. "Hey, Mrs. Tiller." The woman crossed her splayed feet, thereby keeping Meri from seeing up her dark blue muumuu. Her face was bloated, her eyes piggy and mean. Mrs. Tiller hauled herself up, then launched herself towards the door without saying a word.

"Have a good day, Mrs. Tiller." Disheartened, Meri turned and walked towards her vehicle.

Meri went home, unloaded her van, then emptied and refilled the dishwasher. She stared at the contents of her refrigerator, but nothing looked appetizing. She realized she craved chocolate, plus her sister had called. So, she went to steal chocolate from Libby.

Meri parked around back and found her sister in the sweet shop's kitchen, dipping apples in caramel. "Sit down. Pecan and chocolate?"

"Sure." Meri put her head in her hands.

"You look as exhausted as I am." Libby used a towel to punch a button on the microwave. The smell of strong coffee and chocolate filled the air. "I was going to call you." Libby expertly stuck the popsicle sticks in, dipped them in caramel, then rolled them in crushed pecans.

The microwave dinged, and Meri went to the microwave and took out two tiny cups of espresso. "Bless you." Meri sat down and began to sip. "I just came from the Tiller house."

Libby drizzled the last apple with chocolate, sliced it up, plated it, and handed it to Meri. "I am so frustrated with that woman I could scream. Why have three kids if you don't want them?"

Meri sighed, took an apple slice. "Was she a good mom before Jacob died?"

"No. Not in the least."

"I suspect that she started hiring people to do what her husband used to do before he died so she wouldn't get arrested."

Libby finished the tray of apples. "Baby daddy Jacob was a really weird guy."

"No one was surprised when he won the Darwin Award for driving Venture Pass in the rain on that ancient bike of his." The Darwin Award, an imaginary award for dying stupidly, was accurate in this case. Venture Pass had over a dozen hairpin turns; only Jacob Tillman would have been idiotic enough to ride it in the pouring rain. He had been killed instantly after he hit a branch and went airborne a month before his youngest child was born.

"Omigod. You make the best caramel-pecan apples."

"I do. Do you feel like cooking? I don't." Libby put the tray of apples in the refrigerator, poured the rest of the caramel and chocolate over a tray of peanut butter fudge, then put the tray in the refrigerator. She took Meri's plate, rinsed it in the sink, and turned on the dishwasher for the last time.

"I have no urge to be in a kitchen at all. No offense." Meri wiped down the table, then washed her hands.

Libby grinned. "None taken."

They ended up in Libby's apartment, and ordered a mozzarella basil pizza with pesto, mushrooms, and red bell pepper. Libby brought out two cherry sodas and they clinked cans. "So, you tried to talk to me this morning. What was it about?"

"Dinner with Nat."

Meri put her feet on the recliner. "I had lunch with Nat."

Libby raised an eyebrow. "Really. Do tell?"

"Nat wants to date me." Meri laughed. "I never even looked at Nat that way, you know? Jock and all. But we started working out, sweating together…"

"I like how Nat moves." Libby grinned.

"Wait, do you want to date Nat too?"

"The fool didn't tell you?"

"Tell me what?"

"Nat wants to date us both."

Meri stared at her sister, goggle-eyed. "Wait. What?"

Libby snorted. "Might as well date us both, find out which of us fits better as a pair."

"That's..." said Meri, speechless.

"Well, we went together to meet some of our bear prospects."

"Yeah, and that worked out so well."

"Well, let's see if either one of us is compatible. Are you feeling any jealousy?"

Meri stared at her cherry soda. "No, not really. I mean, Nat could end up as crazy as Jordan Racca."

Libby laughed. "No one is as crazy as Jordan."

"Do you remember when that idiot left me stranded on the mountain? I didn't even know on which side Jordan's house was! I had to go bear, and a hunter could have taken me out!"

Libby waved a hand. "I remember when Jordan woke me up at three in the morning squealing about some fight with Carrie. Carrie said she hadn't spoken to Jordan in over a week." Carrie was Jordan's roommate. The two had loved to fight.

Meri finished her last piece of pizza. "I guess it isn't a bad idea. We can compare notes, see if there's any crazy going on."

"We need some ground rules. We keep each other's secrets, don't talk about sex, and don't hurt each other."

Meri nodded. "And no jealousy or games." They bumped fists and grinned at each other.

HAPPY TRAILS

*L*ibby parked at the trailhead and called her brother Len again. "Are you sure you don't want to go hiking? We can go bear."

"The word is still 'no.' Back-to-back clients. Just had one, waiting on the next one, behind Dad's barn. So, I'll see you when you get back."

Libby blew out a breath. "Hate you," she said cheerfully, and hung up. She stretched, and was shocked to see Nat walk up. "Whatcha doin'?"

"Heard from Meri you were planning on hiking this trail. I'll go somewhere else if…"

Libby shook her head. "Nope. I'm planning on doing the ridge hike. Minimal steepness, inclines are pretty gradual."

"Where's the fun in that?" Nat did a double check of his backpack's water and snacks. Their hiking shirts had mesh along the sides; silver and maroon, the local football team's colors over lightweight hiking pants, Libby's in blue, Nat's in a deep olive green that matched his eyes.

They set out with long, gliding steps. Libby led the way. "Day off?"

"Sundays and Mondays. I had this afternoon off because I put in some overtime due to our new schedule, four ten-hour shifts. I arrive earlier, leave later. I'm able to go out on far more calls, so swing and graves aren't so overwhelmed catching up. Weirdly, my other day off is Wednesday, but I get called in for overtime. The county hates paying it, but mainly I cover breaks. Not a full shift."

"Who do you cover lunch for?"

"We have a property room officer who is also the dispatcher, the public information officer, processor of people and things, and helps us get rowdy people into the jail. She also processes dog licenses. Her name is Deputy "House" Howser. That woman needs lunch. Becomes a monster without it. Amir, that's Deputy Cazalos, needs me to keep up with calls while he's on lunch, too. We've also got Leland just over the hill in the next county, Deputy Leland Fortra. Man needs lunch as well, and he's got even more calls than we do. We'll share calls if we're not backed up so he doesn't get overwhelmed. We're on call at night; just rare that we get a call. Amir and I take turns with that, but we'll both get called out if there's a murder, a bad accident, or something like that."

Libby sighed. "I've got weekend people, which sounds weird. I do Saturday or Sunday if anyone gets overwhelmed, but we're mostly busy after school. We don't have a lot of tourists, and we have limited hours both weekend days. If I don't take time off, I get evil." She grinned as they left the dappled trees for a stretch of bright sunlight. "Someone who sells candy can't go to the dark side, unless it's dark chocolate. Great way to lose business permanently."

"Make one mistake, people tend to remember. That's why I tell people to lay off the stupid. People won't look at you the same way again."

Libby stretched out her spine and it audibly cracked. "I remember you leaving to live with Coach Ma."

Nat grinned. "Best thing I ever did. My mother is controlling, needy, and wanted me to be someone she wanted. All male all the time, but I was too short and rangy for her. She wanted a football player, but I liked volleyball, track, and soccer."

"I was lucky. Never for one moment did I believe I wasn't loved. Dad always looked at us with love, and having several moms meant there was always someone to pay attention to us. The only problem was, if you can call it a problem, is that I couldn't get away with too much idiocy. And, my brother Len lost his twin and his dad. They were family friends before my dad married his mom."

"My boss was there for that. Said it was horrible."

Libby sighed. "You lost your dad, so you get it."

"One day there, one day gone. Leaves a loss the size of your heart for years."

"Good news is, I could get angry, yell, cry, hit pillows, just not my brothers. Or Meri, but she did bear the brunt. I went stone crazy, and she went quiet."

"I went...I guess, that's when I got my most blunt. Quiet, but blunt. I got sports crazy, and that helped. Let me kick or hit the shit out of a ball, or run a trail, or something."

They went under the canopy again, and the trail got a little steeper. "We went deep fast."

Nat shrugged. "I am what I am. A vault. I know stuff about people of this town they wouldn't want to share. Who's cross-dressing, who got pulled over for reckless driving because the toddler in the back-seat was having a meltdown, who goes to what meeting."

Libby led them around a curve. "How do you know about the meetings?"

"What do you think pushes people over the edge to finally get help? It often doesn't work, though. Addiction is one of the few diseases that tells you that you are not in trouble."

Libby smiled. "We're lucky; that's not in our genes." This was primarily because bear shifters threw off the effects of alcohol and many drugs so easily. They did get addicted to other things, though. "Hmm. I think...no, I know I'm addicted to chocolate."

Nat laughed. "It's unlikely you'll get arrested for drinking too much of it. Unless you pour hot chocolate on someone else."

"Or serve terrible chocolate, but I'd arrest myself before I did that." Nat laughed. "What I have to do is more hiking, to get rid of my thunder thighs."

Nat sighed. "You do not have thunder thighs. Do you need more muscle and definition, endurance, and flexibility? Yes, you do. Do I? Actually, yes. I would like to bench more. Cardio helps. Can't spend all your time in the gym."

Libby grinned. "First-world problems."

"Exactly. My life is great. I get to meet and talk to people all day long. Solve problems, if I can. I have above-average health care."

Libby groaned. "Expensive for myself and my employees. But, I must offer it. Be a fool to lose good people because I didn't have a plan for them. Have to sell a lot of fudge to cover it, though."

Nat touched her hand, and they both silenced. A doe browsed in the copse to their right. Libby caught her breath as two more deer arrived. They scented the two hikers and bolted. Libby smiled like the sun coming out. "Gorgeous."

Nat grinned. "I love hiking and long-distance running because I get to see wildlife."

The trail narrowed, and they were silent as they huffed and puffed a bit going up. Libby led them to the left, and the path curved. There were wooden beams on the trail stair-stepped as they climbed. Libby and Nat sipped water. They made it to a curve, then Nat touched Libby to stop again. Birds chittered in the trees, squirrels leaped from branch to branch, and there was definitely crashing to their right. The buck leapt over the trail, then crashed off through the underbrush. Libby laughed. "Talk about exiting stage left."

They made it to the lookout. Libby shared her peanut-butter-stuffed protein balls. Nat grinned. "These are amazing. I like your chocolate, apricot, and blackberry ones, too."

Libby passed him another snack. "Tell me how many you want to consume a week, and I'll sell you a box."

Nat nodded. "Sure. May I make a suggestion?"

"Always welcome from you."

"Bring boxes to the gym to sell, or refillable sealed packs of two or three for snacks. They'll sell out in minutes."

Libby pulled out her phone, made a note, put it back in her mesh pocket. "Love increasing my income."

A black bear burst out of the woods. Nat froze. "Don't worry, Nat. They hang out near the house, and they are nearly tame."

"This is not a trick question. Do you know him as a person?"

Libby took several deep breaths. "You know? About shifters?" Nat nodded. Libby stared off into space, then said, "Um, yes, they are. That's my brother Len, the asshat who said he couldn't go hiking today." The bear sat in the middle of the trail. "Either he had a cancellation or he was lying to me." Len raised a paw, and Nat and Libby both raised their hands back. "How do you, um, know?"

"Had the speech when I was hired. Saw a young man shift from human to wolf. Wouldn't have believed it if I hadn't seen it with my own eyes." Nat looked over at Libby. "Ah. High school makes more sense now. No sports despite the fact you were all scouted."

"We kind of have an advantage, even out of bear form. Meri and I both have to taste our food that we cook for others, and we don't like our percentages of body fat. That's the only reason we're going to the gym."

Nat crouched down and looked at the black bear, arms on his knees. The bear snuffled Nat's outstretched hand, then turned towards the path. The bear looked back, as if to say *Why aren't you following me?* Nat stood up and began to follow the bear.

Libby snapped herself out of her shock, caught up, and said, "I was going to tell you on our next date. Although you're really good at dealing with the weirdness of life, I thought that this might be a dealbreaker."

Nat looked at Libby out of the corner of her eye. "The entire family?"

"Kids too, when they turn four or five."

"Oh, wow." Nat walked with purpose, slowly, mind churning. "Do you eat as bears?"

"Not unless we find a beehive or some really good berries. Takes a lot more to fill us up. Better to eat as a human."

"Sweets. It's why you do what you do."

Libby grinned. "It is."

Libby nearly jogged up the trail until she got even with her brother. She put her hand on his fur. Nat sighed. "I have to prevent myself from rushing forward to rescue you."

Libby laughed. "Safe as can be. Len wouldn't hurt anyone in either form. Although he did lie and say he wasn't coming."

They ambled up the trail until Len stopped for blackberries. Libby and Nat risked catching their clothes on the thorns and ate a handful each. They washed their hands in a small stream. Libby touched Nat's hand. "I hate to do this to you..."

Nat grinned. "I bet you want to go bear."

"In both senses." Nat laughed. "I know this is our first date..."

"I've never seen a naked woman before." Nat pretended to be in complete jaw-dropping shock. Libby doubled over with a belly laugh.

They reached the top of the rise. Libby pointed ahead then back the way they came. "There are two ways down. You can turn around, go down and keep heading right, and it will drop you off where we entered the trail. Or, you can circumnavigate the peak by going forward and rotating right until you end up at the fork we didn't take."

"Cool."

Libby grinned. "Wait for the magic." She took off her pack, stripped down, put her socks into her shoes, and put her shoes on the bottom of her pack, followed by her clothes. Libby wore a pink camisole with a shelf bra and matching boy shorts. She stripped down further until she wore only a smile, put the underwear in her pack, and slung one of the loops over her neck and hung it behind her. Nat looked at her eyes, caught not a whiff of self-consciousness. Nat felt his heart thud in his chest, his palms begin to sweat. Then, Libby got on all fours. There was light, and then a bear stood in front of Nat.

The bear shuffled over, and Nat helped Libby as a bear adjust her pack more solidly on her back. Libby snuffled Nat's hand and gave a lick. Then, she ambled over to her brother. Libby and Len both raised a paw, and Nat held up a hand. Then, they took off into the forest.

Nat snorted, then laughed. *My girlfriend just went gorgeous-naked, turned into a bear, and abandoned me to run in the forest with her brother.* Nat decided to forge ahead and circumnavigate the mountain. The views were stunning, the mountains a thousand shades of green. Nat ate a nut and fruit bar and stopped at three separate overlooks.

Nat saw Vic Camber coming up the trail and waved to him. "Hey, Nat. Have you seen Libby or Len?"

Nat decided to blow his mind. "They're in bear form. Up there."

Vic goggled. "You know? About us?"

Nat laughed. "I found out about the wolf shifters when I took this job. Yes, I know, and yes, I'll keep the secret."

Vic coughed. "Um, okay. We're having a cookout. You're invited. I will try to get those two out of bear form and down the mountain. Just cross the street at the bottom and go straight."

"Sure. Have fun finding the family." Nat continued walking down the mountain.

At the bottom Nat heard crashing, turned, and saw one bear with no bag and a second with a bag batting at each other. Vic, in human form, followed them. "Hi, guys. Libby, your brother Vic invited me to the party. Is it okay if I go?" Nat addressed the bear with the pack. Libby raised a paw, and pointed straight ahead with a claw. "I'll take that as an okay." Nat looked both ways, crossed the road, and jogged down the trail, following the scent of barbecue.

Lynette raised an eyebrow when Nat showed up with two bears in tow. "She couldn't resist walking with Len, huh?"

"Nope. Our second date, and she abandoned me to turn into a bear and walk with her brother."

Lynette burst into laughter. "I bet you never expected to put those words together in that particular order."

"Not ever." Nat pointed. "Vic got the bears down."

"I can see that." Lynette turned to the bears. "You two get changed and dressed. Oh, fudge, too late." Two cubs came flying down the hill and barrelled into the two bears. The one on the right got a paw entangled into Libby's pack. The baby bear howled. "Excuse me! Gotta go!" Lynette ran over, disentangled the cub, and took the pack off. "I'll put these inside, Libby." The cubs pawed their aunt and uncle.

Nat had to laugh. It was weird, thinking of them as bears and people simultaneously. He walked up the slight rise to the picnic tables. "Nat!" Meri said. She looked over at the bears, then back at Nat. "So, you know?"

"It would seem so." Nat grinned at Meri's nonplussed expression. "I was read in when I became a deputy on the shapeshifter thing."

Meri grinned. "I thought that would be a more difficult conversation. And that there would be sex first."

Nat burst out laughing. "No, none of that yet. With either one of you."

Meri raised her eyebrows. "You were on a date with my sister when she changed."

"Just a hike, but, yeah. I saw her naked and everything."

Meri burst out laughing. "Bet that wasn't how you thought that would go."

Nat shrugged. "Not exactly, no. She saw Len and got furry."

Meri nodded. "You have to help with the salads."

"Okay. I only cook grilled cheese, pasta, and breakfast, and I can tear lettuce. I can also put sugar equivalents on berries and call that dessert." Nat shrugged again.

"Oh, you poor dear. We'll get you straightened out." Nat mock-glared at her. Meri led Nat to the outdoor sink and they washed up.

Adam crashed into Nat's leg. "You are my ref. Do you want to play soccer?"

"I'm supposed to make a salad."

"We'll pay you to go with him." Vic panted, half-jogging up to them.

"Don't need pay. I like kids." Nat looked down at Adam. "Do you need a player or a ref?"

"Ref. The girls want to play as bears, and we don't let them because they spike the ball with their paws."

"No paw spiking of balls. Good rule." Nat followed Adam to where he was ready to face off with his brother. Nat took the ball, then dropped it. Adam kicked it hard and ran after it. Bobby followed him. Nat used his fingers for a whistle when Bobby kicked his brother, called a penalty. They ran up and down the side yard. The goals were small and not close to regulation, but the boys had fun.

Sure enough, the cubs came up, wanting to play. Nat pointed at the huge farmhouse. "Go in the house and change. Come out in clothes and shoes." He received a halfhearted swipe for his trouble. "None of that. I can't change like you, and if you damage me, I'll be really upset." The swiping bear hung her head, then both the girls changed and ran naked into the house, giggling like loons. Lynette sighed and went in to make them dress.

"Well, that was something," Vic came over and handed Nat a glass bottle. "I'm hearing you like this stuff. Some sort of spiced apple drink." He used a key and popped off the top for Nat.

"I do. I'm never really off duty." Nat handed back the bottle, ran after an out-of-bounds ball, threw the ball back in play, and took back the bottle.

"So, you're courting my sisters?"

"If that means I'm dating them, yes, I am." Nat, parched, took a pull from the bottle, and whistled and called a penalty as Adam body-checked Bobby. "Rough, aren't they?"

Vic laughed. "Bears. If they're not scrapping, they're eating sweet stuff." He sighed. "The girls went bear early. Surprised us all."

"You have a problem with me dating your sisters?"

Vic shook his head. "Never tell a female who she should or should not date." He barked out a laugh. "Just surprised. Unless you're religious, most people don't court two people at the same time."

"Well, it's a matter of demographics."

Vic snorted. "I guess that's true."

"Also, might as well find out if I'm not compatible with one or both of them. Saves time."

Vic stared at Nat. "You are so strange."

Nat shrugged. "Been hearing that all my life."

Vic nodded. "I know your mom. She's a bit...pointy with her disregard."

"Directed at me."

"Ah. Explains some things."

"We can't be in the same room." Nat took another pull on the bottle. "You're gonna warn me to treat your sisters right?" Nat called the score as Adam scored again. Bobby pouted while Nat crossed over to throw the ball in between the boys.

"No," Vic said when Nat rejoined him. "Those females will kill you if you hurt them. In either form."

Nat nodded. "Not that easy to kill. Ex-National Guard."

"Awesome. Knew you went away to college."

"Criminal justice. I tried to be a PE teacher, but found out I do better teaching one-on-one. Plus, I blew out my knee."

"Sucks. Playing soccer?"

"Cycling race. Hit by a car. No longer cycling, and I got my degree in criminal justice and became a cop. Guy who did it..." Nat whistled, and Bobby got a penalty for shoving his brother. "He was drunk and playing with his cell phone at the same time, and he went through a barrier. Nearly killed another cyclist. I got his plate number. They caught him one state over."

"That really sucks. You got run over, blew out your knee, and still got a plate number?"

"And got disentangled from my bike enough to drag my leg behind me to help the other cyclist. She ended up becoming a champion three years later. I almost became an EMT, but nailing the guy who hit us helped me solidify my decision. Besides, I had too much physical therapy to want to be a physical therapist or EMT and I had some PTSD. Got some meds and some therapy, nightmares gone within six months."

"My admiration for you blooms."

"I'm also very blunt and apparently see the world in too much black and white."

Vic snorted. "So do I sometimes."

There was one loud whistle, and the kids abandoned the ball and headed towards the food. Vic pointed to the picnic area. "Food time. Let's get washed up." They walked towards the giant picnic tables groaning with food and washed their hands at the outdoor sink. There were fruit, potato, Caesar, and pasta salads at one end of the table. There were tortillas, grilled chicken and fish, and bowls of regular and mango salsas, cheddar cheese, and sour cream in the middle. They passed the tortillas first, then filled them up.

Nat stood between Meri and Libby, listened to them sing, sat, and let the wash of family news pass over him—soccer games, hikes, the swim when the girls attempted to drown themselves by forgetting to change into bears first, a possible camping trip on the next weekend. The plans for a camping trip had to be checked and double-checked, with the route, the camping site, and a list of things people tended to forget.

Lynette sighed. "I forgot underwear for one kid once. Heaven forfend sharing."

Jetta laughed. "My bad. I didn't check to see if someone was trying to take his brother's stuff out and put it away."

"Sabotage," Meri said, cheerfully. "I once deliberately took out Libby's pet mouse. Stuffed, not real," she explained to Nat. "But I forgot that she couldn't sleep without it. I got no sleep because she didn't. I quit sabotaging after that."

Jetta grinned. "Bobby had a meltdown about sharing clean underwear. I explained to him that sabotage has negative results."

Nat couldn't help laughing. "Not the problem between Celia and I. She has far more wiry hair than mine, so we couldn't share a lot of products. We wore different clothes and loved different colors. So, we didn't fight over the same things." He sighed. "My mom manufactured stuff for us to fight about. Stupid and pointless. I refused to participate."

Meri nodded. "I can see that."

Nat took a bite of his Caesar salad as Vic talked about his brother Davis. "I kept switching out the Legos. That worked until Mom made us keep all our Legos in the same bin."

After lunch, the kids ran around in bear form. Meri walked Nat back to his car. "I've got to do fascinating chores like laundry." Nat grinned, then hugged Meri.

Meri nodded. "I've got to sweep and mop. Then a very long nap."

Libby ran up to Nat. "I'm sorry I bailed on you."

Nat laughed. "If you've gotta go furry…"

Libby hit Nat on the shoulder. "Yeah, well. Anyway, we can do something…"

Meri snorted. "We can do chores at each other's houses."

Nat waved a hand. "I have a better idea. Meet up tonight? Pizza?"

Meri nodded. "Seven?"

Libby snorted. "Six."

Nat nodded. "Cool. Meeting up or staying at home?"

Libby raised a hand. "Over my shop. I've got to go to bed early."

"Movies." Meri held up her phone. "We have a streaming service."

Nat gave both sisters a little wave. "Okay. See you later."

～

*M*at came with a case of the cinnamon apple drink and two liters of soda, and took the pizza from the pizza delivery driver, one vegetarian, one meat lover's, at the bottom of Libby's stairs. Nat walked up the stairs, and Meri opened the door. The smells of acetone and nail polish warred with cinnamon and chocolate. "Come in. Pizza!" Meri took the pizzas and brought them over to the coffee table. Nat put the drinks in the kitchen, and took out a bottle. Libby handed Nat a bottle opener.

Meri held up a VR rig. "We can go VR."

Libby shook her head. "Maybe later. Chick flicks?"

Meri pulled up the streaming menu. "Horror?"

Libby pointed at a picture of two lovebirds staring into each other's eyes. "Romantic comedy?"

Nat sought a compromise. "Action with romantic subplot."

Libby grinned. "Good idea." They sorted out their drinks, sat down, and chose their pizza slices. Libby also had little cinnamon chocolate bites that they all loved. They watched a movie about magical thieves and the cop with special mental powers who tracked them down, then fell in love with a coworker from another realm. They wolfed down pizza and cinnamon chocolate, cracked jokes, and made fun of the bad guys.

Libby fell asleep as the credits rolled. "Early sleeper." Nat covered her with a blanket.

Meri nodded. "I'll put her cell phone under her pillow. She wakes up to it shaking. If you have an alarm, she'll throw it. Broke numerous alarm clocks and a cell phone or two that way."

Nat grinned. "I never knew she was so violent."

Meri snorted out a laugh. "Let's go."

"When are we meeting again?" Nat asked as they put on their shoes, slipped out the door, and walked down the metal stairs.

Meri stepped aside as she reached the bottom of the stairs. "I'm so busy. And tired. I plan on sleeping tomorrow."

"I also plan to sleep tomorrow. Very exciting life. I'm so busy I can't do any work during the week. I did the dusting this afternoon and sprayed everything down. Mopping and laundry are tomorrow, and meal prep."

"So, we can do it in the same place? Or meet afterward?"

"You're persistent."

"I am." Nat hugged Meri, gave her a half-smile, waved goodbye, then jogged down the street.

HELP

$\mathcal{L}$ibby came over to Meri's at ten in the morning. "I'm here to help. My place is so small I did all the cleaning, mopping, dusting, and the laundry. I'm tempted to go into the shop, and that's a bad idea. My people have it well in hand."

Meri handed her a basket full of laundry. "Fold this." Libby sat down and started matching socks. Meri put a wet load in the dryer, and put another load in the washer. She danced backwards to the bathroom, and sang off-key as she cleaned. Libby cringed, put on rock to drown out the singing, finished the laundry, and started on the dusting. She then swept and vacuumed, and Meri did the mopping.

Libby sighed. "I am so bored. Getting up at the crack of dawn on weekends is bad."

Meri snorted. "I got up an hour ago." She sighed. "Bored as well."

"Let's go to the gym."

Meri stared at Libby. "Who are you, and what have you done with my sister?"

"No, really. I want to lift something heavy."

Meri sighed. "Fine. You folded my workout clothes." She grabbed yoga pants and a sports bra and went to change. She came back out in a t-shirt with a cute kitten on it and workout shorts.

Libby filled up water bottles and handed one to Meri. "Shall we call Nat?"

Meri sighed again. "Not yet."

They slung their sports bags over their shoulders and walked to the sports center just behind the high school. The day was sunny and clear. They saw Nat going into the gym, and followed the deputy in. "What are you doing here?" Libby asked Nat.

"Training. Got my chores done last night. Want to join in?"

Meri grinned. "Why not?" There were teen girls on one side and adult women on the other.

"Practice with my peeps." Nat pointed. "We've got the giant rope, the giant balls, medicine balls which are weighted, weight bars, box steps or jumps, and mats for aerobic kickboxing. We rotate through the moves. Did you bring your gloves?" Meri and Libby fished them out of their bags and put them on. "Okay, this is the plan. Meri, Libby, watch what I do. I'll help you modify it if you need it." They took out their water bottles and put their bags against the wall. "Let's do this." They rotated through. Nat helped Meri and Libby keep proper form.

By the time they were done, Meri and Libby were gasping, puffing, and red-faced. Nat patted each of them on the shoulder. "Good work."

Libby put her hands on her knees and gasped. "That. Was. Horrifying."

Meri wiped her face with a towel. "It was. We stink. We need showers."

Nat pointed at the showers. "I'll help put this stuff back while you two shower." Meri and Libby staggered to the showers, gasping like fish.

Nat met them outside after putting the stuff away and taking a super-fast shower of his own. Libby and Meri left their sports bags in their lockers at the gym. "Let's get some low-carb food."

Meri shook her head. "Church ladies. Fighting them for food."

Nat nodded. "Crab Shack has a salmon steak with veggies."

Libby smiled, and Meri nodded. "Lead the way," Libby said.

They walked there, and got a table before the church ladies descended on the humble shack. They all ordered the salmon plate with asparagus with lemon sun tea. Meri waved a hand at Nat. "So, the gym thing."

Libby chimed in. "Helped after Nat's dad died."

"And you left your mom because…"

"A little diggy," Libby chastened Meri.

"Sorry."

Libby glared at Meri. "She's not sorry."

Nat laughed. "I became an emancipated minor and moved in with my coach. That's what you're asking about?"

Meri nodded. "Yes. Do tell." Libby rolled her eyes. The salmon came, and they dug in.

"Well, Mama didn't want me to play volleyball. I broke my wrist, and, to be fair, she really didn't have the money or time to be dealing with my injuries. But volleyball kept me from getting in trouble. I was so angry after losing my dad. She didn't get that. Wanted me to 'give up this nonsense' that I couldn't give up without losing part of my identity. She wanted me to be a boy and play football. I never cared about gender, which drove my mother insane."

Libby passed Meri the pepper grinder. "So, no child abuse."

"Physically, no. Coach Ma kept telling my mother she was irrevocably damaging her relationship with me. I left, and Mama told Delia, my sister, not to talk to me until I moved back. Delia and I didn't reconnect until she turned eighteen."

"That's sucky." Meri passed the salt to Nat.

Libby snorted. "Stupid. If any of my moms or my dad tried to drive a wedge between us…"

"Wouldn't happen," Meri assured Libby.

"My mama began driving a wedge between Delia since we were little, praising her, putting me down. Then, she yelled at me for not being manly enough."

Libby sighed. "We're fraternal twins. No one ever expected us to act, look, or like things the same way."

"Libby's sweet, I'm more matter-of-fact. She hates alarms, I have three. I love chicken, she prefers fish. We both love honey and cooking." Meri grinned at her sister.

Libby grinned back. "We do. How are you with your sister now?"

"She's dating an ex of mine."

Meri raised an eyebrow. "That's...wait, the firefighter? The one that moved away?"

"Yep." Nat ate an asparagus spear.

Libby cut her asparagus. "I'm cool with that. But what happens if Meri wants to date a girl?"

Nat shrugged. "Cross that bridge when we come to it."

Libby snorted. "Be weird in a small town."

Nat squeezed more lemon juice on the fish. "Be weird to date two women at the same time, no matter where I lived. But, it's faster this way. Rule each other in or out."

"If we break up, are you going to turn evil or crazy on us?" Meri asked. Libby elbowed her.

"Nope. At least, no more so than normal. Probably lift too many weights, maybe eat too many carbs, go on super-long hikes."

Meri laughed. "Sounds like my last breakup."

"So, weirded out yet?" Nat waved his fork around.

Meri shook her head. "Nope."

Libby speared the last piece of her asparagus. "Not yet."

"Okay, then. I'm off Wednesday evening. Anyone want to get together?"

Libby nodded. "Plan on it. I'm in bed early, though."

"So, early dinner." Nat took his last bite of fish.

"Walk, maybe." Meri sipped her tea.

Libby groaned. "No walking, too tired after work."

"So, Meri and I walk, and I meet you at your shop on Wednesday."

Meri nodded. "Sounds good."

Libby shrugged. "Okay."

They paid the bill. "Walk around a little," Meri suggested. "My legs will cramp up if I don't move." Nat nodded, and held the door open for them.

They stepped aside for Farrah, who was going in, wearing her church clothes. "You!" Farrah screamed.

Nat stepped in front of Meri and Libby. "Yes, ma'am?"

"You heathen!" Farrah screamed at Nat.

Nat raised one eyebrow. "That's a new one."

"You fornicator!"

Nat raised both his eyebrows. "That's a really new one. We're blocking the door."

"We are," Libby stepped away, dragging Meri with her.

Nat let the door go. "Have a nice day, ma'am." He turned to walk away.

"I'm not done!" Farrah screamed, her helmet hair holding steady despite her bright red, sweating face.

Nat turned around, very slowly. "I am."

Farrah's veins stood out on the side of her neck. "I'm calling the sheriff! I'm reporting you for lewd acts!"

"I would say go ahead, but you'd be wasting his time, and he won't like that." Nat kept his hands out, his voice low and steady.

Farrah pulled out her phone and called 911. Nat sighed. "Guys, I'm sorry this person is disrupting our day."

"So you admit it!" Farrah screamed.

Meri stepped forward. "Admit what? That we ate lunch together? We did!"

"You are doing unnatural things!" Farrah screamed.

Meri's eyes flashed. "Wow. Acting ugly in public to me and to my sister, and my friend. Is there a charge we can make against her for that?"

Nat nodded. "Hate speech, disrupting a business."

Jack Macy, the owner of the Crab Shack, came out, an apron over his khakis and blue shirt, his brown hair slicked back. "Why are you screaming, Farrah? Such a foul mouth, too. If you don't get away from my business, I'm calling the sheriff. By the way, you're not welcome here. Been kicked out of nearly everywhere else, and now you can't eat here, too."

Nat saw flashing lights. "Too late."

Deputy Amir Cazalos drove up and exited his vehicle. He had a narrow patrician nose, black hair, and very dark shades. There were obvious muscles under his uniform. He walked up to Nat. "What's going on?"

Farrah wrinkled her nose and jabbed a finger towards Cazalos. "Where's the sheriff? I elected him!"

"Ma'am, the people of this town elected him." Deputy Cazalos took out his pad and began poking it.

Farrah glared. "Don't need no darky taking down my information." Jack, Libby, and Meri sucked in air through their teeth.

Amir remained calm. "Ma'am, I'll call him, but I still have to fill out my paperwork. What seems to be the problem here?" Deputy Cazalos let Farrah go off on her rant while he filled out his forms.

Sheriff MorganTaylor pulled up and he unfolded himself from his vehicle. His eyes sported deep wrinkles from the sun. "Zip that over to me, Amir, and I'll do the rest." The sheriff turned to Farrah. "Ma'am. Apparently you believe that my deputy is dating someone?"

"Your deputy is doing unnatural acts!" Farrah screamed.

"First of all, that's legal in this country, unless my deputy did something in the streets to scare the children or the horses." The sheriff paraphrased Mae West.

"Arrest her and these lesbos!" Farrah hissed.

"I was born male, but whatever." Nat shrugged.

Jack waved a meaty hand. "I'd like to swear out a complaint against Farrah here for damaging my business."

Deputy Cazalos nodded. "Come with me, Jack." They went over to the deputy's vehicle.

"He can't do that!" Farrah screeched.

"You are under arrest. You have the right to remain silent. Anything you say can and will be used against you in a court of law…" Sheriff Taylor read Farrah's rights to her.

Farrah turned a shade of crimson not normally seen on anyone except after a workout. "Arrest her!" she pointed at Nat.

Sheriff Taylor finished reading Farrah her rights. "You're disturbing the peace. And overly obsessed with gender. Nat, did you turn on your glasses?"

Nat nodded. "When we stepped away from the door, yes, sir."

"Good. Give the footage and your report to Amir."

"Yes, sir."

Meri held up a hand, pointed to her sunglasses. "I was recording, too."

Libby's eyes teared. "I forgot."

Meri rubbed her sister's arm. "We'll give reports and footage, too."

Taylor put plasticuffs on Farrah. "For your information, I don't care if my officers date one person or twelve people if everyone's consenting adults, what gender they are, where they come from, what language they speak, or what color their skin is. Your prejudice is getting you arrested. Don't know what got your panties in a twist today, but you might want to let go of the hate." He looked over at Jack. "Besides, you'll have to cook at home from now on. No one else will let you eat there."

Farrah literally howled and tried to sit down on the sidewalk. The sheriff pulled up on the twist tie and frog-marched her to Amir's vehicle. Amir opened the door and held down her head. Once in the car, she began kicking the seat in front of her.

Sheriff Taylor got the mesh on her, stood, shut the door, and walked back over. "I am so sorry you had to hear such filth. I can't prevent her from acting like an idiot. Her daughter's given up, won't talk to her. The church ladies avoid her. I can only hope we get her some help, but she's refused any and all assistance so far."

Libby shook her head. "Sad. But she can't think her behavior is normal."

"Her daddy was...let's just say, to her, this is normal." The sheriff's eyes betrayed a hint of frustration.

They gave their reports, and the cop cars drove off. Wordlessly, Libby held out her hands. Meri took one, and Nat the other. Libby pointed down the street. "Let's go to the park. We can walk around and get the cobwebs out of our minds."

Meri nodded. "Okay." Nat just gave a small, sad smile. They got almond milk strawberry ice cream from a vendor at the entrance to the park and ate their cones under the shade of a huge oak tree.

Libby sighed. "I have no idea why she thought that was acceptable behavior."

Nat sighed. "I am so sorry you had to hear that."

Meri shrugged. "People will never understand what we are. It is what it is."

Nat nodded. "Sometimes education doesn't work. Especially if you had a bad educator, like a parent."

Libby finished her ice cream and stuffed the napkin into a nearby trash can. "I can't believe…" She choked a little. "I can't believe such hatred exists."

Nat stepped forward and wiped away the tears falling down Libby's face. "She's a broken person. Broken people hate. The amount of energy it takes to keep that going is…"

"Exhausting." Meri pulled her sister into her embrace. "I love you, BooBoo."

Libby laughed. "Love you back, Yogi."

Nat snorted. "You love old cartoons?"

Meri grinned. "Our dad loves them."

"Come on in." Libby pulled on Nat's arm. He stepped in, and they hugged.

The park was huge, with giant oaks, maples, and trails winding among them. The entire left corner side had a variety of workout machines and an enormous playground with a fort on one end and a corkscrew slide on the other, with bridges, slides, and a fake rock wall. There was a rubberized surface on the ground underneath to prevent a steady stream of kids from falls and therefore trips to urgent care. Normally, the park was full of shouts, screams, and laughter. The kids were still in church or after-church Sunday dinner, or were playing video games somewhere. Off to the side there was a steep hill the kids used to toboggan and sled down in winter. The center provided greenspace for people to play soccer and flag football, throw balls and frisbees for dogs, and have picnics. There was a sandy volleyball pit on the other side, the net sagging a bit in the middle.

"We've got to have a picnic here before it gets hotter." Libby looked around and dried her tears.

"Would be awesome," Nat agreed. They circumnavigated the park, talking about nothing much. Soon it would be summer, hot and humid, kids running around everywhere. After a sizzling summer, the trees would completely change, the leaf peepers would drive through, and the writers and leaf peepers would move into the tiny houses spotted all over town. Birders would come through, too, watching birds fly south for the winter.

Meri turned to her sister. "When are you going to get that wall knocked out in between the ice cream shop and your store? Seriously, the two businesses complement each other so much."

"Sales are really good, even on slow weekends. Very steady. Anyway, I'm looking at winter when Penny closes up, probably November."

Meri tilted her head. "Wait. Doesn't she start serving peppermint stick ice cream in winter? And serve it with hot chocolate?"

"There's room for a little play area; she's going to consider having that installed, too."

Nat grinned. "Whoa. That's cool. What, with a ball pit and a little slide, and those tube things for the kids to crawl around in?"

Libby nodded. "Exactly. Draw even more parents in. Probably do that later; the remodel will be expensive enough."

They got all the way around the park, and Libby took their hands again. "I don't want to separate. Let's do something."

"Miniature golf, grab food at the sports bar, movie..." Nat ticked choices off on his fingers.

Libby jumped up and down like a three-year-old. "All three!"

Meri laughed. "My sister likes being a kid." So, they went to the miniature golf place. Libby was silly with her shots but lucky, Meri was precise, and Nat was accurate. They laughed their heads off, and then won some stuffed animal keychains at the carnival games section. Kids ran around screaming, hyper from huge lunches and liberal doses of sugar.

Meri, Nat, and Libby played video baseball in the batting cages in the corner. Libby had a great eye, and hit several homers while Nat and Libby cheered her on. Then they went to the sports bar and watched soccer while Nat pointed out the good players. They had bar food, stuffed mushrooms, mozzarella sticks, and mini barbecue chicken sandwiches. Libby tried Nat's apple juice and liked it, while Meri turned up her nose and stuck to soda.

They walked back to Libby's place; she was beginning to yawn and stretch. "I had a great time."

Nat bent down and kissed Libby's head, then her lips. They were soft, pliable, gentle. "Good night." Libby clanged up the stairs, sports bag over her shoulder, and waved.

Nat walked Meri to her vehicle. "I had a good time, too." Meri instigated her own kiss, deep and smoky. The kiss lingered, deepened.

Nat stepped back, and smiled. "Looks like we don't have compatibility issues."

"Doesn't seem to be a problem." Meri waved and got into her vehicle.

Nat turned and walked away, hands in his pockets, whistling. Nat walked back to the bar, watched one more game, had another apple drink, then headed around back and walked two blocks home. Once there, Nat petted Spooky and gave her more food. Spooky responded with purrs, startling Nat. "You like me now, huh?" Spooky hopped down, twined around Nat's legs, and led the way to bed.

RIVER

*T*hey floated, Meri in a kayak, Libby up front and Nat in back of a canoe. The Twelve Points River flowed, twisted back on itself, then wound its way forward again. The canoes had Ritchie's Rainbow written inside a rainbow arch in the front of each boat that sliced through the water. Nat took in the scents of Libby's strawberry shampoo, citrus mosquito repellent, the slight whiff of plastic from the little cooler that held their drinks and sandwiches. Clouds of gnats hung in clouds just above the water. Willows dipped their pale green fronds into the water. Frogs chatted to each other, and the whine of insects was nearly deafening at times. The day was hot, the air so thick and humid the prow of the canoe seemed to be cutting through it. The water was a deep green-blue and housed catfish, rainbow trout, striped bass, and hundreds of minnows zipping around. Fisherfolk were on the bank in lawn chairs drinking from cans as they tried their luck. Other canoes skated past or pulled over to climb the fall of rocks to see the waterfall up above, one of the many creeks that fed the river.

They didn't bother talking. What was there to say? Besides, they might scare the fish, who liked to jump, showing silver bellies before plunging back into the river.

It just felt...right.

Meri pointed her prow at the rope hanging from a thick tree branch that leaned out over one of the deep swimming holes. Nat steered while Libby got them turned. They pulled the watercraft completely out of the river and Nat used heavy stones to hold the craft in place.

Meri raised an eyebrow. "Overkill much?"

Nat shrugged. "Hefty hike to the road from here. Besides, Ritchie and Millie would charge us for their watercraft if we lost them."

Libby grinned. "On another cautious note..." She pulled out twin spray bottles from her cutoff shorts and pointed them as if she were about to enter the O.K. Corral. "Who's first?"

Nat grinned, shoved the last rock in place with his left foot, and stepped forward. "Be gentle."

Libby snorted. "Take off your shirt." Nat pulled off his battered blue sleeveless shirt with a picture of a starship with "My ride is faster" written underneath. He lowered his knees so she could shoot him in the face, and then Libby shot him on his neck, back, and shoulders with sunscreen. He rubbed the sunscreen into his face, then held out each leg to be shot. He rubbed in the sunscreen while Libby shot her sister. Then, it was time for Nat to shoot Libby with the sunscreen. Under her pale blue t-shirt with a picture of a cat reading a book with the legend "Catastrophes" she had a crimson bandeau top. She slid off her shorts and Nat nearly had a heart attack when he saw her matching boy-shorts bikini bottom.

Meri laughed. "Nat, your eyes went completely out of your head."

Libby looked over her shoulder at Nat, who was shooting her back with sunscreen.

Meri laughed again. "Ooga ooga eyes. The deputy can't keep his eyes off of you."

Nat choked, then said, "I'll get you, ma pretty." He chased Meri over the rocks with the sunscreen and shot her legs and arms.

Libby doubled over laughing. "Good shot."

Meri snarled and stripped down to her cobalt blue tankini. She rolled up her crimson top and cutoffs and put them in the kayak.

Libby stopped laughing long enough for Nat to put his shirt back on. She put her own top and shorts in the canoe. "Last one up goes last!" She darted up the hill the sycamore tree had created with its roots. She tested the rope swing, made sure to aim for the deepest part of the river, swung out, and let go with a whoop. She came up gasping.

"You okay?" Nat was last because Meri moved like she had springs in her feet.

Libby choked, then laughed. "Cold. Spring was too short. Guess the river's telling me where it comes from."

Meri grinned. "Snowmelt, originally." She grinned, waved her sister out of the way, and swung out. She landed with a whoop and a huge splash.

Nat couldn't enter the water because Meri and Libby decided to get into a splashing contest and he didn't want to land on their heads. "Move, ladies, coming in." Meri and Libby floated slightly downriver to get out of the water, and Nat jumped in. He scrambled out again as soon as possible because Libby was right. The water was freezing. He got out just in time to see the women make it up to the top, their hair glistening with water. He lost his breath, righted himself, got out as Meri went first this time with another whoop. Libby followed with a madcap giggle that had him laughing. Nat swung in, and found himself rising to the challenge.

Nat managed to finally make it up to the top before either woman jumped. "I'm getting tired! How are you two still running up here? Do you have batteries in your legs?"

Meri laughed. "This is the best place to go bear. We used to be able to before Ritchie and Mille started with the canoe thing. We hop in, hold our feet, paddle around. Plus, fish. And blackberries." She pointed to a blackberry thicket along the bank.

Nat laughed. "I can just see you in the water, holding your feet. Both of you." He smiled. "Your bears are beautiful." He grinned. "And big. No making you mad."

Meri smiled. "You better stay on the right path, Nat. Making a bear woman mad is a bad idea." She laughed as Libby went flying out over the water.

Nat looked upriver and sighed. "Ladies, we've gotta get out of here. We're about to be invaded."

Meri looked at the fleet of canoes heading toward them. "Libby! Company!" She pointed.

Libby sighed. "Damn." Meri swung in, then Nat. They got out, dried off, and shot each other with the sunblock and mosquito repellent while the other canoes landed just upstream of the swimming hole.

"Coach Nat!" A young girl with freckles, her midnight-blue hair in a braid, waved. Nat waved back.

"Coach Nat?" Meri asked, perplexed.

"Helped Coach Ma a lot, before she followed her daughter to Malaysia." Nat pointed to their watercraft. "Let's get out of here before we get overrun."

"I hear you." Meri pulled the kayak into the water, hopped in, and started paddling, Libby and Nat right behind her. They heard the screaming and splashing kids for two entire bends in the river.

Ritchie was waiting for them by the picnic tables in Marchand Waterfront Park. He was built like an orangutan, all bandy legs and arms, and had the red hair and windburned skin to match. He expertly dragged the watercraft out, checked them for leaks, and flipped them. Nat and Meri helped him carry them to the truck. He already had several inner tubes on giant spikes on the top. Libby carried their towels and the cooler to a picnic table under a giant oak, laid the towels out to dry, and took out their chicken salad sandwiches, can of potato chips, and cans of soda. They sat down and ate in absolute silence.

Nat finished first, and cleaned up. "That was…"

"Perfect." Libby grinned.

"Exhausting." Meri stretched. "I'm so tired I can lay down right here."

Nat laughed. "We could lay our towels under that oak there. Ritchie won't be going anywhere until those teens get here anyway."

Libby grinned. "All right. Let's do that." They lay there, heads together, looking up through the tree branches at the clouds floating by. "They look like cotton candy up there," Libby observed.

Nat grinned. "That they do. At night, more so. All golden and candy-crush pink."

Meri laughed. "Did you just reference a video game?"

Nat shrugged. "Best one to play when you want to clear your head for five or ten minutes."

Libby grinned. "I don't do this enough. Or ever, really."

Nat looked at her out of the corner of his eyes. "What? Lay around looking at the sky?"

Meri nodded. "We used to do this all the time on the farm. Lay around on a lazy summer day. Read books, or just nap."

Nat smiled. "Rest, you two. I'll keep the little darlings from attacking you when they show up."

Meri grinned. "Okay." Nat felt the women go boneless, one by one, slipping off into sleep. He grinned, let the sun hammer down on him, the two most interesting women in town on either side of him. He propped his head up on his elbow and watched the clouds go by.

❧

The thundering herd of preteens left Libby's shop. She nearly fell down with exhaustion. She'd barely had a minute to breathe since the store opened. She knew Penny next door had the same problem. The kiddies liked to mix Libby's goodies and ice cream, so there was tremendous traffic between the two businesses. "I need a hole. Right there." Libby pointed at the wall.

Mary Beth grinned. "I know." She pointed to the tiny office. "Make a deposit in the safe, sit, eat. I'll get this place cleaned up."

Libby nodded. "I can't even..."

Mary Beth shoved her boss. "Go. Be free."

Libby opened the tiny refrigerator under her desk and ate her chicken curry egg salad sandwich as fast as possible. She ate her potato chips so fast she barely tasted the salt. Mary Beth reached in with an espresso, and Libby grinned. "Nectar of the gods." Once it cooled somewhat, she downed it like a shot of Jack. She grinned, stood, washed up, sent Mary Beth on her break, and grinned when the lacrosse team came in, all banged up and sweaty, with pints of ice cream to share from next door. Libby sold out of the mint fudge, butter brickle, and both the peanut butter and the cashew white chocolate toffee. She cleaned up, brought out more trays, and filled up the marshmallow treats before they disappeared. She even sold out of her gluten-free snacks.

The last line ended, and Mary Beth stumbled over and turned the sign to Closed. "I am so sorry."

Libby shook her head. "No, I'm sorry. You get an hour off tomorrow. Run before someone tries to sneak in." Jeb snorted from his table. "And no comments from the peanut gallery."

"Wouldn't dream of it." He looked up from his e-reader. "Aren't you violating the law by letting that one work late?"

Nat entered despite the Closed sign. "Who's breaking the law?"

Libby locked the door behind him and sighed. "I did. I didn't notice the time, and Mary Beth stayed nearly forty-five minutes past her time."

Nat laughed. "I'll have to arrest you. Did you run your register report, or may I purchase some toffee and a cinnamon cappuccino?"

Libby sighed. "Okay, but last customer."

Nat raised his eyebrows. "I'm sorry. I can just…"

Libby shook her head. "It's all right. I'm just so tired I'll need to be carried home."

Nat laughed. "Promise?"

Jeb made a choking noise. "Too much information." He brought the plate with the crumbs of his orange chocolate chip scone and the tea tray to the sideboard. "I'll pretend I heard nothing."

Nat laughed. "Sorry, Jeb."

Jeb waved his hand. "S'all right. See you tomorrow, Libby." He let himself out, and Nat locked the door behind him.

Libby plated the toffee. "Thanks, Nat!" She ran the cappuccino machine, plated everything, and waved for Nat to take it to his table himself. She charged him, then whirled around like a tornado. She cleared out the empty trays, sprayed down the counters and display cases, swept and mopped, deposited the money in the safe, and went in back to make sure everything was cleaned and prepped for the next day. She came out to get Nat's plate and cup before running the dishwasher, and found him waving at her from the other side of the door. She locked the door and checked her messages. *I'll bring food. Thai?*

Libby grinned. *As long as I don't have to cook or clean up, I don't care.* She finished cleaning up and propelled herself to the bank then back home for a shower.

Nat arrived with a Thai chicken pizza, a side of peanut sauce, sodas, and a small salad. Libby sat, staring at the screen. There was some sort of space opera on, aliens fighting alongside their human allies. Nat plated everything and put it on the coffee table. "Long day?"

Libby nodded once, head lolling. "I have no idea how I survived. You?"

"Eat."

Libby nibbled on her pizza, sighed. "This is awesome."

"The peanut sauce pushes it over the top." Nat drizzled some on the top of his own pizza. "In answer to your question, my day was full of calls. The cows got out on ReRe's farm again."

"That son of hers does not know how to repair a fence."

Nat nodded. "I told her there would be a fine next time, and I gave her Indira's number. Girl can fix fencing with one hand tied behind her back in a downpour." He grinned. "I saw the downpour thing, and I saw the one-handed thing because Betsy wanted out. Now."

Libby put down her pizza and laughed so hard she snorted. "That cow does get insistent." Indira and her mother Anvi had a small farmhouse and glass kiln where Anvi blew glass and Indira worked with wooden and glass beads. And, apparently, mended fences.

"Okay. So, your day had farm animals." Libby put her salad on her pizza, and kept eating.

Nat followed suit. "Hmm. Good." He poured more peanut sauce on the pizza. "Well, I also worked my way through a mound of reports, helped Rhonda move two prisoners around, and went out on a lot more calls." He sighed and stretched his back. "I keep thinking things will slow down in summer, but the heat seems to melt people's brains."

Meri let herself in, kicked off her shoes, and went to wash her hands. "Pizza. Peanut sauce. Why did you put salad on pizza?"

Nat shrugged. "Libby made me."

Libby poked him with her elbow. "Did not."

"Did too."

"Children!" Meri sounded exasperated. "Play nice."

Libby pointed at Nat. "He started it." Nat grinned.

Meri took her pizza, sprinkled salad on it, poured on the peanut sauce, and bit in. "Hey, not bad." She grinned. "I thought we were meeting to work out if we're going camping."

Libby sighed. "So busy."

Nat shook his head. "Too busy. I'm also covering for vacations now. Working twelve-hour days a lot."

Meri grunted. "How are we supposed to get to know each other better under these conditions? We'll all be asleep the minute this movie ends because we're getting run off our feet. What the hell are we watching, anyway?"

Libby grunted. "The blue-skinned guys like our human soldiers. They're both trying to kill the purple-black things with teeth."

"Well, of course they are." Meri popped her soda top, and lay back, her hip against Nat. Libby leaned against Nat on the other side, obviously exhausted. "Anyone going to ask about my day?"

Libby pointed at herself. "Broke the law. He didn't arrest me."

Meri snorted. "You'll just have Meri Beth come in late again."

Libby pointed at Nat. "Escaping cow."

Meri nodded. "Betsy?"

Nat shook her head. "Betsy's down by Rhode Holler. This was Daisy and Flapjack tried to get out too."

Meri shook her head. "ReRe's son Vonn has nothing in his skull. Boy better get himself together or she's gonna kick him out."

Nat carefully kept his face blank. "Yeah."

Meri took another slice of pizza and doctored it. She knew that look. Nat wouldn't say a thing, but Meri suspected Vonn had already been kicked out so hard he was probably over the state line by now. "I drove around town three times. Got more clients now that people are falling down, playing sports, getting stung or bitten, or just working on being stupid."

Nat sighed. "I can verify the stupid."

Libby finished her pizza, washed up, sat back down. "I like camping on a platform. With little twinkle lights. A fire in the ceramic fire pit. Those squishy things on the cots. Very nice." She sat down and lay her head down on Nat's shoulder again.

"You mean Big Cedar Outpost." Meri grinned. "Don't have to cook, either. They have barbecue. You just order up what you want. They will give you the fixings for s'mores. Or make s'mores cookies if you don't want to cook your own marshmallows on a stick."

Nat sighed. "You want to go glamping." Glamorous camping was not his thing. He liked to hike to a beautiful ridge and sleep in the special tent-hammock hybrid he'd gotten on sale. There was a matching sack to hold the food up in the tree away from bears. He'd ordered a second one. Maybe he and Meri could... He looked down. Libby was snoring softly. He kissed her hair, smelled the strawberry shampoo. "Whatever you want, baby."

Meri grinned. "What about what I want?"

Nat turned to her. "What do you want, if we magically had time and were wide awake?" He reached for another can of soda, careful not to awaken Libby.

"A cabin. One of those tiny houses so we can sleep in the loft. Someplace on shifter property so we can go bear. You can hike, fish, whatever you want."

"Not into fishing, but hiking, yeah." He explained about the tent hammocks and grinned. "So you go bear, leave me to my own devices, then crash back through the underbrush to see me later?"

Meri looked at Nat out of the corner of her eye. "Essentially, yeah."

Nat grinned. "Tell me more."

*N*at knew the Fourth would trip him up. He had to work. The parade needed watching. Despite warnings from the newspaper, radio station, town websites, and flyers in all the businesses and the availability of park-and-ride buses and vans, people insisted on trying to park or drive on the parade route.

The parks were full of picnickers and soccer, volleyball, and baseball games. There were three separate concerts--a bluegrass festival down by the river with amazing barbecue and cornbread, a square dance held in someone's barn that included an indoor-outdoor picnic, and a benefit to help the various schools pay for new band equipment featuring both kids and their parents, with the help of various religious and spiritual organizations.

Nat needed four clones to break up the fistfights, drunken arguments, attempted vehicular homicide, parade and outdoor concert attendees' falls out of trees, baseball injuries to parked vehicles, and two fathers fighting over whose kid pushed whom, even after both kids had made up. He was run ragged from eight in the morning until the fireworks started down by the river to close out the bluegrass festival.

Nat met Amir on the waterfront and helped him break up a fight between two women over an amused guy. "Ladies, walk it off. In different directions." Nat ducked a punch, and had the woman in flexicuffs before she could swing again. "Just had to have me fill out your arrest report, didn't you?"

Her sobbing friend ran up to Nat, dressed in a silvery crushed-velvet dress entirely inappropriate for the scalding summer night. "Let her go! Police violence!"

Victor Farnsworth came up on his bowed legs, cowboy hat in hand. "Michelle, I saw Stormie here try to punch the officer. Now, let him do his job and get her to the drunk tank."

Stormie stood, swayed. Her platinum wig stayed put. "Think I'm gonna be..." Nat had the woman next to the bushes before she could be sick. He sighed, pulled out a pack of wet tissues, and took off the cuffs so she could wipe her face.

Victor sighed. "Stormie's not usually like this, Nat."

Stormie stood, tears streaming down her face, then gratefully took a wet tissue and scrubbed her face. "Officer, if I promise to have Michelle take me home, can I go with a warning?"

Nat shook his head. "Absolutely not. I want you to call a rideshare and for you to go home alone."

Stormie nodded and swiped at her tears. "Absolutely. I will stand right here and link in front of you."

Nat let the woman go. She weaved a bit, stood straighter, then linked. "My friend Bobbie will pick me up on her cart." She pointed to the road. "Right there."

Nat nodded at Amir. Amir nodded back, and herded Michelle away.

Nat pointed. "Lead the way. " He handed Stormie a bottle of water.

Stormie took it gratefully, rinsed her mouth, spat, then drank it as she hiked up to meet her friend with the cart. "I am so sorry. I was swinging at Michelle, not Casra, the one pushing me."

"I guessed. What did the tearful Michelle want?"

Stormie laughed regretfully. "A fight to watch. She told Casra I said things I didn't. And I was the dumbass who swung back."

Nat sighed. "Lady, get a better class of friends."

Stormie nodded. "Thank you." She sighed. "I should be saving up for my top surgery and working on my dresses for the Summer Ball, but no, I'm here acting the fool. Once again, deputy, I'm sorry."

Bobbie, a short red-hairedwoman dressed in jeans and a cowboy shirt, looked over at Stormie's torn red dress. "Girl, you get an attack of the stupid?"

Stormie nodded. "I am the biggest idiot on the planet."

Bobbie patted the seat next to her. "Girl, don't go talking to my friend like that. Let Bobbie take you home."

Nat helped Stormie get into the cart. "Ma'am, stop off for coffee then get her home safely."

Bobbie grinned. "Yes, Deputy. I thank you for taking care of Stormie here. Sometimes she forgets to do that herself." Bobbie zipped off.

Amir came up behind Nat. "Chief says we can go. People are dispersing now that the fireworks are over." People flowed up and down the boardwalk like ants, heading towards their shuttles or rides.

Nat sighed. "I will greatly enjoy sleeping in tomorrow."

Amir adjusted his baseball cap. "You've got two women you don't see. How do you pull that off?"

Nat closed his eyes, opened them. "Stolen moments, mostly. I've never had a busier summer." He and Amir scanned the crowd, looking for issues, but everyone seemed to keep themselves in order. "I hate that the bits and pieces are so short. But, they're busy too." And that his women needed time to be bears, but he didn't say that. Amir already thought Nat was crazy for dating two women at the same time. Throw in their busy summer schedules, Nat's volunteering as a ref, and Libby and Meri's need to be with family and have time to go bear, and they rarely saw each other. They all had cut back on working out. They were just so overwhelmed. The precious lazy days of early summer seemed like a distant memory.

Amir nodded. "Nat, don't give up. I've known the Cambers since we were all young, and so have you. Great family."

Nat barked out a laugh. "Better than mine."

Amir nodded. "You said it, I didn't." He grimaced. "Just remember, this time won't last forever. We're past the halfway point. Before we all know it, the leaves will change and life will settle into a simpler groove."

Nat nodded. "Thanks, bud."

Amir grinned. "Someone's gotta keep you in line." He pointed to the parking lot. "Let's go, deputy."

Nat groaned. "Will you push me there?"

Amir laughed. "Nope. We both have to walk to the police station lot and file our reports." Nat groaned, and they trudged down the street.

～

*C*amping Trip #1 was rained out--a huge line of thunderstorms that brought down power trees and power lines, stranded motorists, and took out the middle of the Rock Park Bridge. Luckily, no one was stupid enough to be wandering around in the park during the massive lighting storms. Lightning took out a transformer, and two counties were without power for eighteen hours. No one died, but Nat was kept hopping. He spent two days in bed with the flu after helping Mrs. Botham to safety after her car slid into a ditch. Nat used a guide rope and sure feet, and got Mrs. Botham to her granddaughter's house safely.

The second planned camping trip was the glamping one. Nat had been able to cancel the food order and move the deposit. He ordered everything Libby liked--barbecued chicken in a very easy to eat sandwich format, homemade potato chips, blackberry lemonade, and a combo of snickerdoodles and s'mores cookies.

The ground was wet and spongy; there had been two rain showers since the storm. The parking lot ended at a trailhead; Nat booked the scenic one overlooking the creek that had swollen to river size rather than the gorgeous outlook over the valley that was much higher up. The trail to the creek site was relatively flat. He came early to remove any branches in the way. Fifty minutes' work, and he had the trail cleared, clean sheets on the beds, citronella candles burning to keep away mosquitoes, and a crackling fire in the ceramic fire pit.

Libby arrived very late, apologies spilling from her lips. "Sorry! Sorry! I got into the bank just before it closed, then forgot to code the campsite into the vehicle, and I had to look it up." She looked at the fire, the small table and two chairs on the platform set up with the food on cobalt plastic plates, lemonade beginning to lose its sweat. "What the...is this for me?" she asked wonderingly.

Nat laughed. "I had two rock stars and a drummer supermodel cancel, so, yes, it's for you."

Libby wrinkled her nose. "You're lying. Supermodels aren't drummers." She dropped her knapsack just past the tent flap, turned, and sat down at the table. "This smells amazing!

Nat grinned. "We have barbecued chicken, homemade kettle chips, and blackberry lemonade." He poured her a glass, then him.

"I am so hungry!" Libby sat down, and they fell on their food as if they hadn't eaten for days. Libby grinned. "Fire."

Nat laughed. "And cookies."

Libby held out her hand. "Gimme." Nat laughed.

They talked about the rain, the car accidents, the damage to the town. Libby paused to reach for more chips. "Dad and all four moms took turns watching after kids, put on gloves, and joined the Neighbor Team." The Neighbor Team was a countywide group of do-gooders who helped with repairs after a storm or other crisis. Funded by the churches, synagogues, mosque, and temples and the Atheist Association, with healthy anonymous donations from Pack funds, working groups were sent out after each storm. "Cut up fallen trees and removed them, repaired fences, barns, and outbuildings. The bridge in Rock Creek Park's gonna need more intervention, though." Libby held up her hands. "Bruised two knuckes, but got the barn dealt with. Meri's amazing with a chainsaw."

Nat sighed. "Wish I could join the team, but emergencies come first." He sighed. "The city is not supposed to be paying this much overtime. But, it looks like what we're doing right now." He grinned. "That last game was wild, wasn't it?"

Libby snorted. "I don't think the parents were expecting their children to take a mud bath." Libby sighed. "I used half a pack of wet wipes cleaning up the table after the game." She grinned. "My sister and I are making plenty of money on the snacks, though. I'm saving up for a hole in the wall in between my shop and Penny's."

Nat nodded. "Makes sense. You have the candy goodies, she has the ice cream."

Libby chewed a snickerdoodle cookie. "The problem is, we're both seasonal. That makes it really hard to save up enough money for the expansion. It has to be done right. We want to make the space super inviting. We also want to change the bathrooms to unisex, and have kiddie and adult bathrooms."

Nat took a s'more cookie. "That's going to take a lot of work. Have you considered unifying the color scheme?"

Libby nodded. "There are some really cute lights that I found on sale. Part of what I'm trying to do right now is save up money for this expansion. Having teens work on Saturday so my sister and I can sell the snacks allows me to raise more money more quickly."

Nat grinned. "My money goes to my gym membership. I don't have a business to run."

Libby brushed the crumbs off her hands, stood, and stretched. Her back popped audibly. "I know you set up this wonderful event, but I haven't been able to go bear in two and a half weeks. I'm late every-where I go, and I'm so overwhelmed and exhausted. Going bear should help the feeling like I have ants under my skin that are trying to escape."

Nat stood and wrinkled his nose. "That sounds really annoying. I'll clean up here and you go. Just get back here in time to see the sunset."

Libby grinned. She took off her clothes, folded them, put them on her pack, and changed. She held up a paw, waved, and slid down this muddy slope to the river sitting down, her front paws on her back ones. Nat laughed so hard that he thought he was going to explode.

Nat cleaned up the detritus from the meal and had the delivery person pick up the empties. She came up on a dirt bike wearing mud-splattered black jeans, a summer weight black racing jacket, and black motorcycle boots. The teen hopped off the bike, took off and stowed her hemet, showing a closely cropped head of dark hair, a slash of a mouth, and high, wide cheekbones. She shoved the empties into her saddlebags. "Was it delicious?"

Nat laughed. "Perfect."

The girl pulled up a screen and poked it. "Would you like to order breakfast?"

Nat grinned. "Blueberry bagels, strawberry cream cheese, and salmon for the lady. One egg poached hard, a walnut bagel with pecan cream cheese, and four pieces of extra crispy bacon made into a breakfast sandwich. A carafe of orange juice and one of very strong black coffee."

The teen poked in the order, and nodded. "Thank you, sir."

Nat grinned, then lost his grin when the teen stiffened. "What..." He looked behind him and saw Libby splashing in the creek. "Oh, that's a female bear, no cubs. She likes to eat blackberries." He pointed at the blackberry bushes on the opposite shore. "She likes those." Sure enough, there were bear tracks in the mud by the bushes.

"Do you have bear spray, sir?"

Nat patted his pocket. "Never leave home without it."

The girl nodded. "I took away the food containers. Make sure there's nothing for the bear to get into. There's a food locker if you brought any snacks." She pointed to a box located halfway up a nearby tree.

Nat grinned. "Thank you. What's your name?"

"Debbie. Don't get mauled, sir." Debbie put her full-face helmet that made her look like a bug on her head.

"Wouldn't dream of it." Debbie snorted, got on her bike, and zipped off down the trail.

Nat fished out his and Libby's toiletries kit and put them in the enclosed outdoor shower. Nat applied sunscreen and mosquito repellent and went on his own muddy way to the top of the rise. He had enough time to get up there and back down before his girlfriend stopped playing bear.

The ridge overlooked the valley. He could see tiny houses, farms, winding roads, rivers, and trees in a hundred shades of green. He drank from his water bottle, turned, and slowly made his way back down. It was slippery, so he took a fallen branch and turned it into a walking stick.

He heard the water running, and smiled. "Would that be the lovely Libby?"

Libby poked her head out, then laughed. "You're muddier than I am!"

Nat snorted. "You spend time playing in the river. I didn't." He crossed over to the tent, pulled off his muddy shoes, pulled out his laundry bag, and stuffed his clothes inside. "May I join you?"

Libby giggled. "I thought you'd never ask."

Nat slipped behind the rock wall enclosing the shower inlaid with little pieces of glass, bottle caps, and other shiny things. Libby excelled at scrubbing the gooey mud off Nat's body, which made him grin like a madman. She reached down and pulled. "Hey! Important bits there!"

Libby grinned. "I know. I'm just way too tired to play with it standing here."

They toweled dry and ran to the tent in the gloaming of twilight. Nat made sure the mosquito netting was secure.

Libby hung up the towels to dry. "We're not seeing the sunset?"

Nat smiled, pulled back the sheets, and pointed to the little lantern he had placed on the floor. "If you can see the lantern…"

Libby sighed. "It gets dark fast here." They slid in under the sheets.

"It does." Nat kissed his way down her neck, ears, throat. Libby gasped and kissed back. He was working his way down each delectable collarbone when he realized Libby had slipped into sleep. He laughed at himself, held her close, and slid under with her, hoping to find her in his dreams.

~

*C*oach Ma's voice came through loud and clear. Nat listened to Spook's complaints while he opened a can for her and put the bowl on the floor. The cat dug in with a purr.

Coach Ma looked bright and cheerful, her blueblack straight hair falling in a curtain beside wide cheekbones. "How was the Fourth?"

Nat grimaced. "Busy. Another late night for me, actually, or swing shift couldn't have gotten all the calls done. It's lunchtime in Kuala Lumpur, right?" He pulled off his boots and put them by the door, washed his hands, then made himself a grilled cheese sandwich and shoved it into the panini maker.

"It is. What are you doing eating so late at night?"

Nat groaned. "Barbecue was lunchtime. Nothing since. I've been bouncing around like a ping pong ball since then." He pulled out a bag of Cool Ranch Doritos and opened it. "How's Aminah doing?"

"Biggest, smartest, most beautiful grandbaby yet." Coach held up a picture of a chubby-cheeked little girl, a smile on her baby face. Coach had followed her daughter Marissa to be her nanny when twins were born, then another girl arrived eighteen months later. Husband Rayyan was delighted, but both parents were overwhelmed running their technical supply business in addition to raising three adorable but demanding daughters.

Nat oohed and aahed over the picture. "Nice family you've got there."

Coach Ma put the picture down and pointed at Nat. "You sound both tired and discouraged. Speak."

Nat sighed. "For the first camping trip, we both fell asleep just as night fell. We had a lovely morning along with breakfast, but then there was some sort of problem with a soccer game that had been canceled being on again. She provides the halftime juice and end-of-game food wih her sister Meri, so she had to leave. I had another good day of hiking, and she came back a few hours later and we hiked together. Then I got called into work because of a double traffic accident caused by a small rock slide. No one was killed, but everyone needed transportation to the hospital. Libby went home to sleep."

Coach Ma grinned. "At least you got to see each other, and spend some time together. That seems to be what you were lacking."

"Then Meri wanted to try sleeping in a tree. I reserved a tree house, and I'm incredibly glad that I brought both my hanging sleep tent hammocks."

Coach Ma raised her eyebrows. "Did the treehouse fall out of its tree?"

"No, a puma and her kits had taken up residence. They usually use caves. The mother must have decided the treehouse was some sort of hanging cave."

Coach Ma let out a peal of laughter. "And then you had to sleep separately, I take it? I don't remember those hanging tents being for two people."

Nat laughed at himself. "We tried. It didn't end well."

Coach Ma laughed so hard that she cried. "Oh!" She wiped away her tears. "So, have you made a decision? Have you chosen one female over the other?"

Nat shook his head. "They are so good-natured, despite the problems. They both put a zing in my life, and they make me laugh."

Coach Ma pointed a finger at Nat. "You are not some khan or rajah who would do well with fifteen wives. I have no urge to tell you how to live your life. But, I would be very careful here. If you treat one badly, the other will kill you. And treating both people equally is out of the question. Everyone has different needs and desires.

Nat nodded. "I know."

Coach Ma waved her hand. "I did not teach you to give up. If you want these women, then do so, but be very careful. Human hearts are very fragile."

Nat nodded. "These are two of the strongest women I've ever known. But, I see your point. Thank you."

Coach Ma nodded. "You're welcome. Eat and get some sleep. Call me next week. I want an update. None of my other baby birds who have flown away have such interesting lives!"

Nat grinned. "You flew away from me, but for an excellent reason. Family is everything."

Twin girls toddled up to Coach Ma. They had wide dark eyes and beautiful smiles. "Family is indeed everything. Alya! Zara!" Coach Ma picked them up and kissed them, making the toddlers giggle. Nat laughed and dropped the call.

Nat didn't have a functional family. He wondered if he could build one.

AMBUSH

Their occasional Wednesday date night never materialized. No walk, no movie, for anyone. Nat called Libby first. "I'll make this quick."

"Since I've got a line ten people long, that's good."

"You'll read about it in the papers, but I'll be working overtime for a few days."

"I'll let Meri know. Stay safe."

"Meri knows. Everyone's going to be a lot safer now."

Nat dropped the link and looked at Meri. "Your entire family's going to surround the wagons, right?"

Meri let out a shuddering breath. "Yeah, once the shit hits the fan."

"I hate to do this to you, but please tell me what you told Deputy Cazalos."

Meri nodded. "The truck was on manual. I know because it side-swiped me." She nodded to herself. "I've got a really good van, and I wear mesh. Our entire family does after…" She took a breath.

"After a drunk guy texting while driving on manual killed Len's brother and father." Nat patted Meri's arm. "I know you like blunt talk."

"I do. No reason to have anything on manual unless your vehicle's GPS doesn't work, or..."

Nat waved a hand. "You want to go somewhere illegal." Meri nodded. "Please describe the vehicle again, how fast it was going, and where it was headed."

Meri pointed down the road. "There's a firebreak road up there. I saw the truck go up there. It was pretty wide, but not a dually with the double tires. Really old, blue paint, with a lot of mud on the bottom, both wet and dry. My car hit the ditch and bottomed out, as you can see."

"So, the driver ran you off the road and didn't stop. Then, you looked up, and saw the truck go down the fire break road."

"Exactly."

Deputy Cazalos hiked back from the road. "Firefighters all have the code to the e-lock for the gate to the fire road. The perps who have it wouldn't have to mow down the gate. Watched the footage." He pointed to the van. "Happened exactly as she said it did. Called the sheriff and he's ordering a drone flyover."

Clancy rode up in his truck, the one with a tow chain on the front. The man could turn his vehicle into a snowplow, a ditch digger, and a variety of farm machines with 3D-printed attachments. He hopped out. "Your GPS go wonky? See you're not scraped up. You need me to get you to Urgent Care?"

Meri shook her head. "No, I've got deliveries, then I'll take myself then." Nat nodded approvingly.

"Well then, daylight's burning," Clancy put the skids under the back tires, hooked up the hook and chain, and slowly backed up. Within minutes Meri's vehicle was back on the road, only complaining of chipped paint. Deputy Cazalos had already taken paint samples. "Well there, it is my responsibility to report any illegal vehicle-related activity. Deputy Sandawan, I do believe this car has been sideswiped by someone on manual. The fact that no one answered my GPS question means you want me to keep this quiet."

Nat nodded. "That would be a good idea. Please give me your

report so that Meri can finish her deliveries and get to the urgent care."

Clancy gave his report while Meri checked on her hot and cold boxes with her HUD, then manually. "Done reported the poisoned runoff, the dead grass, the increased number of deer on my property, the snakes coming down from the mountain, and the bobcats. Thought you would have found them already with flyovers."

Nat pointed at the sky and mimicked a drone flyover with one hand. "We have looked, but they're well hidden. But now we have a direction, and we've ordered an ATF drone that's good at finding hidey-holes despite camouflage. You tell your cousins not to go anywhere near Cold Creek, you hear?"

"Got it. Now I'll git. Meri, you tell your family the same."

Meri nodded. "They've been looking, but haven't seen the nest. They say it smells wrong up there, and found some carcasses that shouldn't exist. Hunters would dress and take away their kills. They reported it, too, and quit going up there. Afraid of some idiot with a carbine."

"As we all should be until that nest of vipers gets cleaned out." Clancy tapped Meri's arm. "Take care of yourself, you hear?"

"Will do." Meri got in her car, and drove away. Clancy went in the opposite direction.

Deputy Cazalos pointed upward. "Drone's on its way. One of the silent types." The problem with drones is that no matter how quiet the motor, air itself is loud. The Department of Alcohol, Tobacco, Firearms, and Explosives had tiny drones that sounded like insects. The drone of insects in the mountains was so loud it was sometimes oppressive. "Called them, 'cause with dead wildlife, that means illegal activity on federal land."

"Be fine with them doing all the work, taking all the credit, and leaving us with all the paperwork if we can get the land back to rights. Do you think it's pot growers up there?" Nat pulled up a map program, zeroed in on the road.

Cazalos nodded. "The reported smell makes me suspect meth, but they could be growing poppy plants, coca leaves, anything if they have a good system for it." Hydroponics and vertical farming combined with 3D printing had enabled nearly anyone to grow crops. That also meant people could grow illegal ones. If they planted the illegal crops in soil, they tended to use cheap and wildy illegal pesticides that destroyed the land and poisoned wildlife. They tended to use public, untamed land in the back hills to do their dirty deeds.

The nearby valleys had clawed their way out of poverty using their lands for hiking, tiny houses, tent colonies on platforms, and blinds for nature lovers, birdwatchers, and back-to-nature types. Unless a descent into addiction was involved, these days even the poorest families in the valleys had food on the table, shoes on their feet, and their kids in school. They also used solar, wind, and geothermal power, and sold electricity back to the grid. So, anyone up there was probably not local unless they were stupid or crazy, and very likely armed. Stupid and/or crazy people tended to flap their lips in bars and there had been no whisper of these people hiding on the mountain, so they were probably cartel.

Nat blew out a breath. "We're going to need guns and body armor. I'll go down and get our equipment if you want to speak to the feds, or vice versa."

"I'll stay," Deputy Cazalos shook his head. "Be good to get this whole thing over by nightfall. They'll be spooked, sure as the sun rises and sets. I'll get the warrants while I wait."

They didn't have to go anywhere. Nat was walking to his vehicle when Sheriff Taylor spoke into his ear. "Deputies Sandawan and Cazalos, stay put. I'm bringing body armor, weapons, and a former military person I've deputized. We've got to get this rolled up right now, before sunset. We let this go, they'll just pack up and pop up somewhere else. I'm putting this on gas mask protocol so I'm bringing those too. On my way. Sheriff Taylor out."

"Thorough." Amir nodded approvingly.

"Should have thought of the masks myself. You want to work on the warrants while I use our maps so we can block off the roads?"

"On it." Amir filled out the paperwork and called some judges.

They had a halfway-decent plan by the time the sheriff showed up.

They donned their armor, told the sheriff the nascent plan, and were nailing it down when Charlie Camber showed up. "Chief. Deputies." He wore green-dappled fatigues under green-dappled body armor, face paint, gloves with reinforced Kevlar knuckles, a helmet, and combat boots. He had weapons belts criss-crossed over his shoulders and belly. He had stun grenades, flash-bangs, a combat knife, a Glock, and a rifle, along with a gas mask. "I'm a sharpshooter. Nothing I've got will start a fire if it's thrown on concrete. Plus, I've got a camera on the helmet."

"I'll get your feed into our system." Deputy Cazalos poked at his pad.

Sheriff Taylor nodded. "Come over here and I'll tell you the plan. We may have a hazardous site up there. These people are either using pesticides or some very volatile chemicals to make meth, flakka, or even designer drugs."

"I'll pretend this is a chemical weapons plant." He surveyed their probable routes. "Good plan, except there's trails that lead up here and over there." Charlie highlighted the sections on the map. "These people tend to make trails where they feel like it once they get above a certain height. Look for trash dumps. These asswipes leave them anywhere it pleases them."

Deputy Cazalos pointed to his screen. "We've got drone footage."

"Can I get control?" Charlie asked.

"Of an expensive ATF drone?" Amir snorted.

"Well, that agency works with the DEA all the time, so they do know what to look for. Trash heaps, yeah, above this trail, here." Charlie marked it on the map. "Just where I said they would be."

The sheriff grimaced. "Don't get cocky, Camber." Charlie grinned.

"Blinds," Amir pointed out on his HUD and lit up the screen blue.

"Two shooters each, I reckon." There was a glint on the feed, probably from a gun sight. "Cheap but efficient guns. We can sneak up behind them, here." Charlie pointed to a rabbit trail.

Sheriff Taylor nodded. "Do it, you and Deputy Sandawan."

"Another blind, other side," Deputy Cazalos pointed out, and turned the suspected blind blue.

"There's trash. My guess is this depressed shit in the middle is a bunker. Probably a tunnel leading somewhere, too." Charlie stared at the map. "Bet it comes out into that gully, there." He pointed to a spot to the north and west.

Deputy Cazalos pointed at the edge of the map. "I've got the gully. I've got my own stunners and a lot of bullets."

"You get all the fun, Amir," Nat complained. Cazalos laughed and clapped his partner on the shoulder.

"That puts me on the other blind." Sheriff Taylor pointed towards the gully. "Amir, get your vehicle over there. Don't start a forest fire."

"Done." Deputy Cazalos put on his own bandolier, stuffed it full of stunners and ammunition, and headed off.

Sheriff Taylor blew out a breath. "I'll be blunt, because you two can take it. Charlie, I suspect my deputy is dating one or both of your daughters. If you want me to take Nat with me, I'll do it."

"I think you should, not because I have any opinion other than relief than my daughters are dating someone I can get my head around." Nat and the sheriff snorted. "You should have seen some of the bears they dated." Charlie grimaced.

Sheriff Taylor grinned. "Knew you were a bear of a man."

Charlie guffawed. "I am. No, I want you to take Nat because I have more military experience than you, and Nat trained in the military too."

The sheriff nodded. "Okay, Nat, you're with me. Let's do this. Remember, if the ATF and/or the DEA want to stomp their big feet over this, I will let them if they can get here by nightfall. Since I know damn well they won't, and those sons of bitches up on that mountain are gonna bug out, we have the field."

Charlie nodded. "Let's do this." Nat checked his weapons and followed his boss into the trees.

They crept up, Taylor having grown up a barefoot boy in the woods and Nat military trained, so they were silent. They found the blinds with netting and weapons pointing out. Once everyone was in position, they counted down from ten. Nat threw the stunner in, then a boomer when he saw that they were still upright. The blind shook, and those inside fell. Nat eeled in, removed their weapons, and trussed them up, hands and feet. The perpetrators were one man and one woman, both with dark stringy hair and stank to high heaven.

Then, Nat and his commanding officer ran towards the shouting. Nat used his stunner, took out one guy with his machine gun on full auto, going for the neck because he was wearing body armor and a helmet. The shooter fell like a tree. Nat went around the corner, jabbed, hit armor, aimed upward, and shot the woman with a stun round. The woman fell. Nat trussed her up and took the woman's weapons. Nat circled, hitting one rabbiting perp, then two. The last one collapsed right at Nat's feet. Nat knelt, took aim, and took the sharpshooter off the top of the blind, a slim figure, not Charlie.

The fleeing perpetrators streamed out of the middle hole. Apparently they had figured out their escape tunnel was cut off. Sheriff Taylor and Nat kept up withering stunner fire, dropping first the ones in hazmat suits, then the ones in bras and panties that counted the money. The last one went down, and Nat zip-tied them all, did an initial weapons check, then circled the area while the sheriff and Charlie went room-by-room underneath.

They came out in a hurry. "Dead bodies down there." Sheriff Taylor looked annoyed and slightly rattled. "And a bunch of stuff that can go boom."

Nat nodded. "We've got to get these ones all arrested and processed, and we should get the hell out of here if the mountain is going to blow."

"Already called two paddy wagons." Sheriff Taylor referred to law enforcement criminal transport vans. "Then I called a prison bus."

"Let's get 'em processed." Nat stepped to the nearest body, slapped the fingers on a scan plate. "Jacko Phillips. Wanted for armed robbery. Long history of violence, carjacking at eighteen. Probably a sealed juvenile record." The man had a thin, pockmarked face, stringy hair held back in a band, and lacked muscle. Nat checked his physical state, gave him a careful check for hidden weapons, and was annoyed to find a knife hidden in a boot sole. "I think this one's been taking the product."

"Would explain at least some of his actions." Taylor checked a woman in a black bra, panties, and paper shoes for injury. He checked her hair and grunted. He used the tip of a pen to unwind the garotte. "Lovely lady."

Nat carefully checked the prisoners on the right side, while Sheriff Taylor did the left, and Charlie kept a weapon trained on all the arrestees. There was some crashing, and Deputy Leland Fortra from the next county came up. "Got four loaded for Deputy Cazalos. Can take two more."

"Take this bad 'un." Taylor pointed to Jacko Phillips. "Charlie, haul him for Leland here. Guy has a very long record."

"I can..." Leland began to say.

Taylor pointed. "Take that skinny woman there. I just got a garotte out of her hair, so hang for another minute while I check..." He pulled a clip out of her hair, pushed a button, and a tiny but very sharp blade popped out. "Lovely. Let's make sure she can't raise her arms. I bet she's wild as hell when awake."

Nat finished his checks, and found knives hidden in boots and hair. He scanned for prints, took pictures, and ran facial recognition. Most of them were complete unknowns, but he got some matches from the cartel database. None of the people under arrest were there legally, except Jacko and a tiny woman with dirty blonde hair wearing a vinyl suit and gloved hands named Velma Pierce who had been underground, probably a chemist. Sure enough, she had an undergrad in chemistry from a small backwoods college and had taken mostly online classes except for her labs.

The DEA called when Charlie and Leland came back for another round of prisoner transport. "This is Special Agent Diane Dakota," said a woman with a clipped voice into Nat's ear. "You are Deputy Nat Sandawan, and you apparently have a lot of people in custody we want to talk to."

"We do." Nat calmly shot a suspect who began to move with a knockout round. "We brought some of them to our jail, but we'll get most of them to the county facility."

"May I access all of your camera footage?"

"Access anything you so desire." Nat lined up another shot and pulled the trigger. Then he authorized the agent to see his camera footage. "How soon can you have people on the ground here?"

"I'll put two in a car right this minute. I've got a meeting, and I'll head out about an hour after them. Be three, four hours."

"Bring people in hazmat suits. We need your equipment to secure the site."

"On it." Special Agent Dakota rang off.

Rhonda Meyota made it into the clearing, swearing and sweating. "Hoo-ee." She stood there gasping, hands on her hips. "Okay." She straightened, her eyes clear. "I see now why you called me. Y'all won't have enough room in your house, gotta take 'em to county lockup to be processed."

Nat nodded. "Thanks for coming, Rhonda. Leland will help us get the people into the prison bus. Gotta get them in and processed. Checked them all, found most of them loaded with weapons, some well hidden."

"Well then, let's have a look-see. Can't have none of that foolishness on my bus." Rhonda began methodically re-checking the prisoners, and she and Leland carried the stunned prisoners to the road and into the prison transport.

Charlie came back and did one more reconnoiter of the premises. "Seems clear. You stay here and I'll circle the area."

"Good." Nat stretched, panned so his body cam got the area, and began separating weapons into piles. He began the first of the avalanche of forms he'd have to fill out in the coming days.

ATF arrived first in the form of two agents from Columbia, Missouri. "I'm Ford, she's Madrados," said the taller agent. Ford had a sticklike body, but moved with an elegant grace. She had tattoos on her neck, and wore the standard jeans, heavy shirt, boots, and jacket. Madrados wore the same, and both hauled black backpacks. Madrados was much shorter, stocky, and had hard, dark eyes that missed nothing. Ford blipped their credentials to Nat, who used his camera to check their identifications and faces. They were who they said they were.

Ford grimaced. "Sorry we didn't make it to the party. We sincerely apologize."

Nat shrugged. "Had backup."

"Met your mountain man. Military, I take it." Madrados had a raspy voice that sounded like she'd been smoking since she was six years old.

"Yes. Weapons here." Nat pointed to the line of weapons carefully laid out. "Charlie and the sheriff say there's four rooms underground." Nat pointed out the hatches. "Four shipping containers, and we think probably an old camper or two." Nat pointed to pipes sticking up out of the ground, then towards the two blinds. "Blinds there and there. Took out the nests first. Anyway, we think what's down there could go boom."

Madrados held up some sort of wand and took a reading. "Gotta do this fast, Ford."

"Agreed." Ford turned to Nat. "Special Agent Dakota's got herself plugged into your feed, and has seen your paperwork so far. If you want to make tracks out of here..."

Nat shook his head. "I've been at this for hours. Day off is already blown. Might as well finish off what paperwork I can and see if I can give you all a hand."

"Fine, but scoot when the hazmat guys get here. We're going in, collecting evidence." Ford took off a pack and put on a vinyl suit. Madrados checked her seals while Ford got the air supply on her back, got the mask on properly, and gave Madrados a thumbs-up. Then, Madrados put on her suit, and Ford checked her partner's seals. They headed into the hatch on the right.

Nat continued cataloguing weapons, then went to the blind on the right to do the same, then the one on the left. Nat didn't bother with Amir's tunnel; he would have filled out the requisite forms while waiting for the van.

Charlie whistled and the hazmat guys came in, backpacks on their backs. "I'm Carvey, and that's Agajanian." Carvey pointed to himself, then his partner. Both were stocky men, and obviously ex-military. Carvey had wavy light brown hair and Agajanian very close-cut black hair. Carvey pointed behind him. "Met your Charlie. We'll let you two go. The rest of our team will be here really soon."

"Where's Madrados and Ford?" Agajanian asked. Nat pointed to the hatch on the right. "Okay, let's link with them before we get shot."

Nat nodded at the men. "Do you have the feed to my camera and forms?"

Carvey pointed at his pad. "I…"

There was a muffled boom, and Nat bounced on the ground. When the shaking stopped, Nat jumped up, pulled up his mask, then ran toward the hatch. Smoke poured out of the pipes. Nat jumped in, climbed down the ladder, and found the tunnel filled with reeking smoke. On one side was a mess of shattered glass, obviously the lab. Forward was a counting room, blown-up money floating down like a green shower. One of the few remaining uses for paper money was to buy drugs; Nat had written a paper on it in college.

Nat looked to his right, saw one suited figure pulling on another one, then realized it was Ford holding up Madrados. Nat pulled Madrados up. made long strides, the other woman lurching behind her. Nat pushed himself, struggled to breathe, let his legs pull them forward. The tunnel went down, then up. They stumbled out into fresh mountain air. Nat stumbled to the creek and went down on a knee, Madrados hanging onto him. In front of him was a dam made out of some sort of white foam. He gritted his teeth; they had dammed the creek to get fresh water. They had also been poisoning it; green algae ran amok in the previously clear stream.

Charlie whistled twice, got a long whistle from above. Carvey came crashing out of the woods, then a white box with a red cross on it came sailing through the air. Nat turned, caught the box, and realized that Madrados had a ripped vinyl suit and her shoulder was bleeding. Nat concentrated on expelling what was in his lungs into the already-polluted creek. He accepted an inhaler from Charlie, who took the first aid box and began to work on Madrados' wounds.

Ford took her mask off. "Luisa," she croaked. "If you die, I'll kill you."

Charlie gave a half-smile. "Now that makes sense."

Carvey made it down the steep incline without face-planting. Charlie put a hand on Ford's gun hand. "Chill."

Nat accepted the breathing mask out of the kit as Carvey knelt and worked on Madrados. "Her shoulder's a mess."

Nat called for transport by entering a code into his communicator. He wanted to cough more than breathe in, and knew he was in serious trouble despite having worn a mask into the tunnel.

Carvey sprayed something in Nat's face, then shoved the mask back on. "Counteragent. You'll live."

Nat gave a thumbs-up. He heard a whoop-whoop, and knew Amir had their backs.

RECOVERY

at woke up to Charlie's worried face. Nat reached up and found that his hand had an IV and a pulse oxygen monitor and his face had a breathing mask. Nat looked up at Charlie. "Hey there, deputy." Nat snorted. "Good, you're awake. You're hooked up to oxygen and chelating chemicals that will repair your lungs and get that crap you breathed in out of there. Your mask blocked most of the particles, or you'd be in an oxygen tent, maybe have to grow you a new set of lungs."

Nat wrote on Charlie's giant, beefy hand with a finger. *The agent.*

Charlie nodded. "She's a mess. They photographed and collected evidence. That was those black boxes behind us at the creekside." Nat tried to remember if he'd seen them; he didn't think he had, and that bothered him. "She had a real good surgeon after they stabilized her and got her to Columbia. She has a long road ahead, but she'll be fine."

Nat nodded, then wrote on Charlie's hand again. *The case.* "Your case is fine. The sheriff was in here, left to go deal with the agency soup. He'll be back in a few and asked me to sit with you. The Feds have it now, and are interrogating everybody. Looks like a cartel thought that our woods were fantastic for making meth, flakka, and some new designer drug with a lot of initials." Nat tapped Charlie's hand, showing that he understood. "Plus, they got some coca to grow down there, too. The plants are still alive after the blast, believe it or not. Major haul."

Sheriff Morgan Taylor stood in the doorway, his face gaunt, dark circles under his eyes. "I told the agencies to bigfoot all they want, take every piece of evidence. Even got Fish and Wildlife up here to add even more charges on their heads with all the land-poisoning shit. They were dumping their toxic chemical waste on the land, and even into their own bathing water. Even if no drug charges stick, they're going down, every single one of them, except for one."

A man with scraggly hair Nat knew as Jacko Phillips stuck his head into the room. "Hey. Up for receiving visitors?" Nat nodded minutely. "My real name's Georgio Cabrera. I look like a bad guy, so ATF all the way. I've only been embedded with the cartel for eight months, started out as a motorcycle guy. They sent me to look after their operations, bring food and guns, so I removed some firing pins and I've been finding the cartel's hidey-holes for a while. Anyway, you did everything by the book, didn't use lethal force, and kept anyone from finding out who or what I am. I want to thank you for going in to assist my wife." Nat opened his eyes wide. "Yeah, we're both ATF. Anyway, you got her out, so if you need me, or help from my agency, just holler."

Nat carefully inclined his head, afraid his mask or maybe his face would fall off if he moved too much. "Get well fast." Cabrera shrugged. "Gotta go, forms to fill out." Nat huffed out a laugh. "Your head start on yours saved us a lot of work. Anyway, I'll do that on my flight to see my wife. Then, it's back on the road to find more of these nasty types."

Nat raised the other hand, and winced. "Don't move that shoulder," Charlie said, too late.

"You pulled a lot of muscles saving that agent, and have some interesting bruises and scrapes. Plus the exposure to toxic substances." Sheriff Taylor grimaced. "Now, take a few weeks off. We've got law enforcement coming out of the woodwork willing to cover your shifts, whatever we need."

Charlie grinned. "You're coming to live with us. All one level, waited on hand and foot, best cooking in the world."

Nat slowly grinned and relaxed. Then, a warm wind of some sort of medicine took the deputy under.

$\approx$

*M*eri sat by Nat's side. She had the puzzle laid out on green felt on Nat's table-tray. Nat used his good hand to nudge a piece in place. The puzzle was of a mountain stream, woodland creatures everywhere. Meri pointed. "That rabbit is hiding in the underbrush." She slid in a piece of a doe's forward-twitching ears.

Nat maneuvered a straw with a hand that felt like it had a mitten on it and sucked. Meri had snuck in Nat's apple drink. The staff had almost taken it away, believing the bottles to be beer, until Meri set them straight. "Woodland creatures are cute. Are you sure you're okay?"

Meri snorted. "I just had a little pain and stiffness the next day. Made all my deliveries just fine. You, on the other hand, pulled muscles and tendons hauling a woman out of an explosion."

"Nothing's broken. Why won't they let me go? I have paperwork to do."

Meri parroted Sheriff Taylor. "Do it when you're less fuzzy on pain medication. Besides, you had cameras on everything you did, and, according to my dad, you were already into the paperwork when things went boom. One more day, remember? Your heat pack is helping?"

"It is. Just not one for laying around."

"Okay, I have a plan. We can call one of your deputy friends to help fill out your paperwork with you."

"No. They're all covering my shifts." He had a thought, surprising because of all the pain meds. "ATF owes me a favor, and they've got to have people on desk duty." Nat groaned. "Like me. Six entire weeks."

Meri said, "On a positive note, you are alive, and so is an ATF agent." She shuddered. "I can't tell if they were brave or stupid."

"Okay, can you put my HUD glasses on me?" Meri did, and Nat sent a message, got a ping back. "They'll send someone. Anything to get their case perfectly situated."

"Good. Now, puzzle."

Nat used his HUD to zoom in on the pieces, slowly worked to get the rabbits hiding in the undergrowth into a more coherent picture. Meri chatted about her day getting food to clients, and her plans for her "slow times" when her injured clients regained their mobility. Some stayed with her service for convenience, but she lost some too.

They both looked up at a polite cough. A man stood in the doorway. "Agent Rafael Marat." He had a thin face with high cheekbones, dark hair to his shoulders, ropy arms under a thin, blue, long-sleeved ATF shirt, and wore black jeans and boots. "Scan me," he said, staring at Nat's HUD. He spoke with a slight accent.

"Oh, my." Meri rolled up the puzzle up in the felt, stowed it in a bag, and smiled at the agent. "I'm Meri Camber, and I'm leaving."

Rafael walked with a distinct limp. He shook Meri's hand. "I'm Rafe to...mostly everybody."

Meri smiled. "Um, Rafe, be sure Nat gets enough to drink, apple juice is there. Nat's voice gets scratchy. Libby will be by with cherry sorbet later."

"Thanks, Meri." Nat smiled at her. Meri gave Nat a quick peck on the cheek, then she was gone.

Rafe nodded. "Let me set up. I need to prop myself up. How did you score a private room?"

"One, supplemental insurance. Two, on the job injury. Three, cop privilege. Four, constant in-and-out of friends and cops would drive a roomie insane."

Rafe sighed. "Far too used to these kinds of places." He arranged himself so the chair faced Nat, and his left leg rested on the unoccupied end of the bed. Nat could see the outline of a brace under the jeans. "So, you're stir crazy, you're not off all the meds yet, you're itching to get something done, and there's a mound of forms from the raid. Ballsy, hitting up a major op with only three officers and a military conscript."

Nat shook a head that felt more like an angry lead balloon a bare millimeter on each side. "We know the area, plus Charlie is a terrain specialist, among other things. They were going to rabbit because whomever sideswiped Meri's car knew they were going to get caught."

"Good to know. So, let's start with the form you were beginning to fill out when the blast went off. Great job of photographing the scene and cataloguing the weapons. Nasty stuff, that."

Nat snorted. "Garottes and knives in boots and in hair. These guys were killers, no doubt."

"Two of them weren't. They were slaves. The cartel threatened their families. They're testifying like crazy. The Mexican authorities with some American help are clearing out a nest of vipers. Your taking all of them out alive gave us a hidden agent, still alive, and former slaves whose intel has been immensely valuable for our investigation."

"I just wanted to punish the guilty in a cage. Dead isn't punished." Nat used his finger to push the button to move slightly more upright. "Which cartel?"

"Los Zetas. You should feel pleased. There are guns, drugs, knives, and people who are alive to testify."

"It's good that this crop of bad guys is gone. It's stellar that they're out of our woods. But, there will always be another cooker making this stuff in a trailer somewhere.I've seen this crap destroy lots of lives, people committing suicide, destroying families, that sort of thing, in my job."

"Not in your family."

"Nope, my mom just doesn't know or accept me." Nat sipped from his cup. "No, they used banned pesticides, poisoned the land and water. They took slaves. The cartels don't care who or what they hurt." Nat sipped more, swallowed. "Shall we get to the forms?"

"We shall. So, the auto-formatter got me all the relevant information. Let's get the drawing of the crime scene down, shall we? We have your bodycam information and the scans."

"Let's get it done." Nat called up the bodycam files, and Rafe drew the scene with remarkable detail.

Charlie came in an hour and a half as they were beginning the last half of the checklist. "Meri gave me boxes to give to you," Charlie said to Nat.

Rafe carefully swung his leg down and stood. "Special Agent Rafael Marat, ATF."

"Charlie Camber, staff sergeant, US Marine Corps. I know who you are. Former Marine, went to ATF when some of the things you saw turned your stomach."

"Yes."

"Good. Now, have you told Nat who you really are now? Your current designation?"

"No, I have not." Rafe turned to Nat. "What Staff Sergeant Camber is not saying is that I was wounded in a raid on a warehouse. They put my leg back together, but it just doesn't have the strength, speed, or reaction time of the real one. I was told I would never walk again, but I pushed my way into walking. I decided to make myself useful, not just get by with desk duty to finish off my twenty years, and I'm no quitter. So, I became a trauma specialist, part of a multi-agency task force. I've helped dozens of agents and police officers who were traumatized in some way."

"I don't have PTSD," Nat growled through clenched teeth. "No nightmares. I can't sleep because of pain and enforced lack of activity. I don't rehash the scene over and over in my head."

Rafe nodded. "PTSD is a series of loops in the brain that the sufferer can't get out of. I doubt you have it, but I was genuinely between jobs, and my checking on you couldn't hurt."

"You could have led with that." Nat bored holes in Rafe with laser eyes.

Rafe nodded. "I should have, but you seemed to be so...gung ho. I wanted to check you out, unguarded, to get the best impressions."

Charlie glared at Rafe. "You were a fool. Nat is the most professional law enforcement officer I've ever met, and I've met a few. Now you've lost what you needed most to succeed."

"Trust. I know. I apologize. I genuinely just wanted to help."

"Help does not mean rummage through my brain without permission." Nat's glare was intense and unyielding.

Rafe stood. "I am sorry. I will be back after lunch to help you complete the paperwork. Nothing more."

Nat glared at Rafe while he turned and walked with that odd shuffling gait with one leg, a straight step with another, until the door shut behind him. "That was..."

Charlie nodded. "It was."

"Had enough shrinks. First because I got diagnosed as Kleinfelter's, XXY, then being agender. My mom is a narcissist. When I went to live with Coach Ma, Coach got me a good person to talk to for a few months. It all boiled down to my mom wanting me to be some ideal guy in her brain. Some giant football guy, I think. No idea, really."

"I never asked. What pronoun do you use?"

Nat sighed. "I'm bio-male, so 'he' and 'him' most of the time. I belong to an agendered group online, and they use words like 'hir' and 'cis'. I just don't think about it."

Charlie nodded. "Okay. Meri had me bring you some food. Baked honey chicken, two cheesy honey butter biscuits, cole slaw, baked apples with cinnamon."

"Bless her." Nat smiled wide as Charlie uncovered the dishes.

"Still hot." Charlie got the chicken, biscuits, and baked apples out of the hot box, then the coleslaw from the cold box. "Glad your right arm works."

Nat grinned at him. "So am I."

Charlie poured more apple juice from Meri's carafe into the drink container with the straw, and Nat ate while Charlie talked about the farm, the goats, the tiny house on wheels that was nearly complete. "Some author wants it, wants to travel south in winter, north in summer. Got two more orders in the pipeline, got to start before winter."

"Good plan."

Charlie put the empties away. "Let the guy Rafe give whatever report he's gonna give. He stumbled, did the wrong thing. Didn't know you when he did it, or he'd have done it some other way."

Nat's face grew stony. "Trust is earned."

"That it is."

"And once lost nearly impossible to get back."

Charlie nodded. "But you're not an ordinary person, now, are you?" That made Nat chuff out a laugh.

Nat had Charlie unroll the puzzle before he left with the empties. By the time Rafe returned, Nat had started work on the edge of the deer hiding behind the bushes. Rafe stared at the puzzle a while. "Nice picture. Hidden world."

"You pull that shit with me ever again, you're out on your ear." Nat found an edge piece, snicked it in.

"Got it." Rafe adjusted himself again. "I know I'll have to earn back your trust."

"Probably impossible."

Rafe nodded. "I like challenges. So, let's finish this list." They got through four forms before Nat carefully stretched what he could, and the nurse changed the pad on Nat's back from warm to cold.

Rafe stood and went through a series of moves designed to stretch his neck, back, and legs while the nurse was doing her thing. Nat snorted. "Recorded you. Gotta learn all those moves for my rehab."

Rafe stood, hands together in prayer position, and bowed. "I'll send you a more extensive video I made to help with post-injury stretching, with a lot of modifications." He tapped his HUD, called it up, and sent it.

"Thank you."

Libby knocked and came in just after the nurse left. "Whoa. Sorry."

"I'm Rafe Marat, Special Agent, ATF." Rafe offered his hand, and Libby took it, then dropped her hand.

"Nice to meet you. You hurt Nat again, I'll hurt you somehow." Libby smiled evilly.

Rafe nodded. "Protective people. I'll bring you breakfast, if you like."

Libby pointed at Rafe. "You'll pick up the scones and tea from my sweet shop. I'm the only one in town, so can't miss me."

"She's bad at taking 'no' for an answer," Nat warned.

"Of course." Rafe bowed his head. "See both of you tomorrow."

After the door closed, Libby bustled getting the food onto the tray while the nurse changed the ice to heat again. After the nurse left, Libby sighed. "That Rafe guy is an idiot."

"No, he's highly intelligent. He just took the absolutely wrong approach with me. I suspect he got rushed and didn't have time to review my file, know who I really am." Nat grinned at the contents of one of the boxes. "Chicken tacos in corn tortillas!" The tacos were small, perfect to eat with one hand.

"I've got cherry sorbet from Penny's shop and some of my butter brickle toffee crumbled on top as soon as you're finished with this."

"What about your shop?" Nat consumed a taco with lime and mango salsa.

Libby laughed. "Have you looked at the time lately?"

He checked his HUD readout. "What the hell?"

"Too busy." Libby smiled. "I had extra help. My brother Len came down and helped mop the front, wonder of wonders. And your doctor is…"

"Like one of your other brothers, except Davis is an orthopedic surgeon and my other doctor, Dr. Gee, specializes in the kind of poisoning I was subjected to. The third brother is an EMT. I've met them all." Nat reached for another taco.

"Davis is the doctor. Suave, debonair. Did time in the military, like you. Vic is the EMT. Len does yoga and is a home health god. You can use him when you go home."

Nat shrugged, swallowed the last bite of salsa. "I was hungrier than I thought."

"Obviously. Now, eat your sorbet, then you get nice drugs and a trip to the bathroom, even a shower."

"A shower would be heavenly. If I pass that test, I will go home tomorrow." He dug into the sorbet, and moaned.

Libby laughed. "That's what I like to hear."

The nurse came in, then they got Nat into the wheelchair, into the bathroom, stripped down, and on a seat. Libby sent the nurse away, stripped down to her own underwear, and washed Nat from head to toe. "Is it weird that I'm turned on and floppy from the medication at the same time?" Nat groaned.

Libby laughed. "I don't have the perfect body."

"I love your curves." Nat moaned as Libby rinsed his hair, then rubbed in the conditioner.

"I love your angularity." Libby dug her fingers into Nat's scalp.

"Angularity is sexy?" Nat moaned as Libby carefully rinsed his hair, then his sore back with hot water.

"You're like a coiled spring. All cougary. Not menacing, but ready to spring if something goes horribly wrong. Like my mother Lynette."

"Wait." Nat felt his eyebrows crawl into his scalp as Libby turned off the water, then took a towel and began drying Nat's hair. "Your mom can..."

"Turn into a mountain lion? Yes." Libby carefully patted Nat's back dry with the towel.

"Get out! Really?"

"Really. Okay, let's get you dried, dressed and back in bed. I've got more butter brickle for you." She got Nat back into the loose pants and top that had Velcro for the doctors to see what was wrong. Libby hummed the song "Lean On Me" as she got Nat back into the wheel-chair and back to bed. Nat's pain stood out in his eyes and he yelped a few times, but he hummed along.

The nurse took out the dirty linens. There were fresh sheets on the bed. Nat got another bump of pain meds, and lay back as Libby fed him brickle and refilled the apple juice. "Thank you," Nat told the nurse, a tiny woman with magenta braids.

"You will be sleeping soon, now. I'm Jeela. Call if you need me." Then, she was gone.

Nat grimaced, waiting for the drugs to do their magic. "You're too good to me. You're taking care of me, and we haven't spent enough time together."

"We will. But sex and pain do not go together."

"Not without safe words," Nat joked. They held hands, and Nat felt something fill him up deep inside. He let go as sleep pulled him down.

*D*avis was gentle with Nat. He was taller than his sisters, and moved with grace and ease. The examinations were quick and to the point. Davis had a magic touch with bone, tissue, and joint damage. In this case, caused by a concussive explosion and exposure to toxic air. "Your range of movement is much better. My brother Len will do very gentle physical therapy with you. You'll be aggressive with him because you're a cop and an athlete who is used to being in prime physical shape. You have to work harder at muscle tone because of the Klienfelter's. Don't act that way. Len gets his marching orders from me, not you. Do you comprehend what I am downloading to you?" Nat nodded, very carefully. "If you do the wrong thing, if you push yourself, you can do some very permanent damage. Then, no more cop. Do you understand?" Nat gave another minute nod. "I understand there are cold cases from all over the county. I also hear that some guy named Rafe, who may or may not be trustworthy, may be able to be your physical body to deal with them."

Nat sighed. "Hard to trust once it is gone, but I do need a body. Kind of a remote control robot."

Davis huffed out a laugh. "Good punishment, don't you think?"

Nat thought about it. "Yes, I suppose it is." He grinned.

"One more thing, off topic. In fact, I never said it."

"Can't hear a thing."

Davis grinned. "I married Kandace, and so did my brothers Len and Vic. Being in a relationship with multiple people is extremely difficult. Being in a relationship with bears involves a lot of sweet food and hard heads. My sisters deserve the best. If you need help on that end, call me, Len, or Vic. Maybe not Vic. Sometimes he's an asshole. But we're here if you need us."

Nat's eyes filled up. *I'm not alone anymore*, he thought. It was a strange feeling.

"That being said, if you deliberately hurt either one of them, I'll have to stop being one of your doctors. And, I'm damn awesome." Nat laughed. Davis waved, then he was gone.

FAMILY

*C*harlie helped Nat use the "recovery chair." "Button for heat is here." Charlie pointed to the little control panel on the side of the chair. "Stay away from the massage buttons. You're not healed enough for that. If you must do it anyway, use this button to set the level to Level One."

"Awesome."

"Here's the power." Charlie used a meaty finger to tap on the side of his smart sunglasses, lightened since he was indoors. He gave Nat control over the television with his HUD. "There's full VR capability," he said, pointing to the VR rig across the room. "I strongly suggest leaving that one alone. You don't want to jump in surprise and wrench your back."

Nat pretended to cringe, but only moved his body a millimeter or two. "I hear you."

"Okay, I moved this chair to be so close to the bathroom that you can practically fall in." Nat snorted. "There's a bell. Someone will answer. The dogs will be with me so you don't trip. They love rolling in sawdust. Go figure."

Nat laughed. "Go on. Bottles are full." He pointed to a bottle of cherry water, and the other bottle of spiced apple juice. "Run away. Be free!"

Charlie laughed from deep in his gut, a rolling sound that filled the room. He whistled, and the corgis pitter-pattered after him. The door shut, and Nat rejoiced in being absolutely alone. No more nurses, doctors, tests, or the steady influx of law enforcement personnel making sure Nat was all in one piece, physically and mentally. Rafe had gone back to...wherever he came from. His last words were, "Get better so you can kick ass." Rafe vanished, taking the scent of denim with him.

Even better than being alone, his forms were done. Nat had testified to Rafe and Chief Taylor, both of whom recorded the whole thing. So, if Nat dropped dead, his testimony was ready to go. Not that the people they'd either arrested or rescued were going to stand trial. Six had already pleaded guilty to a laundry list of charges, and the judge refused to throw out any of the environmental charges. They had text messages that said everyone knew about and had participated in the dumping, except for the money-counters and the chemist. The chemist had so many charges against her that she wasn't getting out of jail for decades.

So, Nat couldn't work because of back and shoulder strain. Nat had four weeks of only very specific timed movements, hot baths, and the pain sticker on his spine. He had a pile of books to read, but the invasive pain made reading for a long time difficult. He couldn't do what he usually did to clear his mind, which was to go to the gym. So, he began looking up how to write an article. Articles wouldn't take long and he could write, edit, and send them to publications.

When he got tired of writing, Nat could watch...well, no horror, because that bored him. He'd seen enough of it in real life. A thriller would make his back seize up if he got tense. Sunny comedies were often just stupid. Action and adventure may make him want to move around. So, that left science fiction and sword-and-sorcery fantasy.

So, Nat wrote an article on how meditation helped him deal with being diagnosed XXY and agendered in high school, and fell asleep mid-sentence. Then he woke up, finished the article, and watched a

VR series where a very young mistreated elf threw off the bonds of her oppressors.

Lynette came in with the dogs. They sat on their doggy behinds while she doled out treats, then they trotted outside to enjoy them on the porch. "Give me a minute to wash up," Lynette called out to Nat.

"No rush." Nat stretched very slowly and carefully, and then moved his body back to where it was.

Lynette washed her hands, dried them on a bright yellow towel, then opened up the refrigerator. "We have pasta with grilled chicken, apples and cheese with red bell pepper hummus, and a goat cheese apple pecan thing with whole-wheat crackers and pears."

"The goat cheese thing, please."

"Good, no reheating." Lynette had a strong face, very dark eyes, and blueblack hair. She brought over the lunch boxes."You want company, or are you so overjoyed with being alone that you're like the dogs with a bone?"

Nat pretended to look at his HUD. "I can fit in fifteen minutes with you, then I've got a nap scheduled."

Lynette laughed. "I will try to stay within that time frame." She opened her own box of the same lunch. "I smell like goats. Not the boys, thank the universe. They're munching kudzu. Make good money on those boys. Really one of the only ways to get rid of that invasive vine, and blackberry bushes too. Those will take over if you let them."

"Good to know." Nat scooped the soft goat cheese on a whole wheat cracker and moaned. "This is good."

"It is. We have a small farm, but a good one. We grow veggies in the ground and in our vertical farm building over there." Lynette pointed out the back window to the red building behind the farmhouse. "The pumpkin crop's going to be big this year. We'll probably sell all over the county. We have a really big field for the pick-your-own daytrippers."

Nat grinned. "Won't be working security this year."

"We've widened the road out back. People can park all along the width of the field, and we've got high school kids with clippers and strong arms and backs and carts to get the pumpkins into the vehicles so the turnover is pretty fast. Point, cut, put in a little cart, count, pay, go. There will be cinnamon apple cider and hot chocolate with the little marshmallows."

"Awesome."

"If you feel good enough, you can sit in an armchair and click people in. They wave their electronic payments, get in that way. Few people use cash anymore."

"Libby's stocking the event?" Nat raised an eyebrow.

"No, the various county organizations are. The middle schoolers are selling candy bars, the elementary schoolers created hand-stamped gift wrap for Christmas, the high schoolers have a coffee bar for all the winter camps and trips, and the churches, temple, and mosque are having a bake sale. Price of a pumpkin drops if you bring food for the food bank. They'll all be in booths. You can be near-immobile and still put in a shift. How are you at sales patter?"

Nat took in a deep breath, then said, "Get your candy bars, get your candy bars here! Deep, dark chocolate from the rainforest, folks! With your choice of nuts or dark cherries!"

"Wow, that's pretty good." Lynette laughed. "Wait, I know that sale. High school football, soccer, track, and volleyball teams, picked the best chocolate ever, made a fortune."

"I investigated the cocoa-to-chocolate site in Costa Rica, worked out a contract with Coach Ma. We got enough money for all the school athletic programs for three years." Nat slightly tilted his head to the side. "In fact, I'm stunned no one ever stole the money. Some of the guys were hitting the hash pipe very heavily in those days. One of them got kicked off the team."

"That...wait, Ryland Lee."

"Kind of an asswipe then."

"Still is. Became a used vehicle dealer two towns over."

Nat raised his eyebrows. "Someone gave him a job?"

"His uncle's dealership."

"You are a font of information," Nat observed. "Do you remember the robberies that stopped four years ago?"

"I do," Lynette said. "Wait, if it's a college student..."

"They may begin again if said college student has trouble paying for things."

Lynette nodded. "I'll listen to gossip. That's a very good theory."

"Thank you." They sat silently, munching on their food.

Lynette took the empties. "I hid Libby's contribution to lunch. My husband would consume an entire container of nearly anything Libby makes, then act surprised and stunned if someone called him out on it." She grinned, stood on a short ladder, and fished out a white box with Libby's logo in gold on its side.

"How did Libby and Meri both end up making food?"

Lynette laughed, then climbed off the ladder. She put the box down, then opened up the freezer. "Lime, cherry, or both?"

"Both, please."

"Okay. Anyway, as you can guess with teenage boys in the house, let alone girls in the same growth-spurt predicament, I hired a young man named Randolph Thacker to come in and help us with the massive amounts of food growing wolves need."

"Randy Thacker? The St. Louis celebrity chef?"

"One and the same." Lynette scooped the sherbert into fat plastic cups, opened the white box, then sliced up the almond mint fudge with a paring knife and sprinkled it over the sherbert. She then tied up the box, and hid it in a completely different hiding place, in an old pot.

Nat had to laugh. "I thought Charlie cooked!"

"Grills, mostly. Another reason why we needed Randy. Where was I? Well, Randy found out what everyone liked and hated, then made these color-coded boxes that could be lunch or dinner. Stuffed them with main dishes and sides. Made packing lunch boxes for school a one-minute thing, and you could just change boxes if you got bored. Meri wanted to know how to do it, became his helper, and became adept at one-pot and slow-cooker meals. I cook, and so does Jen, and our manly man does love his grilling. And anything sweet, so he'll make cakes and pies. Getting him to make tartlet or bite-sized things is impossible. But, I digress."

Lynette sat down next to Nat. "Anyway, Randy went to bigger and better things, and we paid Meri to do her thing. Had the groceries delivered, then she cooked three times a week. Made enough to go to business and culinary school once nearby families had their kids eat lunch or dinner with us, stay over for a weekend. We were Randy's free advertising, then Meri's. Now, he is doing quite well for himself." They dug into the treats.

"Wow, this lime with mint is awesome!" Nat sucked on his spoon. "So, that's Meri. What about Libby?"

Lynette laughed. "She had to cook or be cut out of Meri's life." Nat laughed. "No, she did some exotic chocolate-passionfruit thing for a bake sale. Sold like hotcakes. She experimented with fudge, almond bark, that kind of thing. Was asked to bake for every bake sale."

"I was on a no-sugar kick in high school. Still am, mostly, except for long days at work. My apple drink has natural sugars. Sometimes sugar and caffeine are your friends. So I didn't pick up on that one."

"Anyway, she went to a different culinary school specializing in candy and bakery things. She still makes scones and muffins, but draws the line at actual bread. She made lots of high protein, gluten-free, and diabetic stuff. Experimented on us." Lynette cringed.

"That bad?"

"The initial iterations were horrifying. Some things even goats won't eat." Nat laughed.

They finished their treat. "Let me get these empties, and I'll help you get to the bathroom." Lynette stood.

"I have a better idea. I'll start walking, and by the time you're done filling up the dishwasher and have read a novel, I'll be done."

Lynette laughed. "I'll help if you call. Just scream, yell, or send up a smoke signal." Nat snorted out a laugh, washed up, and Lynette helped Nat back to the chair. "Sleep," Lynette suggested, and put an extra pain tab on Nat's shoulder.

Nat shuddered with relief. "Thank you." Lynette arranged the light blanket around Nat, and smiled as he slid into sleep.

A few hours later, Nat awoke to a sloshing noise. He looked over towards the kitchen, and saw Charlie pull ribs out of a pot. "Gotta cook them here, then smoke 'em. Can't get a 3D printer to get the right smoked flavor."

"Got it." Nat smiled sleepily at Charlie.

"Be done in an hour. Go back to sleep."

Nat carefully stretched. "I think I'll finish my article on meditation for sports." He'd edited and sold the other one, to his own shock.

"Suit yourself." Charlie brought the ribs out back, then came back in for bags of marinated chicken and wrapped fish and herbs in packets, and carried them back out.

Nat rewrote the article and put it aside, then watched another episode of the epic fantasy show. The young elf had just cornered the thief when Jen came in.

"Hey. Just getting the veggies."

"Cool." Nat watched as Jen brought out corn and potatoes.

By the time dinner was served, Nat was getting sleepy again. They had dinner at the big table. "Finished the roof, love," Jen told Charlie. "The solar installer is coming tomorrow."

"Excellent. Going to have this thing ready to go soon. The septic system can be installed in two days."

The door opened, and a herd of small feet ran in. "Daddy!" yelled Adam. "I got the job!"

Charlie put his rib down, wiped his hands, and took Adam into his lap. Lynette rushed to get Bobby washed up, and Jen prepared the booster and high chairs.

"You got to write on the board?" Charlie asked his son.

"I did!"

"Let's get you washed up and get you some chicken." Charlie stood, Adam on his hip, and walked Adam towards the bathroom. Jetta came in, got all the coats hung up, washed her hands, and started prepping kid plates.

Bobby came out of the bathroom and announced, "I got a job, too. I get to help put up jackets, coats, and lunches."

"Good job!" Charlie said, and gave him a high-five.

Charlie and Lynette got the kids seated. The girls squalled until they got cut-up chicken and brown sugar carrots. Jen kept the girls fed and babbling the story of their day, which apparently involved a game with ponies. "They're actual ponies," Lynette clarified. "Neighboring farm."

"I roded last year." Bobby crammed chicken into his mouth.

Jen grinned. "Rode, and yes, you did. You did a fine job, too."

The dogs were banned from begging during dinner, and wisely sat down next to the highchairs to catch and eat any falling food. River tried to slip the dogs her carrots; Jen stopped that attempt. Bethany was full of pony stories; apparently her pony was named Rocky Road. "Rocky Road is betterer dan Gitter," she said, clearly.

"Glitter." Jetta grinned.

River shook her head. "Is not. Gitta betta."

Charlie shook his head. "No arguing during dinner, ladies."

"Her is," Bethany pointed out.

"No table," River was quick to add.

Adam puffed out his chest. "I got a better job."

Charlie shook his head again. "A job's a job. Nothing too big or too small, better or worse. Just gotta…"

"Get the job done," both boys said.

Dinner at the table was loud, with questions, answers, quips, and barbs flying around. Nat finished his ribs, fish, potatoes, and carrots, and watched the entire thing as if it were a tennis game. The dogs picked up any spilled or thrown food. They were tremendous vacuum cleaners. The kids got lemon balls rolled in coconut for dessert, and consumed them while the adults cleaned up the meal. Nat got his own lemon balls, and once the thundering army of small children were grappled and dragged off for baths, got his own hot soak.

By the time he got out, dried off, and dressed, the little ones were down for the count and the boys were watching an action cartoon. Jen got up and lurched forward to help Nat get settled. "Don't worry. Storytime soon."

Adam jumped up. "I get to pick."

Bobby crossed his arms over his chest. "No fair."

"How is 'every other day' unfair?" Jetta asked her sons.

Jen rolled her eyes. "They're on a fair/unfair kick."

Nat grinned. "Still on one. Law and order, ma'am."

Jen choked out a laugh. "Good."

Charlie came back down. "I'm going to start reading on my own."

"No, Daddy! My turn to pick!" Adam popped up, and ran right towards Nat. Jen blocked his way and made him circle Nat's chair. "Night, Nat!" Adam ran full-tilt towards his dad.

"No fair." Bobby stuck out his lower lip.

"I can read you a story if you bring one down," Nat offered.

Bobby's eyes lit up. "Be right back, Nat." He ran up the stairs on chubby legs.

"You've earned yourself respect, love, and a new job," Jen warned. "That boy's liable to attach to you like a barnacle."

"I like kids." Nat smiled.

Jen's eyes suddenly teared up. "That's really good."

Bobby came back down, waving a book over his head. "Dinosaurs!"

"Good choice." Nat read the whole book with Bobby and made dinosaur noises too. By the time he was done, Bobby's eyes were at half mast.

"Upsy daisy." Jen got the little boy in her arms, picked up the book, and headed towards the stairs. "Thank you."

"No problem." Nat stood and shuffled to the bathroom before bed. He entered the little downstairs room, and found his water and juice bottles and HUD on the nightstand, the sheets pulled back, pillows propped up for his arm and leg, and pillows up so he could recline. Nat lay down, and Libby called on her HUD.

"How's the patient?" Libby asked.

"Sore. Sleeping really early."

"Better than sleeping with the fishes." Libby used a mobster accent.

"I keep that one at the top of my gratitude list. Just tired, and sore, so that makes me more tired."

Libby sighed gustily. "I am exhausted too. School bus came in from out of town, the entire lacrosse team."

"Oh, my. Lots of work."

"True that. Are you in bed?"

"Yep. Just got comfortable."

"Let's watch something together," Libby suggested.

"I just started watching this thing about an elven girl. She is sweet and tough like you."

Libby snorted, then spoke excitedly. "The Ironwood Circle? I just started watching that too! Let me pull it up. What episode are you on?"

"The second one."

"Wait, I'll see if Meri wants to watch." Libby called Meri, then Libby came back on the line. "Nope, she's cooking. It's just us chickens."

"Let's do this." They pulled up the episode. Nat said, "Three, two, one..." and they got started.

EXPANSION

$\mathcal{M}$eri came by with more boxes, put them in the refrigerator, and put a box in the microwave oven. Nat shuffled out of the bathroom, hair still wet. He stepped over Rascal, the loving corgi, and maneuvered himself onto the recliner. Rascal jumped up to join him, and Nat stroked the dog's silken ears.

Meri came over with a tray. "Down, Rascal." The dog hopped down, then ran out the dog door.

"Love the dogs, lucky I didn't trip over them." Nat breathed deeply. "Omelet?"

Meri put the tray down on the TV tray in front of Nat. "Two little egg cup omelets with sage sausage, cheddar, and red bell pepper in a basil cream sauce, side of very crispy bacon, another side of home fries. Eat up, I've got more people to feed." She grinned.

Nat raised his eyebrows, impressed. "Go on. I can put the dishes in the sink. Can't wash them, and it takes me twenty minutes to walk there, but you can move along."

Meri laughed. "I've got three more deliveries this morning, so I'll take you up on it." Meri took her hot box and scooted out of the house.

Just outside, Meri saw Rafe pull up on his motorcycle. "Hey. Did you eat breakfast?"

"Nope." Rafe took off his gloves, stuffed them in his black full-face helmet, and locked them up under the seat.

"Take out a red box, zap it, and consume. You can put the dishes in the dishwasher."

Rafe grinned, amused. Both Meri and Libby had taken to giving him orders since his colossal slipup with Nat. "Will do." He saluted, and Meri was gone.

Rafe stopped to pet the dogs, knocked in a special way he'd learned during his time in the ATF that identified him as another agent. He entered. "Nat, it's just me."

"Hello, Just Me." Nat had the HUD projected on the giant TV screen, reports on one side of the screen, an evidence bag on the other one. "Haven't you been called back yet?"

"Administrative leave, remember?" Rafe had gone back out into the field and had strongly disagreed with the treatment of an agent, an ex-soldier who had been tortured for four days. Rafe had gone up the chain of command and had been sidelined for it. He didn't regret it; Rivka Kalensong would get much better treatment.

He had elected to help Nat on cold cases as penance for the loss of trust. On the surface, Nat's tasks seemed to be stultifying. Old cases going back ten, twenty, thirty years? But, time and the forward march of technology combined with funds raised specifically for the purpose of examining new evidence allowed for old cases to receive a new look. They were looking at a rash of robberies, two rapes, and three murders. They had sucked in cases from surrounding hollers and even entire counties if the M.O. was the same.

Rafe used a kitchen mitt to bring over his hot plate and his other hand to carry some black cherry soda. He'd gone far past his coffee quota that morning dealing with agents in other time zones who were finishing PTSD treatment.

Rafe stared at the screen. One rape had yielded fibers that matched two other rapes in other counties; they were expanding the search. "Definitely a trucker or traveling salesperson." He put his stuff down on a TV tray and sat. He bit into the home fries, redolent of rosemary and garlic. "Universe sings. Meri can cook."

Nat laughed. "Wait until you taste more of what Libby makes." He finished off one of his mini-omelets, then pointed at the screen. "Our unsub is using specific highways. I've got two more cases. One drop of blood and one cigarette, and I think they'll match if the cigarette is from our perp. One of the victims broke his nose."

"Fighter victims help us close cases." The dogs stared at both men lovingly, hoping for dropped bacon or sage sausage. Rafe snorted at their doggy devotion. "I take it you ordered the tests."

"Actually, they've already been conducted. The reports are…" Nat threw one, then the other DNA test on the screen. "Yesri says we have a match!" Yesri was the DNA analyst for several rural counties. She was methodical and precise. Her company was contracted by the state to help out with a backlog of both regular and second-look unsolved cases. "Okay, this person isn't in the CODIS system." The system matched DNA collected from both crime scenes and perpetrators.

"Well, do we have any fingerprints?"

"We have a partial handprint and a partial thumbprint. We need to go through all these cases to find more. If we can get a full print…"

"Then we're in business." Rafe smiled. That old hum, that feeling in the body when a case started to come together, was in his nervous system. Nat had that same intent look on his face. That clenched jaw, narrowed eyes, and razor-sharp focus made Rafe realize that Nat was all in. "We need something to tie this shitbird to the other assaults."

"Working on it. Hair, fibers. Anything we can take to Yesri's company for a second look is…wait. The Jefferson case. Fibers." Nat pulled them up, and did a fist-pump. "Looks like our shitbird made the mistake of using the same jacket. Blue fibers, artificial."

"A stadium jacket, maybe?" Rafe looked at the reports while slipping the dogs a little bacon. "Look, the Mansel case. One of the guys in the bar that night was wearing a blue jacket."

"We've got bar camera feed," Nat crowed. "Let's find our perp."

*B*y the time Jen came in to prepare lunch, dogs at her feet, both men were having separate phone conversations. "Jasper, we need fingerprints and DNA. Go in, buy the guy a bottled beer or soda, take the bottle back. Yeah, he's scheduled to make the final repair at six tonight at someplace called Quall's." Rafe paced back and forth behind the couch.

"Chief Taylor, Judge Reinghart loves you more." Nat laughed. "Yes, the warrant could be served here, or in the next county. The guy will be at Quall's making repairs. He spends all his time cleaning out and repairing the systems in restaurants and bars, replacing hoses, that sort of thing. We think that's how he trolls for victims. Yes, sir. Thank you, sir." Both men dropped their links.

Lynette stared at them both. "Progress, I take it?"

"Rapist should be in a cage pretty soon. Provided new evidence matches, of course." Nat grinned, then carefully stood. Nat and Rafe bumped fists. "What is for lunch?"

"We have chicken mozzarella sandwiches with Cool Ranch Doritos. I made chicken mozz yesterday, and I have a gorgeous pesto and a lot of French bread." Lynette grinned. "Plus Meri cut up a lot of veggies. Are you staying, Rafe?"

Rafe grinned and patted his growling stomach. "We've got two more cases to work on. I'm heading out before dinner. I've got to put in some gym time."

"Okay. I'll get this started."

Rafe stood. "Let me help."

Lynette grinned. "Be my guest."

Nat made slow progress to the bathroom. Lynette gave the dogs treats so they would stay out from under Nat's feet.

Lunch was incredible. They sat at the kitchen table and polished off the sandwiches with sodas. "Have you guys found the college robber yet?" Lynette asked.

"What?" Rafe raised his eyebrows.

Nat gave a slow shrug. "Making progress, Lynette. I have two suspects. Rafe, I hit you up for the ones with serious jail time. Gotta make things look good on your resume."

Rafe snorted. "Good luck saving that." He took a swig of black cherry cola, and explained the situation to Lynette. "I went over a senior agent's head. He was nickel-and-diming his own agent's treatment. I'm on administrative leave. Nat here gave me a task and I thought I'd hate it. But I found out I enjoy it. I usually go for more determined criminals. Crime is still crime, pain is pain. It's just that some people higher up on the food chain are responsible for nastier things. Or are in control of the events that lead up to them."

Nat nodded. "The last case sidelined me, and I've got to admit I was not a happy camper." Rafe snorted. Nat held up a hand. "Those people were destroying a mountain, making poison, and had actual slaves up there." Lynette looked sick. "Can say that despite the hit I took, it felt great to send these people to justice. I don't regret it, not really. I just hate forced inactivity."

Lynette laughed. "I used to have four teens in the house. Now I've got four littles. So, I get what forced inactivity does to someone who is nearly always in motion."

Nat took more chips from the bowl in the middle of the table. "I look at open-unsolved cases all the time. People should not get away with hurting people." Rafe and Lynette both nodded. "Getting a chance to work on these and really put some people away is rewarding."

Lynette nodded sharply. "Glad your recovery is going well."

Nat sighed. "I should never have chosen a second-floor walkup."

"Where's your place?" Lynette asked.

"I live six blocks from work, four from the firehouse. The sirens are what got me banned from going back home. I could start awake and damage something. Anyway, I live over Jaleesa Jackson's glass shop."

Lynette smiled. "That lamp over there is hers." She pointed at a stained-glass lamp in the style of a hummingbird, way up high where little children couldn't reach it.

"She does good work. Anyway, I'm usually at work, the gym, or being a ref for soccer games." Nat cringed at the inability to do that one. "Anyway, the kilns keep me warm all winter, and it kind of sounds like hissing downstairs. Puts me to sleep."

Rafe grinned. "Can I stay there while I'm here? I'll pay you less than I would pay a hotel, but I'll also keep it clean and dusted."

Nat realized he had to decide whether or not to trust the man. "You trampled my trust."

Rafe lost the grin. "I was an idiot. I'd like a chance to earn back your trust. May I do that?"

"Fine, I'll give you the code. You have to feed my feline. I'll call Myrna and tell her you'll be coming over and that you'll feed the cat."

"Another reason for staying here. Our Kandace tripped over that giant Maine coon cat of hers and set herself back while recovering from being slammed into a cliff while climbing." Lynette poured more soda into her glass.

Both men scrunched up their faces in sympathy. Nat shuddered. "Remind me not to complain. Ever again."

Lynette laughed. "Human nature. Now, eat up. I've got a tiny house to finish. It won't build itself." They dug in.

~

*R*afe was out helping to arrest and file the paperwork for another miscreant on their list in another town when the first Pumpkin Weekend began. Everyone was up at oh-god-thirty. They drank coffee to pry open their eyes and sucked down bacon, sage sausage, egg, and cheese mini casseroles.

After breakfast, Meri put Nat in her vehicle and drove him to the pumpkin patch. She put him in the admissions tent. "Portable potty directly behind you, and this is a semi-reclining seat. Your footstool has hand wipes and toilet paper under its lid." Nat got himself situated in the chair, feet on a box, and Meri covered his legs with a blanket. "Entry fee is two dollars per, kids free. They get a refund of that when they check out if they buy pumpkins. One dollar off for canned or dry goods, the boxes are there." She pointed to the giant blue bins. "The Boy Scouts are selling hot chocolate and apple cider, the Girl Scouts cookies." Nat laughed. "The sports teams have various chocolates and candy, the church people have pies and cakes, and the synagogue people have hot, fresh bagels."

Nat groaned. Meri laughed. "I'll snag you some. Anyway, the mosque people have a falafel cart." Nat groaned again. Meri laughed and smacked his good shoulder. "Be good, or you'll be unable to walk around the house." She held up two carafes. "Hot chocolate in the silver one, coffee in the red one. Got it?" Rafe nodded. "You should have help rotating through, plus one of us will zip through and take excess cash off your hands. Most people will swipe, though, so easy-peasy."

It was not easy-peasy. There were a lot of people. There were babies in papoose packs, octogenarians with walkers or scooters, and everything in between. Families with little ones on their heads, in carriers, in wagons. Bigger ones on bikes with baskets on the front or back. Adults walking, shuffling, laughing, even some singing. They wore sweaters, jackets, jeans, sweats, and the occasional hardy one in shorts. Nat knew many of them. He kept his face in a smile and his eyes level. Everyone knew about the cartel takedown, so he didn't have to explain his injuries. He did have to give an update on how he was, which was healing slowly. His left arm in a sling to keep him from using protesting joints and muscles was a dead giveaway.

Nat grew heartily sick of the beep-beep-beep of the card reader. And, of course, the how-are-you question. There were only so many ways to say "improving slowly but steadily." Many people wanted to congratulate Nat on the takedown. Nat could only say "group effort" once or twice before being hailed as a hero, which drove him insane. He'd gotten himself half blown up and with crap in his lungs. That wasn't heroic.

Sheriff Taylor came by about an hour into Nat's shift. "Love what you've done with the place."

Nat snorted. "Not my doing." He smiled at Mrs. Ledbetter, a stocky woman in a blue sweater, flowered skirt, and sensible shoes as the woman put a can in the donation bin. He made sure she got beeped in with the discount. "Thanks for the donation! Have fun!" Nat gave her a little wave.

Mrs. Ledbetter giggled. "Gotta get a pumpkin, then I'm helping Darla sell cookies!"

"I'm sure you'll sell out before long!"

"On it! Get better soon!"

Sheriff Taylor tried to speak. "Just wanted to tell you that..." He was interrupted by four teen girls who were simultaneously laughing, taking selfies, and paying Nat. All four of them were dressed nearly identically, and looked like dark-haired clones. Nat waved them on. "That the cases..."

A man came up with a toddler on his head and a baby in a papoose pack. "Kids are how much?"

"Free." The father smiled, waved in his fee, and hiked out with the kid on top drumming on his head. "Talk fast," Nat said to his commanding officer.

"Need some help?"

"Yes, sir." Sheriff Taylor came in through the side of the tent, commandeered coffee and a blanket, and waved people through as Nat took a break.

Meri swung by, pressed a falafel and a cup of hot cider into the grateful sheriff's hand. "Bless you."

Meri kissed his cheek. "Eat fast. Not often that one's boss helps you out."

Sheriff Taylor sighed. "We don't shoot our wounded, ma'am."

Nat came back and received his own falafel and cider. "Good boss lady."

"You betcha," said the sheriff. Meri snorted and scooted off.

Nat sat back down. With two of them working, they got the line down until there was a break in it. "What's up?"

"Last of them got convicted. Got every single one of them to plead guilty. Sentencing is final, a decade or more with all the federal charges. Human trafficking got the perpetrators a minimum of twenty-two years. The victims got green cards and counseling and each have good job offers in other cities. Your work, your testimony, was instrumental."

"That was unbelievably fast." Nat drank more cider, and passed on cash to Len who dropped off artichoke bell pepper, apple walnut cinnamon, and sun-dried tomato bagels and three flavors of cream cheese. The men chose their cream cheeses and dug in.

"Special court team now does those high-profile cartel convictions. Makes sense to separate out the nasty cartel people from the people who shoplift or do something stupid while intoxicated." They both snorted; they'd seen that and much more. "The progress you've made on the cold cases hasn't been unnoticed." The sheriff held up a hand. "I know Rafe helped. But, still, got some stuff off our books that have just stuck with me. Thank you, deputy."

Nat shook his head, rang through two more families. "Just doing my job, sir. I got really bored."

The sheriff laughed. "Not much chance of that with us, huh?" He stood, brushed bagel bits off his shirt, folded up the blanket and put it back on the chair. "I've got to get pumpkins for the office and my house. What can I bring you?"

Rich Felter swung by, put two cups of cider and two cookies down right in front of Nat. The man was all lanky bone and muscle, with a broad nose crowding a narrow face. "For the hero cop."

"I'm not...I can't accept..." Nat sputtered.

"My sister, Marie, she's off that crap you arrested those cartel people for two years now. Got her teaching certificate, can you believe it?" Rich's brown eyes filled with tears.

"That's really good," said Sheriff Taylor.

"Amazing," said Nat.

"Deputy, say thank you." The sheriff's stare brooked no argument.

"Thank you." Nat worked to make the words genuine.

"No problem. Have a great day!" Rich went off in search of the perfect pumpkin.

"Deputy, I hereby order you to go against policy and accept the food and drinks these nice people will offer you today. You're off duty, injured, and probably need pain meds. I'll send one of the thousand Cambers here today to bring you some more hot drinks when I leave."

"Yes, sir." Nat handed his boss a cookie and one of the hot ciders. "Thanks for your help with the Halloween pumpkin madness."

"Thank you, Deputy. Have a good one, you hear?" Sheriff Taylor waved and was gone.

~

*V*ic swung by. "Hey, Nat. Was supposed to relieve you an hour ago, but there was a little boy meltdown, followed by a screaming match."

Nat held up a hand, uninterested in the explanation. "Be back." He scooted to the restroom and was almost run down by two boys with small orange pumpkins in their hands. He made it back alive, and was surprised to see Meri at the booth, hands on her hip, glaring at Vic. "Where is Nat's medicine, Vic?"

Vic turned white. "I'm so sorry." He patted his pockets, came up with a small sticker.

"Sit," Meri said to Nat. He sat. Meri gave him a new cup of cinnamon-laced cocoa, and had him sip it while she stuck a sticker under his sweater in between his shoulder blades. "Lunchtime for you." Meri had him lean his good side on her while she maneuvered him into a golf cart. She took off at a good clip. "Damn stoic cop."

"Falafel." He pointed.

Meri sighed and stopped at the tent. "Kebab or falafel?"

"Both, with fries. Chicken. Side of tzatziki sauce."

Yusef overheard the order, shouted it out. In two minutes flat, a boy with dark brown hair cut short and a ready smile came out. "No charge for the hero cop, my father says."

"Tell your father thank you. I'm part of a team. Like you and your dad."

The boy grinned. "I am Berat."

Meri took the food so the boy could shake Nat's hand. "I am Nat. I am so happy your food is here. It is delicious."

Berat grinned that infectious smile of his again. "Father says the after-school program will be funded in a single weekend, if we do not run out of food!"

Meri grinned, handed the food back to Nat, and handed Barat a card. "This is my cell number in blue. If your dad needs help with snacks for the after-school program, give me a call. I know some people."

The boy took the card and smiled. "Thank you." Meri grinned, and took off towards the house, dodging teens texting each other, herds of tweens, and the occasional parent chasing a toddler determined to escape. They passed the corn maze, the pumpkin coloring and carving booth, and the pumpkin pulp/seed removal service. People could get their separated pumpkin guts back for cooking soups, pumpkin pies, breads, and the like, or could donate it. Volunteers were baking with a portable oven and packing the fresh pumpkin-laced food to bring to the food banks, homeless and women's and children's shelters, and soup kitchens all over the county.

"This is a nice operation." Nat gestured with a fry. "Keeps a lot of people doing fun things on the weekends, and raises a lot of money for charity."

"We hire a lot of teens for parking enforcement, too. I think half the high school is working today, as well as the community college in Fullerview."

They finally approached the farmhouse. Len ran down, pried Nat out, bag of food and all, and waved to Meri.

Meri zoomed off. "Where's she going? Is there a national emergency I'm not aware of?"

Len grinned. "It's all hands on deck for pumpkin picking weekends. You get food and a two-hour nap. Then you've got work."

Nat groaned. "No rest for the wicked." Len chuffed a laugh.

GAME NIGHT

*I*t was bonkers all weekend. Everyone spent the week recovering. Finally, Friday rolled around, Game Night. It was half past four in the afternoon when people began to arrive. Jen started in the kitchen. She took out a wide variety of utensils, bowls, cutting boards, baking sheets, and the like, and started to assemble stations. Lynette let the dogs out and began assembling ingredients at the stations. "Almond flour for that one." Jen pointed to the station at the far left.

Frustrated by his slow pace, Nat washed up and walked super-slowly to the office. He stole an office chair that, miraculously, had a footrest and even reclined. Len walked in the door and made a beeline to Nat with that boneless Zen speed of his that made it look like he wasn't moving fast when he was nearly running. He caught Nat's hands and led him around the chair and helped him sit in it. "Not. An. Invalid." Nat made the claim through a haze of breathless pain. Len had been all over Nat with physical therapy. The improvements were slow, with a lot of ice and heat in between. At the end of the day, Nat could feel each bruised muscle.

"You're an idiot, but I can see you want to help. We'll find something you can do one-armed."

Nat snorted. "I. Am not. The one-armed man. Killed. No one's wife."

Len chuckled at the *Fugitive* reference and pushed Nat to the table. "Did you wash your hands?"

"Yes." Len snorted and handed over some hand sanitizer anyway.

Lynette came in, red-cheeked from the chill outside. She shooed the dogs back out with her feet because she had cloth grocery bags in her hands. Len made it over in his eel-like way, took the bags, kissed her cheek, and eeled back. He unloaded the bags of goodies directly onto the kitchen island. Lynette washed up and took out two sets of measuring cups and spoons. She looked up recipes on her cell phone and put the right amount of everything into small bowls.

Lynette removed sweet Italian sausage from its container, put it in a bowl, and placed it in front of Nat. "How do you want this?" Nat asked.

Lynette grinned. "That's for the stuffed mushrooms. Remove the casings and break them up so I can fry them up."

"On it." Nat stabbed each link with a fork, transferred the fork to his left hand, then used a knife to tease the casings off. He used the fork to break up the sausage. Len sat beside Nat, put cream cheese and sour cream into a bowl, and mixed it up. He then added and stirred together scallions, garlic, salt, and pepper in another bowl. Len took the sausage to Jen along with his bowls. Jen washed a mound of veggies while Lynette doled them out. Len brought back a wet wipe, a bowl of rinsed and dried button mushrooms, and two small bowls for Nat. "Save the stems in this bowl." Len pointed. "Can you twist the stems off?"

Nat shrugged. "Never know until you try." The wave of pain was receding, washing out with the ability to help others. He held the mushrooms in his left palm while twisting off the stems with his right finger and thumb. He grinned. "On it."

Charlie came back in with the dogs on his heels, sent the corgis back out with bones, and washed his hands in the sink. "I've got this, darling." He kissed Jen's cheek.

Jen pointed to a skillet on the stove. "Cook up the Italian sausage in some olive oil and a little garlic."

"Stuffed mushrooms? On it, love." The man looked like a giant in the kitchen, but he moved with alacrity and purpose.

Len took Nat's bowl of mushroom stems, diced them, and put them back in the bowl. He walked them over to Charlie. "For you, big man."

"For the stuffed mushrooms? Where are my breadcrumbs and Parmesan?" Len pointed out the little bowls with the pre-measured ingredients, and grabbed refrigerated crescent roll dough and two packages of mini hot dogs. Len put the hot dogs down, cut open the bag, and poured them into a bowl. He put the bowl in front of Nat, and cracked open both canisters of dough with a loud pop. Nat jumped a little although Len was opening them directly in front of him.

Len noticed. "A tiny touch of PTSD concerning loud, sudden noises will pass."

Nat grimaced. "It didn't even sound anything like that. It was more of a *whomp*. It went off underground. Then dust, dirt, fire, and noxious odors."

Charlie nodded. "Your brain is reacting to a stimulus, deputy. It will pass, just like everything else." The garlic sizzling in the butter sounded and smelled amazing. Charlie took out his phone and put on a bizarre music playlist that had everything from Willie Nelson to Jay-Z.

Nat concentrated on getting the dough rolled out. Len scored the dough into smaller pieces, and Nat rolled the dough on the mini-sausages to make tiny "pigs in a blanket." Nat put them on a cookie sheet. Len came over with melted butter and garlic and a tiny brush and brushed the dough. Len put them in the oven, and came back with cooked shrimp on a new cutting board and a knife. Nat cut them up while Len whipped up the cream cheese, sour cream, and mozzarella cheese. Len put the shrimp in the mix, and Lynette came over with scallions to be chopped. "Half in this recipe; need more for the cheddar dip."

Nat looked down at his waist. "I'll be nine hundred pounds if you expect me to eat all of this."

Everyone laughed. "We're just getting started," Charlie boomed. He took the sausage mixture off the heat, scooped it in a bowl, added the other contents, mixed for a bit, then began stuffing mushrooms.

"Meri and Libby are coming." Jen brought over cooked bacon for Nat to crumble. "They bring the desserts."

Nat brightened internally. "I can roll with that."

Libby let the dogs in, and they ran under the table, hoping for dropped food. Libby had two bags full of bakery boxes in hand. "Meri's on her way. She's dropping off dinner for a client on the other side of town. She saw Nat and laughed. "Got you swept up in the doings?"

Nat grinned. "Looks like it."

"I've got pecan and key lime pie, mint fudge, and caramel apple bites." Libby put the pies on the counter. "Plus caramel, chocolate mint, and cinnamon syrups." She stole some bacon.

"I think my heart just stopped from the carbs and sugar." Nat smiled at Libby.

"Screw moderation." Charlie kissed Libby's cheek. "I know you've been working all day, Chef, but the sausage-sour cream-cheddar dip and the bacon cheddar bites aren't finished yet."

Nat came to Libby's defense. "Libby, no, you've been working all day. Bring me whatever Charlie just asked for and sit next to me. You can give me directions."

"Nat has a point." Lynette glared at her husband. "Sit, Libby, I'll get the rest of what Nat needs."

"I'll have Meri bring more sour cream." Lynette sighed. "I swear, we use it by the gallon."

Libby sat next to Nat, and bowls and plates of ingredients appeared as if by magic in front of them, along with paring knives, cutting boards, and utensils. "Goody. I cook for a living, then I just volunteered to do more."

Nat laughed. "Just direct me."

Lynnette grinned and bopped to Gwen Stefani singing about bananas. "This is prep. Your father and I are cooking."

"I'm the runner." Len came by with more items and recipe cards. "Left side, cheddar dip. Right side, bacon bites."

"Right." Nat stole a piece of bacon, split it with Libby, used hand sanitizer, then attacked the bacon. "How was your day?"

Libby grinned, shimmied and hummed to "Sexyback," and deftly began assembling the cheddar dip. "You know. Coffee, sugar and caffeine highs. Kids bouncing off walls. Homework done in corners. Moms sipping the nectar of the gods while their kids sleep, color, or try to eat their fingers. The occasional author or businessperson seeking sugar and caffeine. And you?"

"The usual. Len tortured me. I wrote some articles. Sold two."

"Really! That's terrific! *Law Enforcement Monthly?*"

Nat laughed. "And, oddly, a LGBTQ+ magazine. Money isn't spectacular, but better than nothing."

Libby grinned. "Something is usually better than nothing."

"You all set for tomorrow?"

Nat groaned. "Despite the stellar food, don't remind me." He brightened. "If you bring this chair, a heavier blanket, and a pillow, then I'm in." They were selling the last of the pumpkins the next day.

"Done," boomed Charlie. He took more bacon out of the oven, making everyone salivate. "I'll get it out there tonight before bed, even."

Davis came in and smiled, but looked exhausted. "You need more sleep," Lynette admonished. "Get over here and give me a hug."

"Yes, ma'am." Davis looked like he had just stepped out of a magazine, with both his blue button-down and khaki pants looking freshly ironed. Nat finished with the bacon; Libby handed him a wet wipe. Davis kissed Lynette, Jen, and Libby on the cheek, Charlie slapped Davis' back, and Nat held out his hand for a fist bump.

Davis washed up at the sink and began slicing and dicing the pies into cubes or slivers. He took out the flavored syrups. "Stars above, Libby, are you trying to kill us?" He laughed and liberally applied the sauces to the treats.

"That's exactly it." Libby handed off her bowl to runner Len, and stole Nat's bowl to mix it far more thoroughly than he could with one hand. Soon they had all the food that needed baking in the oven. Libby handed Nat a wet wipe, washed her own hands at the sink, then sat back down next to Nat.

Kandace arrived with Vic. The man looked like he could bench-press trees, all corded muscle. "What do you want to drink, babe?" he asked Kandace.

"Damn, knew I forgot something." Charlie groused, then started hauling sodas out of the pantry and putting them in the refrigerator.

"I'll make mulled cider." Vic strode over to Charlie, received a shoulder slap, and began taking out apple cider and various spices from the cabinet.

Lynette gave Vic a hug. "Large soup pot is in the right bottom cabinet." She took something that smelled heavenly out of the oven.

"I'll clean off the table." Davis got everything cleaned off and squared away.

Kandace got up, and Libby followed her. They began setting up card tables. Vic brought out the games, and Nat scooted over to set up Monopoly. Charlie set up Risk, then there was a fast debate about Splendor, Parcheesi, Taboo, and Uno. Poker had been on the table, literally, until Vic reminded them, "Do you remember when we played for pennies?" The deck went away very quickly then.

Nat tilted his head. "What's with the playing-for-pennies thing?"

Libby grinned. "Jetta, who's got the little ones at a little-girl sleep-over with her mom friend Becca, hates gambling. She's got major respect here, so we mice don't play even when the mama cat is away."

Nat laughed. "Oh. Why doesn't she come back here if the kids are at a sleepover?"

"They know the formula. Run them ragged, food and baths early, then relaxation and wine."

"Ah. Good formula."

Meri came in huffing and puffing, trying not to trip over the dogs. "Got your sour cream. Brought some liters of soda, too."

"Bless you!" Lynette rushed over to take the bags. "Omigod, the kids!" Lynette handed off the bags to Jen. "They'll be fresh off a birthday party. Gotta go!"

Vic nodded. "Good, more food for us." Everyone glared at him. "What? They eat cake at birthday parties!"

The boys ran around in circles screaming like banshees when they got home. Charlie and Len took them upstairs for baths.

Libby explained the setup to Len while putting dip in bowls. "The timer is for fifteen minutes. While we're waiting, point out any game where you don't know the rules."

Nat pointed to Splendor. Libby explained the gem-buying card game. "This looks fun."

"It is. Anyway, the timer dings every fifteen minutes, and we circulate to the right. Pick a seat and sit in that seat at every table. We'll roll you there, or Len will." Len snorted. "We have Monopoly, Risk, Uno, Parcheesi, Splendor, and Taboo. There will be plates of snacks at each table; bring your drink cup with you. Just keep rotating."

"How do you win?"

Libby laughed. "That's not the point." Nat looked around. Len rubbed Kandace's back. Davis helped Lynette put plates of snacks at four places at each table. Lynette laughed at something Davis said. Charlie thundered back down with the boys. Meri brought them their own plate and drinks, and spooled up a superhero movie for the boys. Charlie helped them make a fort of blankets and pillows, and they settled in. Jen brought out a tray of mugs of cider, and Davis rushed over to help. Meri made sure there were wet wipes and napkins at each table.

Nat watched the dance of people and kids, food and drink, and sighed happily. "It's about family, isn't it?"

Libby nodded. "Got it in one."

Charlie brought out cups of hazelnut coffee for the coffee drinkers. The timer dinged, and Game Night officially began.

Nat had major gaming trouble. He was sore, his brain didn't want to work, and he was on pain meds. Yet, he found himself laughing like he hadn't laughed before despite the soreness and mistakes. He landed on Park Place and ended up in jail twice during Monopoly. His army got cut off in Risk. Charlie won that game, of course. Nat laughed himself hoarse playing Taboo, failed to get any patrons in Splendor, and went far too slowly in Parcheesi. He had to Draw Four more times than he normally did with Uno.

But, it just didn't matter. Years of perfectionism fell away with the warmth, laughter, and bizarre playlist that had everything from Jay-Z to Travis Tritt, Jason Mraz to Beyonce. "I'm a Single Lady" had him chair-dancing as the ladies did nearly the entire dance to screaming laughter. When "Don't Worry Be Happy" came up, he realized that he was deliriously happy. He hadn't felt that way before, even winning championships, becoming a deputy, taking down monsters. This was warm, fuzzy, a bright light that filled the empty places inside. Meri was sardonic and obviously exhausted, but she won more than one game. Libby laughed a lot, and her desserts were amazing.

Nat had no idea how he ate so much. He took some dip here, a cheddar bite there, and drank a lot of cinnamon apple cider. He got through an entire plate of Libby's food. The sugar high, along with the laughter and camaraderie, pushed the pain to a nibbling monster hiding in a closet rather than one that was trying to eat him alive.

Someone would tap out, bring a load of empties to the sink, load the dishwasher, then come back with more plates burgeoning with food. Nat wanted to help, but it would be nearly impossible one-handed. Besides, he did manage to collect rent from both his favored women in Monopoly. Atlantic was a pretty good property.

The boys fell asleep after superhero movie two. One had a bat, one a spider, and that seemed to please the boys, who ran around the living room racing pretend bat-motorcycles and slinging webs until they fell asleep in front of the television.

Meri came to him that night after the dishes were put away and the boys carried to their beds. "You were so great." She helped Nat undress, sliding hands over the strong planes of his stomach, his wide hips, his strong shoulders.

Nat snorted. "I lost. A lot. All night."

Meri stripped him down to his boxers and folded up his clothes. "You stepped up last weekend like crazy. Got the boys their soccer game to burn off steam." She laughed. "I've never seen pumpkins used for goals before."

Ned smiled at the memory. "Had the coolest rotating team. Great that we had blue masking tape around to differentiate the players." Ned was a ref with a few others. Parents had come in with their kids, helping little ones make goals. Then they rotated out, bigger and bigger kids stepping in, playing with parents, and finally it was the teens versus parents as the sun began to slide down. Nat remembered sweaty, laughing faces, screams of laughter and cheering, someone passing around water bottles while the light caressed their faces as the harvest moon lay fat on the horizon. Nobody cared who was playing, who won. "That was one of the best days I've had, until tonight. That was incredibly fun."

Meri took off her sweater, smiled at the bright look in Ned's tired eyes. "Sit down, deputy." He sat. "You tell me what you want, and if it hurts. I'll be on top."

"I like my women on top." Ned reached out, freed those gorgeous breasts from their ivory lace prison. He pulled Meri to him, took his time stroking and touching.

Meri closed her eyes, groaned. "Lower," she moaned.

Ned kissed his way down, slipped in with two fingers under lace underwear. They kissed, touched as he made her slick with sweat and dew. He slid his fingers out, took off her underwear. She pulled a condom out of the pocket of her discarded jeans. Ned laughed. "You came prepared."

"No, I came. You haven't yet."

"Sometimes I can't. But I enjoy the ride."

Meri helped Ned take off his boxer shorts. "I haven't ridden you yet, but I promise you will enjoy it."

"I know I will. I have loved everything else we've done." She gently pushed him back, rolled on the condom, mounted. He had to force himself to keep still. Pain was not an aphrodisiac for him. She rode him, made him cry out into her neck. She came with a crash. He tried, but couldn't. But, it didn't really matter. She wrapped himself around his good side, all willing woman. Despite the pain from various abused muscles, he held her close, kissed and stroked her hair. The pain meant nothing to him. This woman did. This woman who saw him, acknowledged him, made him feel strong at his weakest. She took care of him, withdrew when he had enough. She was amazing. He realized he needed to hold on to her, to this feeling. It was like coming home.

HIDDEN FACES

*N*at sipped on his favorite spiced apple drink and dug into a brie salad. "There's trouble."

Meri nodded. "I usually lose clients because they get better, like Denise, the tumbler who moved back home. My regular client Avram Pews cancelled on me. Been with me for four years. Says he can get his business from God-fearing people, not us."

Libby choked on her cherry water. "He what?"

Meri pointed her fork at Libby. "Come on. You told me that Cyrus and his kids stopped coming in last week, then Wendell and Polly Ann."

Nat carefully put down the apple drink. "Both of you are losing business?"

Libby nodded. "Someone's been preaching against us in a revival tent, the Reverend Al Harper who didn't attend any divinity school I know of." Meri snorted. "Looked him up. Used to be a snake handler until his brother didn't milk his snake right and died during a service."

"I am so sorry." Nat took another bite of salad. "Both of you have worked long and hard to build your businesses. We can break up. Go on hiatus, despite the fact I'm a bio-male and we're not kissing in public."

Meri sighed. "The supposed reverend hasn't tweaked to that."

"Do you not want to date us?" Libby glared slitty-eyed at Meri. "You didn't have to tell Nat about the lost business."

"I do want to date you, both of you." Nat looked at Libby. "How much is business down?"

Libby met Nat's steely-eyed gaze. "Twenty percent."

Meri nodded. "I can't tell how much is simple attrition, but about the same."

Nat sighed. "I can't let the two of you suffer. I care about both of you far too much."

Meri shook her head. "First of all, breaking up won't reverse this. Two, we've had some lunches and the occasional dinner out. We don't lean on each other, kiss, or otherwise show affection by more than a quick hug or shoulder touch because you're essentially on duty 24/7. Even if we kissed, we're not doing anything wrong."

Libby looked slitty-eyed at Nat. "What's up with your going back to work after only three and a half weeks?"

"Nothing was broken, I've got a special chair and lap desk, and I'm doing office work only. We're far too shorthanded being a small department. The alphabet soup agencies are long gone, except for the environmental people using seized assets to clean up the mess on the mountain." Nat raised a hand for another apple drink. "I cover lunches for Dispatch, too. I had to get back."

Meri waved a hand. "If you want to date us, date us. We've been tagged as 'whores of Babylon' by that lunatic preacher. Dating or not dating won't change it at this point." Her eyes grew misty. "Kind of better to know who's really got your back, you know?"

Libby nodded. "This is complete bull puckey. I am a baker. What happens when I'm not baking is no one's business."

"I'm probably getting fired next week." Libby hissed out a breath and Meri stared goggle-eyed at Nat. "My boss is furious, won't do it, but the mayor goes shooting with that self-styled preacher, so I'm probably out of a job."

Libby glared. "That's illegal."

Nat sipped his water. "Jaylee Wheeler is on it." Jaylee, an attorney who lived in Columbia, handled employee issues all over the state—discrimination, worker's compensation, and the like. "Pricey, but I don't have a choice. I was injured in the line of duty, and I'll need to sue to be sure the insurance pays for everything."

Libby lowered her voice, but it vibrated with anger. "You are a hero cop. You saved an agent from getting dead. You...ugh!" She threw up her hands.

Meri nodded. "Fight this, please. I know you will. You fought to be on the teams in high school. You fought to get into the military the day you graduated, and you graduated early."

Nat shrugged. "Had to do something on the way to all those away games. Took extra classes and did a lot of homework on buses."

"So you'll fight?" Meri's voice was low, but it had a ribbon of steel in it.

"Never backed down from one yet." Nat gave the server his card, and took the unopened bottle of spiced apple juice. "Movie night?"

Libby nodded. "Nat, you're off earlier than we are. Pick up pizza?"

"On it. Have a great day, ladies. Paperwork awaits." Nat waved and was gone, taking the bottle of cider with him.

~

*N*at brought tandoori chicken pizza and a case of black cherry cola very slowly up Libby's stairs. He kicked off his shoes, put the food and cola on the coffee table, and Nat stroked Libby's shoulders while she sat on a fat pillow on the floor. Meri reclined, and they watched a comedy about the first alien world president. They were finished with the pizza and halfway into the second episode when Libby stood up, took Nat's hand, and dragged Nat to the bedroom. Meri sighed, put the pizza box in the recycling, and headed home when the water in Libby's tiny shower began to run.

Libby was very careful to wash Nat thoroughly. "You're not...put off?" Nat watched with half-lidded eyes as Libby traced the tattoos on his biceps, one of a soldier and a dog, another of a hawk in flight.

Libby snorted. "I saw you naked at the hospital. Similar situation.

If I were going to run screaming from the room, I would have done so then." She waved her hands and made a squeaking noise.

Nat laughed so hard he dropped the pouf he was using to soap up Libby. Her breasts were high, tight, ready to give pleasure. Libby snorted and knelt to retrieve the pouf. "My testicles are low and hard, and my swimmers don't swim."

"Well, that was blunt." Libby handed back the pouf. "Good to not be worried about dropping a baby right this second. In fact, needing extra help is nice. Won't have to worry if I forget my injection." She squeaked again and covered her mouth. "Not romantic, sorry."

Nat laughed. "I'm a cop. You could talk about dead bodies and, ten minutes later, I'd be ready for food."

"Or sex?"

"Sex is food. The most important kind. Pleasure is a wonderful gift, and feeds the body and soul at the same time."

Libby's eyes went all glowy and warm. "Now, that's romantic." She kissed Nat, the hot spray pounding on their backs. She traced his back, and noted the scar along his back. "I didn't ask you about this before when you were in the hospital. You were in so much pain then that I didn't want to bring up bad memories. Kidney transplant?"

Nat grunted. "Attempted kidney transplant. Knifed in the back by a drug dealer. My partner took him down. Nicked some important things, but got to keep the kidney."

"And this one?" She fingered a round puckered scar on Nat's forearm.

"Bullet. Domestic squabble that got out of hand."

"Which one shot you?"

Nat shrugged. "The one with the gun. Sadly, they both went to prison. Found all sorts of items of an illegal nature at their house. The aunt has custody of their two kids." He kissed Libby again, stole her breath. "I'm happy to answer any questions you have, but I don't want to talk about sad things right this minute." Libby stroked downward, and Nat had to keep from slamming his head into the tile of Libby's tiny shower when she found just the right spot. "Oh. My. God."

She grabbed his balls in her hand. "Mine."

"Anything you say." Ned felt the spray on his back, her fingers everywhere, his heart diving out and up. He reached behind him, turned off the spray, then was unable to move. Or think. Or do anything at all except attempt not to collapse. He held himself up with his hand on a slick wall, the other on a soapy shoulder. He tried not to smash his head into the wall as he saw spots behind his eyes. He stood, gasping. He turned the water back on as Libby began to wash him again. He wanted to kiss and lick those delectable breasts, but stooping on his shaky legs wasn't going to work. "Bed."

Libby got them rinsed off and Nat turned off the shower. Nat used all of his training to get out of the shower on wobbly legs, then dried himself off. Libby dragged him to her bed shoved up under the eaves, covered by a beautiful quilt done up in blue and gold. He folded that precious quilt, put it aside. Fell into soft sheets. Libby wanted to be in control, but those breasts were calling him. He got to taste one, then the other, then he reached out with fingers into soft slickness. She grabbed a condom, rolled it on him. Unneeded, since Nat was sterile and had no diseases. He knew Meri and Libby were disease-free; they'd exchanged medical reports when they had begun dating.

Libby groaned, munched on Nat's ear, and climbed on top. Nat found himself screaming out her name as she rode him, reaching out for those lovely breasts, fell into her eyes, felt her damp hair on his neck. He didn't care, just wanted her to never, ever stop what she was doing.

When she did stop, one rolling wave after another having spent them both, Libby lay on his good side, her head on his shoulder. "What. Did. You. Think?"

"Must. Breathe." Ned gasped for air. "I. Didn't. Want. This. To. End."

"Then. I. Was. Okay?" Libby reached for a water bottle, got the top off, drank.

"You. Were amazing." Ned stole the water, drank some, handed it back. He felt sore as hell, like he'd been squashed in a vise, but it was worth it. Way worth it.

~

*L*ibby took Queenie Belson's order. Queenie was in a lime green top that caused her double-Ds to flop around, a magenta pair of pants that encased her ample behind, magenta lipstick, shimmery green eyeshadow, and fluorescent green nail polish to match her top. "I'll have the cherry smoothie. And the peach cobbler bites. And gimme a slice of that key lime pie."

"The cherry pie's real good, too." Miss Hannah Green was ninety-five, and still stood ramrod-straight. She was tiny, but packed a punch. Everyone knew this because Junior Madsen once tried to steal her purse. No one had ever touched her huge white bag with a dandelion clasp without permission ever since.

"And the cherry pie. And put Miss Green on my bill." Queenie looked back and down at Miss Green. "You're a fellow picketer."

"Why, thank you, Queenie. I'll have what she's having, except give me the three-bite platter." Miss Green grinned at Libby. "We're supporting your main squeeze, you know."

Libby tried not to choke out a laugh as she made a double batch of lime smoothies. "Naw, that term's 'significant other,' on account 'a ya don't know no more if someone's dating a dude or a girl, an' ya don't wanna ask. It's rude to ask, you know." Queenie moved to the receiving window and Miss Green followed her. Luckily, the sound of the blender masked Libby's laughter. She tried to pass it off as a coughing fit.

Libby nearly gave up and bellowed a laugh when Miss Green said, "Mayor Eldridge is a weenie."

"Firing someone like that, it's not legal. Plus, hero cop, done make the town look bad." Libby filled up two plates, put everything on a tray, and handed the tray to Queenie. "Come on, Miss Green. We picketers gotta stay together."

Libby kept busy with the picketers who were picketing city hall, right across the street and to the right from the sweets shop. The picketers began with the Diversity in Business members, spread to the Parents of Lesbian, Gay, and Transgender Youth, which had been eye-opening in and of itself, then spread to the League of Women Voters, which had caused a split within their ranks. There were also divisions in church groups, but the tiny mosque and small synagogue's members were well represented when those members completed work in the evenings. Libby hated the divisions in the community, but business was booming.

Libby ran around the counter when the line was finally clear to clean off tables cleaning spray and cloth in hand. "Suzette, you've thrown away the muumuus for good!" Hailey Roth gushed to Suzette Miner. They were League of Women Voters ladies, clones in expensive jeans, soft sweaters, boots, and hair in ponytails.

"Meri Camber got me on this plan. She brings over boxes so I don't have to cook, and I get to eat bacon pizza!" The women were sharing gluten-free dark chocolate almond butter snacks. Libby doubted Hailey had any idea what she was eating was part of a wellness plan.

Hailey grinned. "Sign me up! I hate cooking! So hot in summer. The rest of the year, boring!"

Libby finished her whirlwind cleanup as the women went back out with iced lime drinks to picket. The chanting abruptly cut off as the door closed. She sighed, made sure all the tables were cleaned, then washed the blenders, then the counters.

She had just taken out more of her special vinegar solution when the mayor walked in. Libby froze and slowly lowered the spray bottle, afraid she'd shoot an unarmed man. The mayor looked awful. His short-sleeved blue button-down shirt looked wrinkled, his remaining brown hair stood on end, the black plastic glasses he affected to hide the size of his honker of a nose were smudged, and his normally polished black shoes were scuffed. "What do you want?" Libby was shocked when her voice came out even.

"Iced coffee."

"No."

"What?"

Libby pointed at a sign on the counter that said she could refuse service to anyone. "I don't have to serve you. So, I'm not. You can leave now." Libby walked around the counter, turned her back on the mayor, and sprayed the biggest case.

"What?" Libby ignored him. "Do you know who I am?"

The door made its fake chime sound, and Libby grinned to see Mary Rudolph, the mayor's wife, the local party, wedding, and events planner. She was tall, with a wide face and deep blue eyes framed by razor-cut shoulder length platinum blonde hair that swung freely. She wore a dark blue short-sleeved suit and low heels. "What can I get you?"

Mary Rudolph smiled sunnily at Libby. "Queenie and Miss Green both love your lime ice. I'll have one of those." Libby gave the case a final swipe, went behind the counter, and washed her hands. She took Mary's card, ran it through, took Mary's refillable container, washed it out, and went to make the lime ice.

She could hear Mary's ringing voice over the sound of the blender. "Hello, Dick."

"Richard."

"No, you're a dick. The divorce papers are on your desk. Sign them by the end of the day. The prenup is in place, so that shouldn't be a problem. Oh, and the auditor is already there."

"I didn't order an audit!" the mayor spluttered.

Libby heard the rest crystal-clear as she poured the lime ice into the container. "Yes, you did, when you committed an illegal act and fired a hero cop. Any illegality and the audit is automatically triggered. Oh, and I'm running for mayor. Should you still be in office in two months, I'll run against you." Libby handed the woman the cup, and Mary grinned. She looked fabulous in her navy pleated skirt, pale blue top, and low heels. Her skin glowed with a summer tan that hadn't yet faded. "Libby, I'm so sorry my husband was a dick. Have a good day now!"

"Have a great day!" Libby waved. Mary sailed out the door.

"Make them stop," Mayor Richard Rudolph complained. "I can't get my work done. I can't hear myself think."

"Then hire the hero cop back." Libby grabbed her spray bottle, and approached the gluten-free case, now denuded since Meri had begun spreading the wonders of a gluten-free existence.

"I can't. I'll lose twenty percent of my constituents."

Libby snorted. "You've already lost far more than that. Have you looked outside your office lately?"

"There's only twenty or thirty people out there at one time."

Libby sprayed, wiped, and turned around. "Start looking at their faces. They're coming in shifts." She turned away.

"I want an iced coffee," the mayor whined.

"If you aren't here to eat or drink, and I've already refused to serve you, the door is that way." She pointed, turned, wiped down the case, and listened to the mayor's footsteps as he shuffled out.

~

*L*ibby flipped the sign to closed after a very busy workday, walked out, locked the door, and nearly stepped on her mother.

Lynette had River in her arms and Bethany on her foot. "Aunt Wibby!" River screamed, and launched herself at Libby. Libby caught her, and two legs wrapped around her waist while the arms strangled her. Libby repositioned the little girl's arms until she could breathe.

Lynette pointed with her chin at the Farmer's Market General Store just down the street. Libby nodded, and the two women walked down the busy sidewalk. The next shift of picketers began to arrive, with signs that said "Hero Deputy Fired!" and "Heroes, Not Zeroes." Libby snorted at that one. The veterans were there, and Libby was shocked to see Jeb giving a speech. His tinny voice crossed the two streets between them. "Nat saved my life," he said simply.

"Saved mine, too," Libby said to her mother. "Same incident."

Lynette nodded. "So, you have a hero worship thing going on?"

Libby snorted. "With someone I went to high school with? A jock, no less? No. Not hero worship. Just...Nat is a good person. He pays attention, asks questions."

"Umm humm." Lynette stepped past a protester heading towards the picket line, Wella Chomsky, a grade school music teacher. Wella gave a wave, and Lynette and Libby nodded towards her. "So, courting for a while now. Any conclusions?"

"Gentle, kind, loving, wicked strong. Ready to be helpful, backs off when help isn't asked for." Libby smiled. "So, nothing like my brothers."

Lynette snorted. "They are the first part, I agree not so much on the second part."

"Vic was by this morning to ask how Nat was holding up. Vic got pissed as hell when he found out some of the parents were threatening to withdraw their kids from soccer if Nat continues to be a ref."

Lynette hissed out a breath. "That's...unfortunate." Her voice was honey edged with steel.

Libby looked at her mother out of the corner of her eye. "My sentiments exactly." She stopped at a planter to let her limpet-niece stand up, then Libby turned around to have River ride her back, strangling her in a whole new way.

"Wibby piggy pack." River wiggled her feet, encased in pale pink glittery boots. Libby made it into the bank, and made her deposit. They were out the door into the sunshine in no time.

"So, no divisions over this...situation."

Libby shook her head. "Absolutely not. Nat was worried about Meri and I losing business, but our business has vastly increased. I've got picketers, and half the picketers have weight loss issues or gout or some other thing. Someone, not me I might add, brings up Meri's home delivery service, and she gets an order within a day or two. Haven't seen her in three days. When I was last there, her little half of the duplex had cold and hot boxes waist high all the way through that yellow kitchen of hers."

"She should move into Trust House." Libby stared after her mother as Lynette sailed into the store, put Bethany in a cart with the bottom in the shape of a car so Bethany could "drive," and started her shopping trip.

❧

*L*ibby helped Lynette fill up the car with groceries, then texted Meri to ask if she needed any for her business. Meri sent a list with a bunch of heart emojis, so Libby whipped back through the aisles, free from a strangulation device in the form of a little girl in a pink t-shirt with mauve jeans to match. And, of course, pink glitter boots.

Libby took the fruits and veggies past the library to the duplex Meri shared with Tina Marie Phipps, a librarian and historian just out of college. Meri had a huge kitchen done in shades of yellow, a living room barely large enough for a couch and flat TV hanging on the wall, and a tiny bedroom. Libby cut up the veggies and fruits to order, put them in canisters and labeled them, and put them in the refrigerator. Meri still wasn't home.

A shower sounded good. Libby left, locked up, and was beginning to get into her vehicle when she looked up and saw Nat walking toward her. "Are you here for my sister?"

"No, for you. She told me you texted her. I checked the store first. Dinner yet?"

"No, and if I don't eat, I'll fall down."

Nat grinned. "The Reading Room?"

Libby nodded. "Yes, but I don't want to stay. I've got something to show you. My mom brought it up." They walked quickly, both hungry. "I saw the mayor today. Kept demanding an iced coffee and didn't understand why I refused service."

Nat shrugged. "Consequences. Some people don't understand them."

They approached the Reading Room, a coffeehouse that also served paninis. Libby ordered brie and bacon, Nat a chicken pesto. Nat leaned against a white pillar and surveyed the shop. Readers, writers, and students sat in comfortable wingbacks, some with piles of books next to them, some with pen and paper or index cards as well. The place was deadly silent except for riffling papers, scratching pens, and taps from keyboards as people worked against deadlines and readers read in the back corners. They got their paninis and some cherry lime sodas and Libby led them to the car.

The drive took them just outside a neighborhood. Rolling hills gave way to flat land. "Closest neighbors are here." Libby pointed. The fat farmhouse and ranch-style houses gave way to empty wooded land. Libby stopped at the end of a cul-de-sac. "Two floors, six bedrooms. Three-car garage, basketball hoop." Libby parked under the hoop. "Come on." The door opened with a code. "Entryway, hooks for keys, backpacks, shoes."

Libby kicked off her black sneakers and Nat took off his boots. "Hallway to the living room, kitchen behind." The kitchen was vast, with two refrigerators, two stoves in a center island, counterspace in black and gold granite. "We had to design for both of us living here." Libby put down the sack with the sandwiches, fished out a soda, popped the top, and drank a long pull. "The plan was..."

"For you and Meri to share the house with your spouse or spouses." Libby stared at Nat. "Your parents are poly. You apparently had a plan to live poly sometime in the future."

Libby nodded. "Then we had terrible luck finding bears to date, and Meri soured on finding someone we could both love. So, this house has been sitting empty."

Nat took out his sandwich and drink. "I'm just happy this seems to be working out so far. Not the complicated mess I thought dating two people would be. We're all busy, take time when we can. Nickel tour?"

Libby showed him the three kids' bedrooms, complete with beds and shelf storage. There were master bedrooms with bathrooms on either side. Meri's was done in yellow and cream with pale-stained wooden furniture with clean lines. The other master was obviously Libby's, with a huge platform bed and lots of storage, the furniture in her favorite maroon and gray colors. The bathrooms in the middle had either a fat tub or a shower on the other side of the den.

The mudroom had a spiral staircase. Nat went up, and Libby followed. The bedroom over the garage also had its own bath, a wide closet, and looked down on the basketball hoop on one side, the woods surrounding the house on the other. It had primer on the walls and was devoid of furniture. "This is the spouse's bedroom?"

"It is. It's waiting for someone to put a stamp on it."

Nat kissed Libby. Libby sighed into Nat's mouth. "It's perfect. I see woods everywhere. I know the Camber farm is behind us, way behind us."

"The property is on five acres, and there's a stream back there. Follow it, and you're on Camber land."

"So, you can go bear once you're in the woods."

"If our eventual kids are bears, we'll have to put up a fence so they can change in comfort." Nat raised an eyebrow. "That happens around age five."

"Good to know." Nat kissed Libby again then let her go, walked around the room, hands in the pockets of his jeans. "You two are getting serious about me." Libby nodded. "I think I'm getting serious too." Libby's stomach grumbled. Nat laughed. "We have to get serious about food first."

"Picnic on the deck." Libby clambered down the metal spiral stairs, just like the ones to her apartment. Nat looked around, smiled, and followed her down the stairs towards the kitchen. They looked out at the wide backyard with several huge trees and a wraparound deck. "I'm really jumping the gun here, but Meri is swamped and needs a bigger kitchen, stat. Be a pain in the ass, really. We haven't lived together since high school."

"How can you afford this? You scrimp and save to make sure that your businesses work." Nat threw up his hands. "Sorry, none of my business."

Libby put a hand on his shoulder. "We do scrimp and save for our own businesses. We wanted to make them ourselves without family money. This house...we don't own it. Our family trust does. We call this Trust House. Whether shifters have multiple spouses or not, we tend to have large families and huge get-togethers. My brothers went really big, so this house went to us. I know you're just getting to really know us, Nat. But Meri needs more space, and I've always loved this house."

"Are you asking me to move in with you?"

Libby snorted. "Not yet."

Nat blew out a sigh of relief. "Awesome. What day are you moving?"

"Oh, no you don't. You're still recovering, and I have a lot of big bear brothers. And, have you seen my dad or my moms? They can each bench-press trucks. Carrying baby bears around is no joke."

Nat threw back his head and laughed. "Okay, okay. Lamps only."

Libby planted a kiss on his mouth. "Lamps only. Or kid herder. They'll want to be underfoot. You can ref a soccer game over there." Libby pointed to a spot of yard big enough for a garden, or kids running around.

"Anytime."

RUN

*M*eri took her time walking with Nat. The day was cool. The insects buzzed so loudly they drowned out thought. Bees bumbled in and out of the last flowers on the wooded trail. They were on a flat part of Camber land. "Wish I'd brought the hand weights." Nat did some practice stretches.

Meri glared at Nat. "I have no idea why you went back to work full time after your...hiatus."

Nat opened wide eyes at Meri. "Do you mean when I was fired, was forced to sue, and got hired again by the interim mayor? Still waiting on the back pay."

"But your insurance got covered."

Nat grinned. "Part of the lawsuit. Court costs and any increase in insurance premiums were covered as well. Judge Trask was not happy that his fishing trip was cut short for, and I quote, 'This nonsense.' City Hall's going to have problems, what with the ex-mayor's use of city funds for things like trips, cars, and landscaping for his own house. Interim Mayor Mary sure is cleaning up. She can prove she knew nothing about his thievery, too."

"The Auditor Strikes Back." Meri laughed. The smell of

woodsmoke grew stronger. "Barbecue. You haven't lived until you've tasted my dad's barbecue."

They increased their pace. Meri was delighted that Nat's breathing was even. The evenings were sliding towards cold rather than cool, and all the leaves had gone crimson and gold.

They emerged into the backyard. Bobby came streaking across the lawn and attack-hugged Nat's legs. "We needa ref," he said, with sweaty little boy enthusiasm. He wore his cool-weather soccer clothes, including cleats on his feet.

"Sure. Have the cards in my pocket." Nat started walking forward, Bobby still attached to him. The little boy let out a full-throated laugh.

Meri made a beeline for Jen, who was gesturing with a knife at Len. She broke into a light jog at the slitty-eyed look on Jen's face. It was nearly impossible to get her mad, but once angered, Jen was a heat-seeking cruise missile.

"I had new clients, and Vic threw his schedule around. I had the wrong day." Len held up his hands placatingly.

"You forgot a date with Kandace?" Meri asked. "I can see how that could happen. I've been so busy I forget the day, time, and everything else. Have little ringers on my HUD all day to tell me where I'm supposed to be with what and when."

"No, but thanks for broadcasting that tidbit all over the yard." Len, the Zen one, was actually enraged. "I forgot to pick up Bethany and River from tumbling."

It was Meri's turn to go all slitty-eyed. She understood Jen's knife-waving. She reached over, took the knife, put it on the cutting board, then washed her hands. "Where was everyone else?"

"I was on a roof, Charlie was out of town dropping off a tiny house, Lynette was one town over buying new tiny house stuff, Jetta had the boys, Davis was in surgery, Kandace was at a doctor's appointment, Vic was out on a call, and you and Libby were working." Jen bit out the words from between her teeth.

"Sounds like we need better backup emergency coordination." Meri dried her hands, then began cutting the carrots into matchsticks.

Jen got slitty-eyed again. "A family master schedule."

Meri shook her head. "I have enough trouble figuring out my own tasks. Adding other people's stuff would be a nightmare. No, anyone working with the kids gets six to ten emergency numbers. They just have to work their way down the list."

"That's...doable." Jen pointed at Len. "You were still stupid."

Len shook his head. "Honest mistake, a dumb one I'll admit, but a mistake."

Meri pointed the knife at Len. "You were dumb." She pointed it at Jen. "You failed to find a solution. Now, Len, you have an extra pickup duty this week to make up for it. You, Jen, go make the emergency list for all of us."

"Fine." Len stomped off.

"On it," Jen said. She poked at things only she could see in her HUD. "So, Nat. Back to work full time."

Meri snorted, switched to cucumbers. "Can't tell that one to do anything. Either Nat does it, or not. If Nat says it'll get done, it gets done."

"That's good. Any progress on moving into the Trust House?" Meri pointed at Libby, who was chasing Bethany and River with a bubble wand, making the girls giggle. Meri lifted her foot, and held it in the air. Jen snorted. "Those tiny units you two have aren't good places for adult females whose businesses are taking off."

Meri nodded. "Can't rush Libby. She kind of...oozes."

Nat suddenly took off at a sprint. It took a moment to figure out he was following Vic. "What the..." Meri handed the knife to Jen, and took off for the driveway and her van. Jetta rushed to the girls, her black hair streaming behind her, and caught the bubble wand as Libby dropped it.

Nat and Vic leaped into Nat's vehicle and zoomed off, lights flashing. Meri met Libby at the driveway when Nat's call came through. "Libby, we need your license, right now. Josephine Tiller was smoking in bed and fell asleep. She's being airlifted to the burn unit in Yaeger." Meri hissed out a breath and lunged to her van. Libby ran around and hopped in the passenger side. Libby listened as Nat said. "Not the house, Vic says County General. We're almost..." Nat's voice cut out.

"That's horrible." Libby thought furiously, then called Lynette. "Mom, Josephine Tiller is on her way to the burn unit in Yaeger. Need you to talk to Minnie at the Clothes Swap. I know that's where the boys' clothes are coming from. She'll have Beau, Denver, and Ricky's sizes. Get everything and have someone drop them off at the Trust House."

"On it." Lynette dropped the line.

Nat called back. "Boys have smoke inhalation. On their way to the hospital with kiddie oxygen masks on their faces. House is nada." He dropped the link. Meri put the hospital into the GPS, and the van drove itself just under the speed limit.

Libby waved her hands. "They won't have a thing. If Josephine survives..."

Meri sighed. "Months, even years of recovery. And she just won't be capable of running after three busy boys."

"I feel horrible saying it about someone so severely injured, but she wasn't running after them before this." The van took the fastest route past people out picnicking, shopping, and taking their kids to the community pool. "We've gonna eat first. No sense moving stuff while we're hungry. Both our apartments?"

"I'm paid through the end of the month. Tina Marie will have some college kid in my duplex half by tomorrow morning." The van drove past a herd of minivans heading to a baseball game, bats, balls, and gloves strewn over the seats and poking up in back windows.

"I can have Penny in by Monday night." Libby referred to the woman who had the ice cream shop next door to her business. Libby looked at her sister, then looked away. "I took Nat to see the Trust House." Meri glared at her sister. "What? We had a nice picnic."

Meri pulled up to the hospital, parked. Libby was out the door and into the hospital before Meri could feed the meter. Meri jogged up to the emergency room. The nurses let them back. Vic had Beau on a mask and was using a wet wipe to clean the soot from the boys' face and hairline. Libby stroked Beau's hair, brown turned nearly black with soot and sweat. "You okay, Beau?" Libby asked.

Beau shook his head. "Denver's sleeping. Mama went off in the loud thing."

Vic nodded. "Denver kept taking out his IV and pulling off his mask. They had to sedate him." He made a rotating helicopter blade with his hand behind Beau's head, and then pretended to put an AET tab on, then made his arm jump. So, Josephine had flatlined in the helicopter and had to be revived.

Libby stroked Beau's head again. "You stay here with Uncle Vic. I'm going to check on Denver. Probably have some paperwork to do, too."

"I've got Ricky." Meri followed her sister in.

Deputy Leland Fortra was there in the hallway, face grim. "House went up. Josephine..." He held up his hand and waggled it. "Less than fifty-fifty. They'll be split up if you..."

Libby held up a hand. "License." Leland handed over the pad, and Libby started poking it, then used her own to send over her files.

"Denver?" Leland pointed, and Meri headed off down the hall. Denver was asleep, his head lolling. Ricky was sitting up, eyes wide, breathing into his mask. Meri hurried over. "My brudder..."

"Can go home tonight." The nurse, Iggy Walsh, had springy blonde hair held back in a clip, and wore scrubs with teddy bears on them. "Lynette."

Meri whirled around. "Len dropped me off." Lynette went over to Denver, stroked his hair. "Any of them with lung damage?"

"Scans say no." Iggy pointed to the mask. "We'll send home a nebulizer and breathing treatments. Take them back here if they have trouble breathing. They need massive fluids. Expect sleeping, eating, and food issues, and..." She wiggled her hand up and down to imitate emotional issues.

Meri nodded. "Expected."

"Is." Lynette stroked Denver's cheek. "We've got to get these boys showered, fed, and hydrated. They smell like my husband's grill."

"Release forms will be done in ten." Iggy began poking her pad.

"You're coming home with me and Libby." Meri pointed to herself. "And my mother Lynette, here, is going to help us for a while."

"I want my house." Ricky's black hair was streaked with soot, his blue eyes wide.

Meri shook her head. "It's burned up, love. You get your own room in the new house." Meri held him as he cried.

The boys were wheeled out in small wheelchairs. Meri grinned when she saw that Len had also dropped off and installed three car seats. Lynette unloaded the sleeping Denver first; Deputy Fortra helped with the door. Then, there was Beau in the middle, then while Libby loaded Ricky, Lynette and Meri went to the back to put up the mesh so the empty containers in the van wouldn't slide or tilt towards the boys. Meri got in to drive, Lynette in the passenger seat. Libby took the foldout in back.

Len opened the door to the mudroom for them when Meri pulled into the garage. Meri picked up the heavy Denver, staggered to the door, got Denver's shoes off, then kicked off her own. She slowly staggered to the shower on the right while Lynette and Libby took off their shoes. Ricky thrust out his bottom lip. "Why do I hafta take my shoes off?"

"Dirty." Libby pointed. "See that chart Uncle Len hung on the wall?" She got Beau's shoes off. He kicked them into alignment. "You listen, do your chores, you get stickers."

Len held out a magnet sticker. "Beau looks like he likes Spider Man." He put the magnetized sticker under Shoes Off on the line with Beau's name. "You get to trade these in for TV time, computer time, stuff like that."

Ricky sighed as if he had been asked to climb Mount Everest without a sherpa, but the shoes came off. "Need a liner for the hampers." Libby dragged Ricky down the hall. "Boats. We've got seals and whales, too. For the water." Len had texted them about liberating them from the Camber farm, along with a chore chart and extra magnets.

Meri ignored the seal-versus-whale discussion. She got Beau's clothes off, and Len came in with a garbage bag. Their clothes and shoes were unsalvageable. Meri put the shower on and used a washcloth to get the soot and dirt off the boy. Len came in, and they got him on a towel, dried, and dressed in underwear, socks, gray sweatpants, and a Captain America sweatshirt out of sacks from the clothing store.

Libby came out of the bathroom almost as wet as Beau. Beau had a duck towel on his head, the beak a cowl he could use to dry himself. "Do you want the red, blue, or yellow room?"

Beau pointed to the yellow duck towel on his head. "Yellow. Ricky likes red. Denver doesn't care."

"Blue room it is." Meri staggered under Denver's weight. She leaned against the wall as Len pulled back the blue sheets. Meri slid him in, and covered him with the sheet. Denver's head lolled on the pillows. His skin, dusky with a summer tan, was gray underneath. Lynette came in. "I brought food and drinks. Barbecue and fluids. Bathwater doesn't count."

Len grimaced. "Eww. Shower water was gray."

Libby and Lynette got the boys into sweatpants and sweatshirts while Meri put out the barbecued chicken. She knew Ricky would eat cucumbers but not salad, and that Beau would eat nearly anything. Meri wolfed down her grilled chicken sandwich and salad, and went about labeling lower cabinets while Lynette and Libby cajoled the tired boys into eating. Len got the terrifying story of the fire out of them while Meri got containers out and raided the pantry for things the boys liked they could easily eat—cheddar crackers, carrots, celery, wheat thins. She got them packaged in small containers and put them on the shelves.

Beau's story was heart-stopping "We heard a whoosh, and fire jumped. I was gonna hide under the bed."

"I made him get out." Ricky sat tall, and inhaled his chicken.

"Good move." Len and Ricky bumped fists. "Who got Denver out?"

"We shirted him."

Ricky and Len bumped fists again while Meri tried to parse the sentence. "You dragged him out by his shirt?"

Ricky shook his head. "No, I stole his shirt and he chased me." Libby, Meri, Len, and Lynette exchanged startled glances. They could have lost all three boys who didn't have any idea how to handle an emergency. A stolen shirt had saved Denver's life.

Libby stood. "Plates in the sink, then rinsed, and in the dishwasher. Two steps gets two stickers."

"Iron Man, Superman, or Batman?" Len withdrew all three magnets out of his pocket.

"Denver likes Iron Man, so I'll take that." Ricky grinned ferally.

Len shook his head. "Others before yourself. Family first. So, for that, you can have red and gold Iron Man, but your brother gets black and gold Iron Man."

Libby shook her head. "And he's sleeping and can't decide for himself. Cold, dude." She stood up, took her plate to the sink, rinsed it, and put it in the dishwasher. Beau came over, and she held him up so he could rinse his plate. "Cups in the top, plates in the bottom." She put Beau down. "Good job!" They fist-bumped.

A mulish Ricky did his chores, and stood on Libby's knees to rinse his plate and cup. Len took them to get their stickers.

Meri followed. "You can earn TV time with that, or Lego time. TV time is three, Lego time is two."

"TV," Ricky and Beau chimed together.

"Okay." Len took the chore stickers back. "You get tooth-brushing stickers too. Do that first." Lynette took Len's offered bag of small boy toothbrushes and superhero toothpaste, and Libby followed the boys back for the tooth-brushing.

Len pointed towards the door. "Let's go, Meri. We've got your apartment to move now."

Meri followed Len's truck to her duplex. Len packed her clothes— easy since they were rolled up in boxes on shelves—while Meri packed the contents of her refrigerator and freezer into cold boxes. There were two refrigerators and a freezer at the trust house. Meri grabbed a dolly and began loading her van with the boxes. She came back and packed the tools of her trade—silicone baking dishes, knives, measuring cups, bowls, plastic and wooden cutting boards, microwave, convection oven, mixer, air fryer, and slow cooker. Len dropped off her clothes in the vehicle and came back to pack Meri's glasses, plates, and silverware.

"Furniture stays here, except the rolling cart." Meri pointed. The cart had held her now-packed microwave oven and small convection oven, the blender and smaller appliances inside the bottom doors wrapped in bubble wrap. Meri emptied and cleaned the slow cooker, and the chicken enchiladas went into her hot box while the wrapped slow cooker went into the cart doors. She worked fast and cleaned as she went.

Len kissed her cheek. "Love ya. Dad called from Libby's. I can fit most of this stuff in the van on my way out. See you at your new home."

"Thanks for this."

Len's eyes filled up. "They all could be dead. Or worse. You need a toothbrush at three in the morning, you call me."

Meri nodded. "Rarely an emergency, but yeah. We'll call."

Meri did a last walkthrough, sent a text to her bubbly landlord to say she was moving out, effective immediately. Meri knew there would be a new renter nearly immediately. She made sure all the cabinets and closets were empty, did a super-fast clean although she'd cleaned the day before.

Meri headed off to her van, and took the less curvy main roads to her new home. She hauled out her cases, and got them into the house. Meri filled up the garage freezer and refrigerator first, and put the empty cases in her van. Then she unloaded the rest, taking up part of the kitchen refrigerator.

Meri washed her hands in the sink. The boys were watching a series about a middle school for superhero tweens. Libby had Meri's list for the next day, and was using a spiralizer to cut carrots. "Do you want to move your stuff tonight?"

Libby shook her head. "Dead on my feet. Can you check on the boys?"

"On it." Meri found Lynette gently stroking Denver's hair. Meri waved, and Lynette followed her into the kitchen. Lynette crushed her into a hug.

Meri pushed her mother back, stroked a lock of Lynette's escaping hair. "You can go home now."

Lynette patted her daughter's hand. "Not yet. Your father found a seven-passenger vehicle with storage, netting, mesh, and built-in carseats. You can use that and give your sister your van. Her car isn't gonna cut it."

"What color?" Meri leaned against the doorjamb and stretched.

"Crimson. For the price, it's really easy to have it detailed and painted silver with your logo."

"I'll...no, have the trust buy it. It's for the care and feeding of the boys."

"Good thinking." Lynette very carefully moved a tendril from Meri's forehead. "They're going to be yours, you know. The woman couldn't parent worth excrement before." Meri snorted. "There is no way she'll be capable with her injuries."

"The hospital gave an update?"

"Got nothing but a runaround. Vic called and found out she's still breathing and in a medically induced coma."

Meri sighed. "Not good."

"No. You two have a secret to keep. These three will babble about it the first chance they get. No filters on these ones. We'll come down and spell you so you can go bear at least twice a month."

"Small price." Meri stretched. Her back and neck both audibly popped.

"And Nat? This will throw your deputy lover for a loop. Dating with three kids with no boundaries or filters?"

"Sufficient unto the day." Meri sighed. "Libby is too tired to stand. I'm going to get her stuff. Luckily, she's got an apartment the size of a postage stamp."

"Go. We'll hold down the fort."

Meri nodded, turned away, turned back. "Thank you."

Lynette held up a hand. "We're family. Grandkids are precious. Even if they are marauders."

Meri snorted and headed out.

~

*C*harlie Camber looked ridiculous as he wrapped Libby's favorite blue goblets in bubble wrap, his huge hands able to hold four wrapped glasses at once. Meri filled the box, then hauled a cold box over to the refrigerator. After that, Libby's baking supplies took an entire box and a half. Meri got the kitchen packed, then went to Libby's tiny bedroom. She filled up two suitcases with the contents of the bedroom and miniscule linen closet. She came back out, and put the suitcases next to the boxes by the door. "Let's do this." Meri stretched: her back popped.

Charlie grinned. "Your vehicle has been purchased, and is getting detailed and painted. It'll be delivered late tonight while you are sleeping."

Meri stretched her arms over her head. Her elbows popped. "Sleep like a stone tonight."

Charlie nodded. "Just remember, the name of the game is to get through the next minute. Not a day or an hour. Trust me. On the weekend, we'll take the boys for hikes, soccer games, stuff like that. Wear them out, give you and Libby some much-needed free time. And bear time."

"Okay, thanks. Now, quit slacking off and go downstairs. I'll walk these halfway down, and you get the rest."

"Yes, ma'am." Charlie saluted, picked up two heavy boxes, and walked them down the spiral staircase. Meri took boxes down four steps, left them, then took two more, then walked them down halfway. She went back up, and walked two more down. The suitcases were last; she rolled them out and handed them down by their handles. Meri did a last walkthrough, made sure the door was closed, walked down, and got into her overfilled van. Charlie followed her. They pulled in at Trust House, and Meri parked in the garage. They started a line when Lynette came out to help pass it all into the house. Charlie kissed his wife once the line was done, then dragged her away from the new grandkids to take her home.

Meri stumbled in, washed up, and went over her checklist. Libby had it all done, boxed and color-coded. "Shower."

Libby stood. "Help first." The boys were completely passed out on the couch. Meri hauled Ricky to his bed, and Libby took Beau. Meri got her yoga pants and loose tee from her suitcase and stumbled towards her shower. She used her travel kit, unable to remember where her shampoo and conditioner bottles were located. She stumbled back out. "First shift."

Libby shook her head. "You moved us. I've got the couch."

Meri went to the boys' rooms, made sure the nightlights were on in each one. She turned on both hallway ones, bought for the home visit when Libby got certified to foster or adopt. All the plug protectors were in, cabinets, refrigerators, and freezer locked. The boys could get to food and liquid in their open cabinets on the bottom where they could reach. Libby reclined on the couch, and slipped into sleep.

Meri grinned and covered her sister with a blanket. She went to the kitchen and prepared two kinds of pancake batter and the lattice for the bacon pizza. Then, she slunk to her bedroom. Meri managed to make up the bed with soft sheets, a warm comforter, and soft pillows with smooth pillowcases. Then, she fell into bed and slept just as she pulled up the comforter over her shoulders.

NUCLEAR FAMILY

*L*ynette arrived just as Libby finished wrapping her gluten-free snacks. Lynette rushed to wash her hands and Meri held up both types of pancakes on a plate. "Banana nut or apple cinnamon?"

Denver pointed. "Apple." Meri gave him the pancakes, and Lynette cut them up for him.

"Banana." Beau wriggled in his booster seat.

"Both." Ricky was obviously tired, but very hungry. Meri served them up, Lynette cut them, then Meri served her sister and her mother. She put the plates down and passed around the syrup.

Libby finished packaging her snacks, then came over to the kitchen table. Libby, Lynette, and Meri stood up, sang, then sat down. The boys were nearly done with their pancakes. They had already inhaled their small pieces of bacon pizza covered in cheese and veggies.

Libby grinned. "Eat up. We leave for school in half an hour."

Meri wolfed down her food, then stood. She took the now-empty pancake plate and her own plate and took them to the sink. She rinsed the plates and cups and put them in the dishwasher, then put away the last of the bacon pizza in a container. Lynette brought a stair step; the boys stood in line to put their dishes in the dishwasher. Denver grumbled until Beau explained about the stickers. Lynette rushed to the van to bring in two more step stools for the bathrooms.

The boys brushed their teeth. Meri got Beau into his blue jeans, then held up a red shirt and a blue shirt. "Which one? Red or blue?"

"Blue." Beau got into his shirt, and Meri rolled up the other one and put it back on the shelf. "Why are my clothes not in drawers?"

"Easier to see and get, and they don't get wrinkled. Like my nose." Meri wrinkled her nose, and Beau laughed.

They got all the boys dressed, shoes and jackets on, and into Meri's new vehicle, gleaming from a fresh wash. Meri filled up and left in her old van before Libby pulled out with Lynette in the passenger seat. They arrived, and Lynette helped Libby get the boys to their classes. The school office administrator, Ms. Palci, was relieved that Libby had all the information needed to show the school that Meri and Libby were legal guardians. She was stunned by the number of Meri and Libby's family members allowed to pick up the kids, but was relieved to receive pictures of the family members and an extensive list of emergency numbers as well.

Finally, they jogged to the vehicle. "I'll pick them up." Lynette grinned as Libby sighed in relief. "You might want to tell your sister." Libby pretended to slap herself and sent Meri a text. Libby dropped Lynette off at the Camber house, then went to her shop.

*L*ynette brought the boys home, and had them help her empty moving boxes and take them out for recycling in exchange for earning stickers. They had tacos, and all three chose TV after they cleaned up. Meri came home, hugged Lynette and sent her home, filled up the slow cooker, then brought the veggies and put them, a paring knife, a cutting board, a spiralizer, and both bowls and trays onto the table behind the couch. She cut up all her veggies and had time to fill up her boxes. Denver asked for more juice for his sealed cup. Meri poured more, sealed the cup, and showed the boy where he could get snacks and flavored waters anytime he wanted from his own cabinet. "Really?" Denver's eyes were huge.

Meri grinned. "Of course. You're a growing boy, aren't you?"

"Yeah. I am." Denver got a sticker for asking politely for more juice, which delighted him. He chose to cash two stickers in exchange for Legos, and built them at the kid-sized table in the living room.

Meri gave them a breathing treatment; they all got stickers for sitting quietly for ten minutes. Libby got home, and they ate dinner. The women helped get the boys in the bathtub. A three-way war among a duck, a boat, and a seal ensued, with much splashing of water.

Libby helped get them all clean, then it was storytime. Libby took her own shower while Meri got them dried and in bed. Meri pulled out a book, and found out nearly immediately that Beau was dyslexic. Meri texted Lynette with the information; Vic had math dyslexia, known as dyscalculia. He'd learned to pass his math courses by using a plastic colored filter that "kept the numbers from jumping around." They would have to take Beau to a specialist and find his color.

The boys were all asleep by the time Meri had her shower. She came out to find Nat had found his favorite spiced apple drink in the refrigerator. Meri made herself a cup of hibiscus tea and they sat at the kitchen table. Nat clasped his bottle loosely. "Josephine's hanging in. No fireproof boxes in the ashes, no bank boxes, no lawyers with hidden wills."

"Lovely." Libby filled her own cup with water, and sat with a groan.

Nat sipped his juice, put it down. "Adopting these kids is going to take time."

Meri shook her head, sipped her own tea. "Not as bad as you would think. According to our lawyer, the judge is going to see a severely injured mother known to social workers as someone without parenting skills, who wouldn't take any suggested classes or help.

They'll also see this fine house and school district and a large, tight-knit family known to the community. We've got a doctor, a paramedic, and a Zen master for brothers, and we have our own businesses."

Libby and Meri hired a lawyer named Allie Moreau who specialized in family law. Allie was tough, and great at getting even the most difficult adoptions to go through. Her kind dark eyes, serious demeanor, love of kids and families, and knowledge of the law had swayed many judges to her point of view.

Nat rubbed his neck, sighed. "And, now for the elephant in the living room. We date, but our PDA is very limited to brief hugs or shoulder touches. No kissing in public. We went through a very public situation, including protests, and we're still together, but very low-key. If you think this will impact the adoption, then drop me like a hot potato. I'm expendable. The kids are not." Nat took a swig after that particular speech.

Libby narrowed her eyes at Nat. "You call yourself 'expendable' again, I'm smacking you." Ned grimaced. "I talked to our caseworker today at lunch. Her name is Helen, and she says this state can't discriminate. We're dating a cop, which stands for law and order. We're very low key. Dinners, that sort of thing. We've been far too busy to date much in public these last few weeks. And you, Nat, are back to work full time. Hero cop does carry the day with some judges." Libby put her head in her hands. "Meri, you carried the burden yesterday."

"Family is what it is. Besides, you prepped my client's breakfasts for me." Meri patted her sister's arm, then turned to Nat. "The other elephant in the living room is that we just changed everything, irrevocably. We are adopting, Universe willing, three highly active boys. They're shellshocked and are therefore being good, holding onto the people that have given them food and a roof over their head."

Libby lifted her head and grinned. "And stickers."

"And stickers. This honeymoon won't last. We're going to get three angry, grieving boys whether their mother lives or dies. We've become sudden mothers. If you want to run, the door is over there. We're in this, and we're not giving up on them."

"We know you love kids. You ref with them. We know you're not a child abuser; you've gone through numerous background checks to do what you do. Loving kids and joining a sudden family are two different things." Libby touched Nat's arm. "You're a sweet, thoughtful lover and an amazing person. The question is, do you want a sudden family?"

Meri nodded. "You've gotta be sure. I know I'm coming off like a porcupine. I'm not trying to drive you away. Exact opposite, in fact. You just have to be..."

"Absolutely certain. I get it." Nat looked at both women. "I know how much of a handful they are. I'm the one that was called when Ricky got kicked out of three preschools and Denver gave two kids bloody noses in one day. It broke my heart that their mother didn't care enough to keep them out of trouble, to give them boundaries. They can't make friends this way."

"So you..." Libby's eyes were full of hope.

"I'm ready. Maybe I'm insane, but I live a bit dangerously as a police officer. I nearly got blown up, and had some time to think things through. Family is what's important. I want to move in, if that won't screw up the adoption." He sighed. "Just know, my own mother sucked. Coach Ma was great. I'll consider myself that, a coach, getting the kids ready for life."

"The greatest game of all." Meri grinned, and they all clinked glasses.

Libby nodded. "We're going to have a cop on the premises in a room over the garage. Hero cop, protective, soccer ref. You are still a ref?"

"The preacher's long gone, since his buddy the mayor's probably going to prison. No one filed anything with the soccer association, and a few parents got ostracized." Nat took another pull on the bottle of spiced apple juice. "So, yeah, I'm back in."

"Good." Meri touched Nat on the arm.

"We need to get you some furniture." Libby pulled up her HUD. "I know you may not be ready to move in, but you'll probably spend the night here from time to time.

Nat shook his head. "I've got my own furniture. Old, battered stuff from the church store, but furniture."

"Yeah, not going to work. I know an online furniture discounter." Libby pulled out her pad, pulled up a website, scooted closer to Nat to show him some options.

Meri threw her head back and laughed. Her sister's idea of good furniture was Ikea and a good-sized kitchen table. She pulled up a better website, sent it over. "It's on us. The trust. And don't worry, it's consignment. Not abusing the planet."

"Good to know." Nat grinned.

~

*N*at moved himself in within two weeks. Spooky enjoyed the new special shelves, hammock, window seat, and kitty door Nat installed in the door to his room. The boys were taught how to gently pet the kitty, and were threatened with complete sticker loss if the chatty Spooky was harmed in any way. Spooky liked Beau, and wisely stayed away from Denver and Bobby for the time being. Nat's sports equipment went along the side of the garage on hooks he installed himself. His somewhat meager non-sports belongings fit easily in the room over the garage.

Nat went through the same parenting classes Libby and Meri had. Nat was busy with work, and had to get a four-wheel-drive big enough for two added adults and three wiggly boys with built-in car seats. Charlie stepped in and found an ex-cop vehicle built like a tank. Nat had it painted silver and was able to join the rotation to pick up and drop off kids.

The caseworker, Helen Regis, was over twice. She wore blue pantsuits, liked wearing lavender scent, and had short, choppy dark hair and a blade face. The first time, all was well. The kids did their chores and earned time playing with Legos and a set of plastic and metal cars.

The second time, Denver hit Beau and lost all his daily stickers. He had time out, Beau got ice and a shoulder to cry on, and Ricky started to act up because he felt no one was paying attention to him. Nat took one of Ricky's stickers away and took him out to play soccer, Meri talked with Denver about protecting his brothers, and Libby cuddled with Beau. They got a very high rating for their teamwork, despite the snafus. "Great teamwork in a difficult situation. Also, that's the most impressive larder I've ever seen." Helen Regis pointed at the over-stuffed pantry.

Meri sighed. "It's my job. And, making more food isn't really a problem for me. I bought another slow cooker. Problem solved. Plus, I fed them before. I know exactly what they will and won't eat."

Libby nodded. "Secret weapon. And, I make treats. Everyone likes those. The trick is to use sugar substitutes. Those three do not need to be on a sugar high."

Nat raised his eyebrows. "Don't tell the kids."

Libby laughed. "Don't worry. They don't know what monkfruit and erythritol are anyway."

Helen nodded. "Ned, how soon can you get the parenting classes completed?"

Nat grimaced. He hated having others move around their schedules to accommodate him. He'd chosen Wednesday nights and all day Saturday, which meant he wasn't there to read books to the boys several times a week or ref for soccer. "Two down, six more to go."

"I'll file when we...find out." Everyone winced. Josephine was still in a coma.

$\sim$

*S*ex was...difficult. This made no sense to Nat. There were two attentive, kind, loving women in the house. Meri was clear about what she wanted, and Libby had amazing fingers and teeth. Each woman made his head explode with their inventiveness. But Nat was realizing just how bruised, sore, and exhausted he still was. There were three active boys that needed walks, soccer, and help with chores like raking leaves in the enormous yard. Meri needed help with getting her food prepped; she was far busier than usual. Then, there were the meals, drinks, and snacks hungry boys required. Meri and Libby were training the boys to get, and eventually create, their own food. They had to be careful about letting them use the microwave, though. Nat had moved in to help, and had stayed for the increasing joy he felt at being a parent.

But not today.

Nat unplugged the machine, then shot the sparking microwave with one of the fire extinguishers. The smell of burning plastic and hot metal were not pleasant. Denver laughed out loud. "That was funny!"

Libby opened up the windows so the smoke alarm would stop blaring. Beau came running in. "Did Denver get deaded?" He was terrified, tears running down his face. Libby picked him up, held him. "No, but that's why we don't put metal in the microwave." She took the crying Beau out to the living room. "Let's open the windows, shall we?" Chilly air rushed in.

Nat spoke to Denver in a calm, quiet voice. "Your old house was burned. Do you want that to happen here?"

Denver snorted. "That was funny!"

Nat left the ruined machine alone, washed up, and knelt to talk to Denver. "Causing sparks is scary, not funny. You were really lucky I can move fast. What if I hadn't been here?"

Denver shrugged. "No biggie."

"Yes biggie. You know that fires are real. There are consequences. No stickers for the day, and you'll have to help me clean this up."

Denver's face grew mulish. "Can't make me."

Nat shrugged. "The real world has consequences." He put on heavy gloves, took the dead microwave out to the trash, then came back with kid-sized gardening gloves. "Put these on." He handed over a kid-sized face mask. "Let's clean."

"Don't wanna." Denver put on a not-gonna-do-it face.

"Do you want an early bedtime?" Nat asked. "You can go to bed now. In fact, that may be a good idea. It seems like you have your not-listening ears on. Gloves, or a nap?"

"I'm not a baby!" shouted Denver.

"Inside voice, please. Now, glove up, or a nap. Which one?" Denver grudgingly put on gloves and a mask, and halfheartedly helped clean up the floor. Nat got a fan and plugged it in, then they washed up. Nat got Denver in a coat, brought him outside, and gave him a soccer ball to kick. Ricky came out to play, and Nat gave him another ball. "Ricky, Denver has big feelings today. He needs to shoot goals by himself. Do you want me to show you how to handle throws and shooting from the outside?"

"Sure!" They practiced for nearly an hour until Libby called them in for blue corn soup. The boys loved blue food, so she also served grapes and blueberry five-grain bread and butter. Unsurprisingly, Denver refused to eat more than a little food and wouldn't do his after-dinner chores. Meri took him up for a bath and book, knowing he would be nasty to his brothers if left downstairs.

Nat helped Beau put his dishes in the sink. Beau seemed to have gotten over his earlier shakiness, but he was still confused. "Is Denver in trouble?"

"Sort of." Nat knelt, gave Beau a hug. "He's angry because he did something wrong, then didn't want to fix the mistake. Mistakes are okay. We all make them. But then you clean it up."

Beau nodded. "Like my Legos."

Nat nodded. "Like that. Okay, time to clean off the table. Want to help me?"

"More stickers!"

Nat laughed. "More stickers."

By the time Meri's food for the next day was prepared, the boys were read to and in bed, the living room picked up, and an angry Denver finally asleep, all three parents were exhausted. "I cannot believe that happened." Libby put her feet up and sighed.

"Sorry the zapper bit the dust." Nat stretched out on the recliner end of the couch, and rubbed Libby's shoulders. Libby groaned. Meri came in with tea, and Libby offered a corner of the blanket.

Libby shrugged. "Three of us, three microwave ovens apiece. Luckily, the built-in is too high for them to reach."

Nat shook his head. "They have feet and chairs."

Meri groaned. "Nice thought." She sipped her tea. "We have to think about how three grieving boys can get into trouble and remove any threats we can foresee."

Nat snorted. "We'd be at that for weeks. If these boys want to break stuff because they think it's funny, they will. They're grieving."

"In some ways, Denver is a scientist." Meri covered her feet with the blanket, stretched her feet out on the ottoman.

Nat sighed. "I tried to explain to him that he scared his brother and that was not okay. It just made him madder. We'll have to talk to him later when he gets over his snit."

Libby shook her head, making her hair bounce. "There's no getting over grief."

Meri nodded. "No way out but through."

Nat nodded. "Did you want music or television, or to just chat?"

Libby groaned. "I just want to sit here."

Nat nodded. "Okay, we can do that." Libby put her head on Nat's shoulder, and slipped into sleep. Nat sighed. "I had no idea that becoming a parent and moving in would mean sleeping within an hour of the kids falling asleep."

Meri laughed with a tiny note of hysteria hidden inside. "I thought hey, we'll share you. Switch off nights."

Nat sighed. "We did have a rotation schedule, didn't we?"

"I get it. All three of us have demanding jobs where we interact with people all day, you two more than me. Performing, for lack of a better term."

Nat tilted his head. "Sort of. I try to be real with people, but it is also a performance. Some people you just want to…"

Meri raised her eyebrows. "Shake some sense into them?"

"Exactly."

"You see them when they break the law. I work with people who have been in accidents, even attacked, like my sister-in-law Kandace, and the tumbler that…"

"Tumbled. She saved her own life, you know. I was in on that particular case. The so-called friend that pushed her didn't know she'd been caught on camera."

"Boom." Meri pulled her hands apart to mimic an explosion.

"Exactly. She won't avoid jail time, and has a lot of bills to pay."

"Why are people such idiots?"

Nat sighed. "Wish I knew."

They woke Libby up long enough to get her to bed, then Ned let himself be dragged into Meri's room. "We both have an early day tomorrow."

Meri shrugged. "Sleeping in is a distant dream. All my parents agree that it won't happen with multiple kids until they leave home for college or technical school or whatever."

"Or they start sleeping a lot as teens."

Meri nodded. "I did. Growth spurt." She shut the door, then walked up, put her hand over Nat's mouth. "Kiss me, silently." He did, and she wound her fingers in his hair. He wound his good arm around her, left his hand on her hip. The kiss went on and on. She pulled off his shirt, then stripped. She reached for him as he fumbled with the button on his jeans. She got him unbuttoned, kissed her way down. They fell onto the bed, and Nat returned the favor by kissing his way down her body. Her back arched. He slid his fingers in, stroked her, his thumb on her most sensitive area. He knelt and kissed the inside of her legs. He pulled her to him, then there was a scream.

Nat stood, got his jeans and shirt back on, and ran down the hall. Beau was crying. Nat took the little boy in his arms, rocked. "What happened, buddy?"

"Fire smell! Hot."

The room was cool, no smoke, no fire. They had closed the windows downstairs before dinner after thoroughly airing out the house.

"Buddy, no fire. It was a memory." Nat stroked Beau's back. "It's okay. Look at me. Look at the clock."

"Clock."

"Yes." They both stared at the digital numbers, 10:12. "Let's wash your face, get you some water."

A fully-dressed Meri brought in a washcloth and a glass of water in the room. "Already on it." She wiped his face, had Beau sip from the glass. "Now, you need to close your eyes and dream of Pooh Bear. Can you do that?"

Beau nodded. "Nat stay wif me."

Sorry, Nat mouthed over the boy's head. "Of course I can."

Meri kissed Beau's cheek, then Nat's. "Love both of you. Good night."

Nat sighed. Beau smelled like fear and tears. He held the boy close, rocked him in his arms. Nat realized he was no longer expendable. None of them were.

~

*A*fter weeks of complete silence, Nat's sister Delia asked to meet at their usual restaurant. Nat arrived early, ordered his apple drink. He was perusing the menu when he looked up and saw Delia come in with Nora, their mother. Delia looked crisp and clean in a gold silk shirt under a dark blue duster and maroon pants. Nora wore a heavy white suit and pearls around her neck and in her ears. She walked stiffly and stood just behind Delia.

Nat kept his face impassive. He kissed his sister's cheek and didn't say anything to Delia. "You didn't leave." Nora eyed her offspring.

"I got here, this is my table. I do reserve the right to not order. I can eat later."

"Are you going to be unpleasant?"

"Only if you are." Nat relaxed, took another pull on his drink. The women sat. Delia ordered white wine and Nora a glass of burgundy. Nat looked at Delia. "You asked for this meeting, and didn't inform me our mother was coming. Was there some reason for that?"

Delia shrugged. "You wouldn't have come."

"Good point. Nora, did you have something to say?"

"You aren't going to call me 'mother'?"

"Why?" Nat slowly put her drink down. "You did at least four things on the bad-mother checklist. You never accepted me as I was and am, you set your children up to compete and fight with each other, you put roadblocks in my way when I wanted to do things that were right for me, and you forced me to wear clothes I hated and cut my hair. Shall I continue?"

"I didn't come here to fight. I hear you're adopting children." The server came by with the wine, and Nora sipped hers.

"I am." Nat didn't elaborate.

"I will be a grandmother." Nora put her wine glass down carefully.

Nat shook his head. "No, that would imply participation in their lives. You are not biologically related to them, and I've spoken to their other parents. None of us want you around them. At all. Ever."

"You would choose them over me?" Nora was incredulous.

"I will pick my kids, who are too young to protect themselves, over you any day of the week. I could let you visit with them, then repair the psychological damage you would inflict on them, or I can say no. No is faster, easier, and permanent." Nat finished his drink and stood up. "Delia, I only hang around people I can trust. This little ambush proves to me I can't trust you. Have fun with Nora here. You deserve each other."

"Wait." Nora stood. "What makes you think that I would damage these kids in any way?"

"Why do you want to meet them?"

"What?"

"Why do you want to meet them? I presume that's the reason for this conversation. So you can tell your friends you've made peace with me? You can lie to them if you want, but unless the words 'I'm sorry' are spoken to me, no. Not true. So you can protect them from my influence? Guide them into being like you? Show them off at church?" Nora flinched at that one. "Ah. This is about you, not about how they can benefit from your being in their lives."

Nat called over the server, paid for his drink, and included a considerable tip. "Have a nice day. You can manipulate, lie, cover up, and talk around each other's real wants and needs all you want. For me, that's a waste of my time." Nat walked out, head high.

Delia rushed out after Nat, tottering on her heels. Nat waited until the door shut behind both of them and turned. "Hey! That's our mother! Weren't you a little harsh?"

Nat lowered his voice. "Try being told who you are on a fundamental level is not what your mother, on whom you depend on for love, food, and a roof over your head, wants. Try turning yourself inside out on a daily basis to not be that person. Try having everything you try to do, want to do, rejected over and over. That is the tiniest sliver of what happened. You don't get it. You never will. Like I said, you deserve each other." Nat turned and headed for his new-to-him giant four-wheel drive.

"Wait!"

Nat got in, rolled down the window. "Will any of what you are about to say have an 'I'm sorry' in it?"

Delia looked sheepish, then mulish. "No."

"Have a nice life, Delia. And tell your lover exactly what I said, not something that makes you sound good. We still talk from time to time. It would be nice if the truth got back to me for once." Nat waved and drove off.

⁓

*N*at picked up Ricky; he had chosen Nat and a walk for his parental fun time. Nat fed him a grilled cheese and fries at Hallie's Roadside Stand and had one himself. Then they went home and walked down the trail, the leaves in piles under the trees everywhere. Ricky talked in a spill of words about the school's half-day art camp. "Then, Kelli and I made stamp pictures." He pulled back his sleeve and held out his arm, covered with red, green, and yellow stamps of ducks, trains, airplanes, otters, whales, and dolphins.

"I can see." Nat helped Ricky over a log. "I like your stamps. Very colorful."

"I want a stamp kit. How many stickers 'till I get one?"

Nat thought a minute. "Three, and then it will only take one to use it."

"Kay." Nat walked some more. Nat walked at a snail's pace; Ricky's little legs couldn't remotely match Nat's long-legged ones. "Denver says it's weird that you're not a girl or a boy."

"I was born a boy, but I don't care about that stuff. Do you care about what paper you use for your stamps?"

Ricky shook his head. "Don't care. Can be colored or striped or white. Don't care."

Nat nodded. "Gender, boy or girl, just doesn't matter to me. We're a small part of the population. Some people like blue paper, some red paper, some stripes. I'm like people that want blue diamond paper. Rare, but still a choice."

"Okay. Can we get a dog?"

Nat grinned at the sudden change of subject. "Well, that's an adoption. The dog needs a home, food, water, and walks every day. Lots of love. You have to love, train, and protect the dog. You have to be there with food and water and walks and love, and give that to the dog for as long as the dog is alive."

"Okay. I can do that if the dog is kinda little. Not good when the dog is too big."

"Good thinking. Well, I think we should get your adoption done first. And everyone has to treat the dog with love. Like all you brothers need love, and need to love each other." Nat felt a pang; the boys' mother had no idea what she had in the boys.

"Okay. I'm tired. Can you carry me?"

"Of course I can." Nat knelt. "Back or front?"

"Back, piggy pack." Nat turned, and Ricky scrambled onto Nat's back. Nat was mostly healed. His back gave a giant twinge, then settled. The boy smelled like sweat and loam and his polyester coat. He held on tight, then loosened his grip as Nat walked with a slow gait. "Where are we going?"

"The stream. There are fat fish hiding in it."

"Cool." They found a flat rock. Nat pointed out minnows and trout. He taught Ricky how to look in deep pools for fat fish.

Ricky stood and pointed back down the trail. "I'm hungry."

"Me, too." Nat carried Ricky out of the woods piggyback. They had a snack of juice and string cheese, played a little soccer, and built a Lego building. Libby came home with Denver, sweaty from their kickball game, and Meri came home with pizza and Beau. They were also sweaty after a round of miniature golf. They all ate pizza, showered, and crashed out in front of the TV.

QUESTIONS

*N*at began the day in his favorite way. Meri snuck in at oh-god-thirty. She wrapped herself up in the comforter, then around Nat. Nat felt his body rise, then fall, then rise again as Meri's tender fingers found all the spots that needed loving. Nat kissed, licked, sucked. He felt himself go stiff and rose up to meet her. She slid herself on him, kissed her way down his neck. He wasn't able to complete the action, but it didn't matter. She came several times, gasping so sweetly into his ear. That was the best start to the day he could imagine, even if it was still dark outside.

Afterward, they had a few minutes to talk. A very few. Meri whispered into his ear. "I'm on breakfast duty today. By the time you two have them dressed, the oven will ding."

Nat snorted. "Getting them dressed is an exercise in frustration. Making them take their shoes off when they enter the house and leave them in a line by the front door saves our bacon. Less sweeping and mopping." Meri favored Nat with a long, slow kiss. "What was that for?"

"I do love a man who cleans up the kitchen."

Nat snorted. "Either or both of you would remove my spleen if we had a dirty kitchen."

"That we would." She zipped to his shower. He groaned, pulled himself out of bed, and joined her in the shower. Sadly, there was no slip-sliding sex. Meri had breakfasts to deliver all over the county and she would not be late. Ever. Meri whispered in Nat's ear. "I'll tell you what the lawyer says. It's my turn to get the call." Josephine was not expected to last much longer. She hadn't regained consciousness. So, the adoption was proceeding at its glacial pace.

Nat kissed Meri goodbye, then stumbled to the kids' bedrooms. Beau woke up cheerful, ready to make decisions about which sweater to wear. Ricky and Denver got into an is to-is not argument about who was stupid. Nat shut that one down and made them get dressed. The clothes they were allowed to wear per the weather were rolled up and placed in boxes. The kids just had to grab one pair of jeans and one sweater or sweatshirt, since they slept in socks since the weather turned chilly. Libby had gone on a tear about everything matching so no teachers' eyes were seared. She kept the tops in primary colors and bought a lot of jeans, so that seemed to work.

Breakfast smelled heavenly, so Nat just said the word "bacon" several times to get the boys moving. They fell upon the egg-and-bacon cups with gusto. There was some orange juice/mango twist confusion, but Nat got it sorted out. Ricky lost a stamp for refusing to wear his jacket, but earned it back by helping his brothers with their backpacks. Nat got them to school on time while Libby went to bake at her store.

~

*T*he leaves were gone when Josephine slipped away. School had another round of the dreaded Placement Testing. All three boys needed tutoring, but none got held back.

Denver got into a fight on the first day of regular classes after testing. Nat responded, cop car and all. "Tell me what happened."

Principal Roberts said, "This student..."

Nat held up her hand. "I was asking Denver. In fact, why don't you leave the room."

"This is my office." Nat simply stared until the woman took her hair pulled back so hard it had to have hurt, her black suit—in a grade school!—and her disapproving glare out of the room.

Denver shook his head. "You'll yell at me."

"Have I yelled at you yet?"

Denver stared into space. "No."

"Okay then. What happened? You had science in the morning."

"Science is stupid."

"Science allows you to wear warm clothes and play space games. It isn't stupid, but you have to change your mind to understand it better. We'll work on that later. Okay, after science."

"Ray-Ray pushed me."

"Okay. Let's back up a minute. What were you doing?"

"We were in line for milk. I wanted almond chocolate milk."

"Good to know, I'll have Meri get more on her way home. Okay, you were in line. Did you step in front of Ray-Ray?"

"No. She pushed me."

"Okay. Like this?" Nat put two hands in front and pretended to push someone.

"No. She kinda...." Denver stood from his little yellow chair and fell against Nat.

"Okay, so she fell into you, fell on your body."

"Yeah."

"What did you do?"

"I defended myself like Unca taught me." He mimed a hard shove and sat down, face stony.

"Which uncle was this?"

"Unca Haller. My mama saw him sometimes."

Nat groaned internally. Melvin "Mince" Haller was someone who came sniffing around Josephine after her husband was killed; he had gone to prison on a drug possession charge nearly a year ago. "Okay, I think there's been a communication problem here. I think Ray-Ray tripped. Did she have time to say she was sorry before you pushed her?"

Denver said, "Why say sorry?"

Nat sighed. "I don't think she meant to push you. I think she tripped and fell on you. In fact, she may have been pushed by someone else. You may have attacked the victim rather than protect her from a bully."

"You mean, she didn't push me?"

"No, and you pushed her, which means you attacked her. You see how that could be a problem?"

Denver narrowed his eyes. "I 'fended myself."

"Actually, no, you should have made another choice. You didn't have all the facts. You should have stepped back and asked if Ray-Ray meant to push you. You need a pause button." Nat mimed pushing a button. "In a situation, hit your button. Freeze. Pay real close attention. Find out what's really going on. Ask questions. You can't find the truth if you act first and ask questions later."

"A pause button." Denver mimed pushing a button.

"We all have one, and you need yours working really well. You have some really big feelings." Nat made his hands wide. "Big angry, big sad."

"I ain't sad." Denver folded his arms across his chest.

"Your mama died, your house is gone. That's two big sads. And angry, well, you lost your mama and all your stuff. I'd be really mad."

"Mad sad."

"Yeah. Big mix of those, like chocolate banana swirl ice cream. Anyway, you hit your pause button first, then ask questions. Let's do this over again. I'll be Ray-Ray."

"This is stupid." Denver glared at Nat until Nat got on his knees and fell against Denver. Denver stood up, huffing mad. Nat saw it in his eyes when he realized he was supposed to pause. He pushed his hand in front of him, then reached out, helped Nat upright. "You tryin' ta fall on me?"

Nat made his voice so high it sounded like he was on helium. "Naw, I fell."

Denver let his arms down, cracked a smile. "I used my pause button!"

Nat stood, then sat back down in the visitor's chair, a hardback designed to be tortuous to adult bodies. "Great job!" They bumped fists. "Now, to the hard part. If you fall on someone, what should you do?

Denver looked mulish again. Nat sat quietly until Denver made his decision. "Mama Meri says if you make a mistake, you apologize."

"Yes. Do you remember how to do that?" Denver shook his head. "Okay, how about this? You say, 'You fell on me, and I didn't ask you if you fell on purpose or not. I'm sorry for shoving you. I forgot to hit my pause button.'"

Denver stumbled through part of it. "You feel on me. I...question..."

Nat sighed. "I'm sorry, I got too wordy. Cop problem. Tell her, 'I'm sorry for pushing you. I will listen next time.'"

"I sorry I pushed you. I listen now."

"Close enough." He stood up. "Let's go." Nat walked out of the office, sailed past the sputtering principal, and walked Denver back to class.

They looked in the window. "She's not here," Denver observed.

"School nurse. Follow me." Nat walked Denver down to the school nurse's office. Ray-Ray wore a bright red shirt, red sneakers, and a mulish expression, and held an ice pack on her arm. She stood up, and walked straight up to Denver. "You pushed me!"

Denver looked her in the eye. "I'm sorry. I didn't listen."

"Darn right you didn't. Tia pushed me. She's a jerk. Then you were a jerk for pushing me."

"Pause button," Denver said, pushing the air in front of him.

Nat shook his head. "He already apologized. You don't get to yell at him after he apologizes."

Ray-Ray nodded. "Fair 'nuff. You don't push me anymore."

Denver nodded. "I listen. First."

Ray-Ray nodded. She held out her fist, and Denver bumped it.

"Good, now back to class." Nat opened the door.

Ray-Ray handed back her ice pack. "Come on, Denver. We've got running. I'll show you how to run faster than Tia." They took off down the hall.

"That's impressive." Lori Daughtery wiped down the ice pack with sanitizer, then put it in the freezer. She had on pale blue scrubs, and wore HUD glasses in the same pale blue. "I like the pause button thing. I'll look into it with the school psychologist, Malee Addams."

Nat nodded. "I would like to stay and chat, but I've got another call. Busy day."

Lori nodded. "Thank you for coming by so quickly. And that...that was magic."

Nat grinned. "All part of the service."

Nat was down the hall, nearly to the side entrance, when Principal Roberts waylaid her. She put a hand on Nat's arm. Nat stared at the hand until the principal removed it. "Why did you send that boy back to class? He's suspended!"

"One, 'that boy' has a name. It's Denver. Two, Denver lost his mother, his home, and everything he knew and loved. He is hurting and angry, and has been told a pile of horse puckey in how to deal with people. Three, I took care of it. Denver realized he had a communication problem, and he apologized. Four, Ray-Ray accepted the apology, and offered to teach him to run faster in gym class. Five, if you dare suspend my son, who needs every second of actual instruction he can get, I will sue you, and I will go to the newspaper and television stations as well about profiling and harming a kid who is grieving. Six, a girl named Tia pushed Ray-Ray first. You haven't made a single move to suspend her. That's bias. Now, have I made myself clear?"

Principal Roberts visibly recoiled. "Maybe your son..."

Nat held up a hand. "If you end that sentence with 'isn't the right fit for this school' then you are getting a lawsuit. Everything was explained to you, his counselor, and all his teachers in the meeting after this happened. You have a non-discrimination policy at this school. Is that in effect, or not?" Principal Roberts stared stonily at Nat. "Now, educate, not discriminate against, my son. Give us a chance to work with him to redirect his behaviors and manage his grief. And if I hear one word about his getting suspended, you will be in massive trouble. You can call me, and if I'm not on another call, I will come and sort it out. Have I made myself crystal clear?" Principal Roberts stared at Nat some more. "Have. I. Made. Myself. Clear?"

"Yes," said the principal, through clenched teeth.

"Don't ever test my patience again." Nat smiled ferally at the principal, who recoiled. "Have a nice day, ma'am."

~

*N*at let the boys pick out three things for themselves and three shared things from the used sporting equipment store. He knew perfectly well that was dangerous, but they were going to have to learn to share at some point. The boys argued over the together things; Nat broke the tie at two soccer field goals being one item. Nat helped them pick out baseball gloves, and nixed the hockey sticks until they were out of the worst of their grief. Nat bought a T-ball set for Beau, far too young to try to hit a moving ball. "This bag of t-balls counts as one thing," Nat told Beau. "Why don't you tell your brothers it's the same with the baseballs?"

"Thanks, Nat." Beau attack-hugged Nat, then let go before Nat had no more air. "I'll tell 'em." He ran on his chubby legs towards Denver.

Gus Hoak, used sporting equipment shop owner, sighed. Gus had no hair on his head, but plenty on his bushy red beard. "That kid is ten miles of cute. The other two..." Ricky and Denver stopped their argument when Beau ran up with the bombshell about the bags of baseballs.

"Is. The others, well, I just have to run them ragged. Get them worn out." Nat grabbed a giant bottle of orange-scented insect repellent. "And use a lot of this stuff."

Gus guffawed. "Definitely need that."

Nat was not surprised when Denver and Ricky dragged up a huge bag full of baseballs, three basketballs, three footballs, and two hockey pucks. "Gus, trade me out more baseballs for them pucks, wouldja?"

Gus guffawed again. "Seems I can do that." He fished out the pucks with his meaty hand and put in two more baseballs. The mitts went on the counter, along with helmets, two wooden bats, and a plastic T-ball set. "I'm gonna throw in four bases for five more." Gus pulled out four plastic baseball bases in an orange so bright Nat pulled down shades.

"Done. Ring this up, Gus."

Gus rang them up. "You boys consider Gus's Goods for all your sporting goods needs, ya heah?"

"He says, when you need more balls and bats, he's ready to sell me some for you boys." Nat grinned and started hauling the stuff out. One click of the clicker and Nat and the three boys tossed all the stuff in the back. Nat closed the hatch. "Seats and seat mesh." All three boys scrambled into their seats. Nat checked that the mesh belts were intact, got in front, and set the navigation to get them home.

Once home, Nat set them free, got them on the ground, and passed out sports bags. The boys ran around the house to the backyard. Nat followed and caught Beau's shoulder. Nat knelt to talk to him "Beau, I've got to talk to your brothers for ten minutes. Let me help you first, then your brothers, then I'll come back." Nat showed Beau the correct stance, and how to hit the ball off the tee.

Then, Nat had the boys throw to each other. "I wanna hit balls!" Ricky complained.

Nat grinned. "You need to throw pitches to each other, low and slow, over the plate before you practice hitting. I can take you to the batting cages, but the balls there are too fast for you. You'll get frustrated. Really mad. You practice here, learn how to throw and catch. Then, long, slow pitches where you can learn to hit. Then, batting cages." Nat ignored Ricky's scowl. "Okay, here's how you throw a strike." Nat positioned the brothers close enough to easily catch the balls, and insisted they wear their helmets.

Nat jogged back and helped Beau hit the ball. He tended to go low and knock over the tee. Nat repositioned it and helped him hit it again and again. Nat jogged back and forth, moving the kids to the "pitcher's mound" in the backyard. The mound and first base were much closer together than regulation; the boys needed to learn to pitch and hit. Ricky hit first, and kept popping over his shoulder. Nat corrected his stance, then Ricky hit solidly. Nat set the HUD to go off every ten minutes so they could switch, then jogged back to Beau.

"I'm doing it! I'm really doing it!" Beau crowed after he got three solid hits in a row with no assistance.

"You are. You improved a lot in a very short time."

"Can I get ice cream?"

"Before I answer that question, do you think Ricky and Denver improved too?" They both looked over, and Nat held up a hand as the HUD dinged. They switched places at a jog.

"Yeah." Beau shoved the tip of his shoe into the dirt.

"Okay, do you think they should get ice cream too?"

"Yeah!" Beau held out a fist, and they fist-bumped.

Nat finished them off by having them slow-jog the bases. Denver and Ricky literally ran circles around Nat keeping pace with Beau's little legs. Nat whistled, and had them put all the stuff into the sports organizer on the back porch, complete with u-hooks for the baseball bats and baskets for the balls. "We get ice cream 'cause we 'pwooved!" Beau crowed. They all kicked off their shoes and ran to the freezer, staring at it expectantly. Nat laughed, and they all got caramel bliss cones. They were required to sit at the table and drip on the place-mats. Nat put Meri's chicken bacon casserole in the oven and herded the smelly boys to the bathtub after they inhaled the ice cream.

There was a fierce naval battle. Nat made sure the shampoo was used and the scrubby poofs as well. In between the sinking of the Good Ship Blue by the attack seal, Nat had two out of three scrubbed from head to toe. Ricky had to be threatened with taking away a hard-won playing-fairly sticker to get him washed.

Meri showed up in time to drag Ricky out and get him dry. Denver followed, excited to wear his new Batman pajamas. Beau got a sticker for helping Nat put the bath toys in their corral. Nat got him dried off and in his new Superman pajamas, and soon they were back in the living room. Surprisingly, they all chose Legos and cars, and built a recharging station on the side of a plastic hill.

Meri grinned. "I've got this. The casserole will be out in ten. Get your shower."

"Doth I offend?" Meri held her nose. Nat laughed and made a beeline for the shower.

Nat served while Meri got her shower. The boys were triumphant about a successful baseball situation, and Meri asked lots of questions as she passed out garlic bread after her shower.

After dinner, the boys had homework. Denver's was about light and color, Ricky's was a series of math problems, and Beau read three sentences aloud, then drew a picture of the rabbit-turtle race from the story. Libby got home, and they all had cocoa coconut protein snacks. Libby showered, then hauled the boys in for a half hour of pre-bed television while Nat and Meri sat at the table cutting vegetables. "A full day of calls, and baseball? Do you have topped-off batteries I can borrow?"

Nat snorted, grabbed an apple drink, and groaned as the sweet spiciness went down his throat. "No battery. Surprisingly, no actual punches were thrown. We are still on for Saturday's picnic at Camber House?"

"We are. Nat, I talked to the lawyer today."

Nat tried to gauge Meri's expression. "And?"

"It's going. It's just that..."

"Meri, use your words."

Meri barked out a laugh. "This was supposed to be fun, romantic." She pulled a ring box out of her pocket, then two, then three. "It's just that, in this state, the license takes a while. And we can have a long engagement, but we have to decide which two of us get married. Three people can't get married yet. I'm sorry, I'm doing this wrong. It's not supposed to be some sort of business transaction."

Nat sucked in a breath. "I can legally marry you or Libby."

Libby entered the room, sat down. "One book for them all. Beau's already asleep; the other two have books under the covers." She looked at the ring boxes. "Meri, this is not cool. When you ask someone to marry you, you go somewhere awesome, like a park or a restaurant."

Nat grinned, then sighed. "We do have to do this indoors. It's kind of a mess out there, what with the missing preacher and the ex-mayor." He smiled at each woman. "I love you. Both of you. Like crazy. I love how we switch off parenting. How we trade off nights, and everyone gets a night alone to just relax. I like how you laugh, Meri." Nat reached over and took Meri's hand. "I love how you try to feed us love." Nat reached out, grabbed Libby's hand. "I know you and your family helped get the ball rolling on the picketing. I love that no matter how busy we are, we all help each other. We're gonna be cutting vegetables and emptying the slow cooker tonight, make some gluten-free snacks." Libby and Meri both laughed. "I want to marry you both, but as an officer of the law, I can't do anything illegal. Libby, you're primary on the custody battle, right?"

Libby nodded. "So. We're getting married?"

"We get married, we both adopt the kids. I have one last class; I don't see how I wouldn't get a license." Nat kissed Libby, slow and sweet.

Nat turned to Meri. "I want to marry you legally. Know that I will give you my heart and my bond. Know that the piece of paper is so we become a family, not so one or the other of us is 'more married' than the other one."

Meri brushed aside a tear, then kissed Nat, hard. She stood, let go of Nat's hand, and ran towards her bedroom.

Nat stood. "Can you trade nights?"

Libby nodded. "I'm so sorry. I wouldn't hurt my sister in ten million years."

Nat nodded. "We're pushing for equality here, and working toward making those boys safe and whole. We have a meaning and purpose far greater than just us."

"This sucks." Tears spilled down Libby's face.

Nat hugged her and wiped her tears. "Love you."

Libby smiled wetly. "Love you more."

Meri hadn't even made it to the bed; she was crying on the floor with her back to the bed. Nat grabbed the box of tissues, sat down next to her, and handed her a tissue.

Meri dabbed at her tears. "I'm sorry. I'm acting like a nutcase. I really screwed this up."

Nat put an arm around her shoulder and held her close. Meri sobbed into his chest. "You're not screwing anything up."

Three tissues later, Meri stumbled to the bathroom and washed her face. Nat sat down in the wing-backed chair at the end of the wide bed. Meri came back out and sat on the end of her bed, knees touching Nat's. "Before I met you, I met all sorts of people living in all kinds of places. Most wanted to stay where they were. Bears make a home and stay there." She sighed. "I never in a million years considered you. I thought you were a standoffish jock. I had no idea your mother was such a..."

"She sucked as a mother."

Meri nodded. "She did. I knew you lived with Coach Ma, but I didn't get why. Some people live with others because of school district issues; I figured it was to get more coaching. I was kind of oblivious back then." Meri snorted out a laugh. "That's kind of a definition of a teenager, isn't it?"

Nat nodded. "I was as well. I was so busy refusing to get my hair cut military-short, informing my mother I wasn't going to play football, and refusing to go to her kooky church that a marching band could have walked through my life and I wouldn't have noticed it."

Meri barked out a laugh. "What a pair we are. The point is, I want both of us to be married to you in the eyes of the law. I also know you are a cop, and can't break the law. Libby has the best shot, I can have guardianship papers, and then we can all be a family."

"Ah. This is about guardianship. You won't be the mom on paper."

"You'll be a legal parent, and I won't. Friends do adopt together; it's happened. Siblings have adopted together, too, but the paperwork is a mess. It just skips a lot of steps if you marry Libby before the final adoption papers." Meri looked at Nat with swollen eyes. "I love you, Nat. I love our family. This is such a tiny price to pay that I wonder why I'm crying about it. It's just that we were sudden parents. Libby and I talked about adopting them if the state took them away and Josephine didn't care enough to get them back. We looked into it about two years ago, took the classes. Then you came along...:

"And threw a wrench into the works."

Meri took both Nat's hands in hers. "No, you made it a thousand times better. Each of us has someone to hold at night, to talk about our day, the kids. Someone to take up the slack, laugh with, joke around. Someone to have our backs, help with the laundry and cleaning."

"About that. We need to get Consuela in here to clean. I hear she has an opening. With all three of us working, we should be able to spring for it. And the kids would get someone from their previous life here."

Meri nodded, then pushed the subject away with one hand. She held onto Nat's hand again. "Quit being practical and shut up." Nat laughed at her with his eyes. "The point is, we don't want to let you go, not for one second. We love you, need you, want you in our lives. Will you marry us?"

Nat kissed Meri gently, then with heat. Nat leaned back. "Of course I will. And know that I would marry you both in the eyes of the law if I could."

Meri nodded. "You and Kandace need to talk. A bear handfasting is in order. We're supposed to be handfasted for a year before doing the legal marriage thing, but there are extenuating circumstances. And other shifters are invited to watch, so the boys can't be there. They'll tell everyone at school. The other Camber kids know not to change in front of the boys, or talk about what they are."

"It drives them crazy not to tell, doesn't it?" Nat leaned back in the chair, letting Meri's fingers go. "I hate covering things up. I really do. I don't like not trusting our kids."

Meri sighed. "Neither do I." She sighed. "I have a mountain of veggies to cut before bedtime, and I'm stone tired."

Nat stood, and dragged Meri up to standing with her. "Let's see how far Libby's gotten doing it." Nat held Meri close. "We'll make it work."

"Absolutely." Meri kissed Nat, then they both went out to help. Each one of them put on a glistening sapphire and titanium engagement ring before going to bed.

JOINING

*D*enver and Ricky ran bases. Nat stepped back as Beau hit the heck out of a T-ball. "Good job, Beau!" Nat's HUD pinged. A sleek silver car pulled into the driveway. Nat sighed. He was alone with the kids. A quick scan of the family schedule found Len without any clients. Nat pinged him to get over to their backyard, double time.

Nat's sister Delia stepped out of the car. Nat relaxed his shoulders when Delia stepped forward, alone. Nat canceled his 911 to Len, watched Delia ring the doorbell, then peer in the windows. Denver and Ricky yelled at each other when Denver tripped over Ricky's leg. Nat watched Delia use the porch to walk around the house with one eye and kept the other eye on Denver and Ricky, who decided to get into a shoving match. Nat held up a sticker and the boys separated. Nat pointed to Denver, then the catcher's base, and to Ricky and the pitcher's mound. The boys separated and jogged to their places.

Nat was mildly impressed that Delia was willing to walk across the frozen backyard in heels. They were low-slung black heels, and Delia was wearing a grass-green pantsuit under a long black coat, so it should be all right as long as no sweaty boys launched themselves at her. "Keep at it," Nat told Beau. He walked towards his sister.

Delia held up a hand. "I come in peace. I am sorry." Nat stared at her as if she'd grown three heads. "My lover called me a stupid cow and yelled at me for how I treated you. It's just that Mom gets under my skin."

"If you want to hang out with her, then do that. But, I don't want to hear a single word about her or your relationship with Nora."

Delia raised an eyebrow. "Because I brought her to our meeting?"

"No, because she's needy, controlling, manipulative, underhanded, and untrustworthy. She doesn't say what she means and mean what she says. You never have any idea where you stand with her until she stabs you with a verbal knife."

Delia raised her eyebrows again. "At least I can rely on you to be clear with me."

Nat laughed. "Say what you mean, mean what you say. And, with me, what you see is what you get." Nat's HUD pinged. He whistled and pointed to Ricky. Ricky dropped the catcher's mitt, ran forward, and grabbed the bat. The boys catcalled each other a bit, then Ricky headed to the mound and threw a nice grounder that Denver hit. "Nice one!" Nat called out.

"You know, I thought this parenthood thing was batshit crazy on your part, but you're their coach, aren't you?"

Nat barked out a laugh. "I like the new, blunt you."

Delia grimaced. "I might as well do it now. No one I know can see or hear us."

Nat looked at Delia out of the corner of his eyes. "Are we gonna keep sneaking out of both our towns to see each other?"

"No, I'm gonna come here and talk straight to you. It's kinda refreshing."

Nat barked out another laugh. "The way my future wives cook, you'll have to make a date with some gym equipment if you keep coming here."

Delia blew out a breath. "That's completely insane, marrying two people." She held up a hand at Nat's slitted eyes. "But if anyone can handle it, you can."

Nat nodded. "I can. I am. I'm marrying Libby. I can invite you to the wedding. It'll be small, mostly the Cambers. They live that way if you go through the woods and jump the creek." Nat pointed.

"I'd like that."

"And you can come to the adoption party. It'll be at the Cambers' farm because they have really good barbecue and the kids like playing with each other."

"Should I bring something?"

Nat nodded. "Yourself. If you want a relationship with some wild and sweaty boys..." Nat whistled, and Ricky and Denver changed places. Beau stopped to drink some water, and then ran in between second and third base.

"Not in these clothes."

"Do yourself a favor, pack some jeans and a sweatshirt when you come here. Anyway, if you want a relationship with them, we're building up a present closet. They can trade in a lot of stickers for something from the closet. I suggest going to Gus' Goods in town and buying a certificate. Hauling sports equipment around isn't your thing. Or kids' books. Go to a yard sale and buy a whole box. I know you scout for stuff for staging your properties."

Delia nodded. "I can do that."

"You can stay for dinner. The bacon chicken pasta is amazing, hands down the best ever. Yours is pretty good, but you'll want the recipe for the sauce. Both Meri and Libby learned from a now-famous chef. Oh, and Libby makes gluten-free things that taste amazing."

"Can I avoid hugs until the boys are less sweaty?"

Nat laughed. "My room is over the garage. Go get some jeans or sweats on. That way, you can be clean and pressed when you leave."

"We're not teens anymore at all, are we?"

Nat laughed. "I hope not."

Nat had the boys jog the bases, then they all earned stickers for bringing the balls, bats, and gloves to the porch and racking them. Nat put the chicken in to bake and got the boys snacks and showers while Delia did something in Nat's room. Nat put the chicken together while the boys did their homework, just in time for Meri to return. Meri kissed Nat's cheek. "Good, you got the chicken penne ready."

"Homework is done."

Meri whirled when Delia came down the stairs in Nat's gray-and-yellow Mizzou sweats and sweatshirt. "Delia, meet Meri, one of my fiancees. Meri, my sister Delia."

"I apologized." Delia was taken aback when Meri hugged her.

Nat grinned. "Let's eat." Meri had the boys set the table while Nat introduced Delia. "Delia is my sister."

"Hey." Ricky waved.

"Yo." Denver got out another place setting for Delia.

"Hey, Auntie." Beau hugged her legs. Delia's eyes went wide. She patted Beau's back.

They ate, and the boys told their parents and Delia about their day. "And we did our homework already." Denver grinned.

Ricky grinned. "Got two stickers for doin' it early, too. Earned some racing time." The boys were slowly earning a racetrack for their toy cars. They had one loop so far.

Meri nodded. "Good job. You know you only need two stickers each to earn the second loop." Pooling their stickers got them more stuff. The boys were getting rather good at math and sharing—and goading each other to do little tasks to earn more stickers.

Denver nodded. "Can you check my work? I organized the paper stuff." The boys now had art supplies in a specialized box with many compartments.

Meri smiled and touched Denver's shoulder. "Sure."

"I already checked Beau's labels for the shoes." Nat grinned. Delia looked at the back door where her black pumps sat, all alone. She had Nat's thick socks on her feet.

Ricky groaned. "I need a project!"

Meri nodded. "You can help me mix up snacks after dinner."

"Good." Ricky gave Meri a thumbs-up.

The boys cleaned up, and Meri checked Denver's work. Nat checked Meri's list and brought a cutting board, veggies, and supplies into the living room while Denver and Beau bought the new track with their stamps, got it out of the closet, and put the new track sections together. Ricky helped by putting on gloves and getting the cut veggies into the correct box, eager to finish so he could join his brothers.

Delia stared. "This is..."

"Strangely quiet?" Nat chuffed. "Wait until Libby comes home with treats. Then it's not so quiet."

"Domesticated."

Nat snorted. "Families are families. Ours works pretty well."

"I can see that." Delia smiled.

~

$\mathcal{N}$at put an envelope on Chief Taylor's desk, then sat down. "Chief."

"Deputy Sandawan, this better not be your resignation."

"No, but it does mean my life will change."

The chief opened the envelope, and went perfectly still. "I take it that the adoption team knows about it?"

"They suggested it."

"You're marrying both of them, though?"

"Committed to one, married to the other. Operatively speaking, yes, married to both. Legally, hell no."

Taylor nodded his head. "Okay. I'll be there. What do I bring?"

"Nothing. Unless you want to bring something for the boys. The adoption's right after that."

"You got Judge Fisk to agree to that?"

"She's officiating the ceremony, so, yeah."

Chief Taylor stared at Nat. "You want me to shut this town down for at least half an hour so all of us can be there."

"Great wedding present."

Taylor guffawed. "I agree. Okay, set it up. Get with the surrounding towns. It's at four, so that's good. Then, we'll have some overtime catching up. But, doable as long as one follows the other quickly."

"Same half an hour. The judge promised me."

"Okay, we're on."

~

The entire Camber family in their jeans and sweaters took over Judge Fisk's courtroom. The cops showed up in full gear and turned down their radios. Since Nat had worked over lunch, he was in uniform as well. Charlie walked his daughter to Nat. Libby wore a soft white dress that flared on the bottom, silky with long sleeves, a white rose in her hair, and a huge smile. No one objected, and they became spouses after a scorching kiss.

The adoption ceremony began immediately after the wedding. Judge Fisk, the presiding judge in their adoption proceedings, asked Denver, Ricky, and Beau who they wanted as their parents. The judge explained the boys choosing all three parents as "Meri the sister" was also involved. The judge signed off on all the paperwork, including the guardianship papers so any of them could pick the kids up from school, attend parent-teacher conferences, and the like. "Then, I declare Denver, Beau, and Ricky Tiller to be Cambers." They had decided not to pointlessly saddle the kids with Nat's long last name, Sandawan. That brought out a cheer from the crowded gallery. They posed for photos.

"Barbecue!" Charlie crowed.

Libby laughed. "Dad, it's always a barbecue day for you."

"Can I have corn?" asked Denver.

"Absolutely." Meri stood. "Let's go. This judge is busy enough without us cluttering up the courtroom." Everyone hugged and some cried joyful tears while Meri herded them out the door.

Beau was confused. "Mommy isn't coming back?" They had explained it to him, but Beau still didn't understand what had happened.

Meri knelt down. "Mommy is in Heaven." She choked on the statement; she knew no such thing. "Libby and I are going to be your mommies now." Nat rubbed Libby's back as tears streamed down her cheeks.

"Okay. Can I have cake?"

Meri grinned. "You sure can. Chocolate and cherry. With ice cream."

Beau grabbed Meri's hand and started pulling. Everyone laughed.

The cops dispersed, and the real party began. Everyone piled into SUVs, trucks, and minivans, and went to the Camber farm. Nat got out of uniform and changed into jeans and a blue sweater, Libby hung up her dress and got into jeans and a soft red sweater, the kids chased each other, and Charlie began the barbecue. Nat's sister Delia hadn't come, but Nat was good with that. Baby steps forward for all of them. Nat packed food and sodas for the cops, and Amir Cazalos swung by to pick it up.

Jetta pulled Meri aside. "I know you're unhappy not being the legal wife. The trust paid for a lot of paperwork; the three other parents are on the paperwork if I die or I'm incapacitated. Getting married would cut down on the paperwork that already exists. Just...it mattered in my guts, at first. Then it just didn't matter. We love each other. Charlie is their dad. I'm his wife. End of story."

Meri sighed. "Yeah, head and guts weren't the same thing for a minute. Now I'm on the same page. Or will be tonight after the ceremony. I really wish the kids could be there."

"They're yours. Roll with that. The rest will come." Meri hugged Jetta, then both women laughed as Len and Nat ran outside, chased the boys, and corralled them to put on their coats. Beau found watching his brothers get chased down so funny that he couldn't catch his breath. Davis jogged up, worried he was having an asthma attack, but Beau demanded a piggyback ride from Davis instead. Davis agreed, and soon Denver was on Len's back and Ricky on Nat's back. Davis grabbed a kickball, and soon they were throwing a ball around, making the kids laugh. Jetta's four kids rushed out to join them in their winter gear.

Jetta smiled softly. "They needed a family."

"They did. They have one." Meri wiped her eyes, and so did Jetta.

Jen walked by and bellowed, "There's no crying at wedding receptions!" The women laughed.

~

*U*nder cover of darkness, an enormous great horned owl flew low, and landed. A wolf came out of the woods and sat. A puma came to the edge of the clearing and lay down in the moonlight. Everyone else was in human form. Nat wore boots, black jeans, and a black sweater with a leather duster, and so did Meri, except her sweater was silver. Libby wore a white, beaded dress, a silvery beaded duster, and pale pink cowboy boots. Her sleeves covered her wrists; her titanium wedding and sapphire engagement rings twinkled in the light of the torches. Both Nat and Meri wore the glistening titanium rings as well. They hated leaving the kids asleep under Kandace's watchful eyes, but they needed to keep the secret a little longer. They would share the shifter reality with their kids when the boys had worked past the grief.

Jen led the singing. Nat stood still, his shoulder still smarting from the tattoo of two bears on his shoulder surrounded by secret symbols worked into a tribal knot. There was snow on the ground, but only a dusting as they'd had a warm snap a few days before.

Jen stepped forward. The circle tightened in response. "Spirit moves me to bring one not of our number into our family. Does anyone have Spirit speaking to them about this?"

Meri stepped forward. "This man has shown great compassion and humility, taking in three boys not his own. He has kept our secrets. He also refuses to take any crap from the school system." Everyone chuffed a laugh.

Charlie stepped forward. "He has shown an amazing ability to heal damaged minds and hearts. I have seen this with my own eyes. Those boys were wild, and now they accept direction." He stepped back.

Libby stepped forward. "This man can learn, travel in new directions, and excel. He knows our hearts." She stepped back.

Lynette stepped forward. "This man was literally blown up. But, he accepted the pain, moved past it. He will endure." She stepped back.

Jetta stepped forward. "He is steady as a rock. He thinks of his family first. He gives to others. He keeps our laws and secrets." She stepped back.

"Spirit moves me to accept this man as our own, to keep our secrets, even at the price of his own life. To stand by us, help in times of need. To raise our children with our laws and strictures." She looked out at the shifters in attendance. "Do the Changed Clans object?" The wolf bowed its head. The owl was seemingly inert. The puma was absolutely still. Jen took in two more breaths, then said, "Therefore, by the Spirit that moves within us all, I accept him."

"I accept him," said the rest.

The wolf slunk off, the owl took flight with great beats of enormous wings that made the torches flicker, and the puma melted into the night.

Jen smiled. "Well, shall we begin?"

They drew inward. Meri stood at Nat's left hand, and Libby on her right. Each lifted a hand, and took Nat's hands in theirs. Jen bound their hands with red and gold ribbons. She stepped back. "Please watch and observe. You will be called upon to support them in any way they need." Her voice carried on the wind.

Charlie, Lynette, Jetta, Len, Davis, and Vic surrounded the triad. "We watch and observe, and will give our support."

Jen's voice rang out. "I pledge to you my heart, hearth, and troth." Meri, Nat, and Libby repeated the ancient words. "I pledge to join with you in times of sadness, joy, and all in between." They repeated again, voices solemn. "I bind myself to you until the winter of our lives buries us under its snows, to rise again with the spring." They repeated the last words together, Nat's voice steady and clear, Meri strong, and Libby with tears streaming down her face.

Jen decided to let her own tears fall. "Then, with great joy, I recommend you to the Spirit that lies within us all, that your spirits be joined in this life, and that you find each other in the next." Jen unbound their cords, then braided them together to hang over their door. She led them in the ancient chant. Nat had memorized most of it, and clearly said the words that rang through the ages with vows of secrecy, family, and in finding joy in one another.

Charlie and Vic gathered the torches. Charlie gave one to Jen and another to Lynette, and took up the rear with the last torch as they all hiked back to the house. There, they had a huge dinner of roast pork with apples and honey, brown sugar carrots, biscuits with butter and honey, and pie for dessert, sweet things for a sweet life together.

Nat pulled Lynette aside as they finished the last of the caramel apple pie. Jen stole their plates, and Nat ushered Lynette out into the mudroom. Lynette laughed, snagged two random parkas, made Nat put on his boots while she zipped up her own black ones, then dragged Nat onto the porch. They fumbled with putting the parkas on and zipping them up.

Lynette shivered, pulled the parka hood up. "Why are we out here?"

Nat snorted. "Bear hearing."

Lynette tilted her head. "What do you want to tell me that you don't want to tell the rest of our clan?

Nat stomped his feet. "I told you about a case. A cold case. A thief."

"One you were close to catching. Is it a clan person?"

Nat shook his head. "No. The person went to the military. Supports young family members. I found out the person had a rocky start, but is a good soldier. The person was a juvenile when it happened, and is a buttoned-down soldier now. No point in pursuing this cold case. It will be closed in a solved way, no blowback on a reformed non-juvenile citizen."

Lynette nodded. "Oh. It must be Jackie. I'll contact the Service Committee." Specialist Jackie Haless had a sick mother and had apparently become a thief while in high school to support her two younger brothers, now living with a cousin. The Service Committee worked with all the service and religious organizations in the community to help those in need. "Let's get the pressure off the soldier, shall we?"

Nat smiled. "Thank you."

Lynette hugged Nat. "No, thank you. It is always good to be of service. I am so happy you joined the family."

Kandace stomped out in her boots. She handed Nat his parka. "Yours. Give me mine back."

Meri spilled out of the house without a parka, a giggling Libby on her arm. "Time to change! You two are still good with watching the zoo here?"

Nat grinned. "Sure." Nat kissed both wives, and then Kandace and Nat stepped back while the others took off their clothes and went furry. Two black bears waved at Nat; Nat waved back.

Kandace grinned. "They'll be back. They need the whole communing with nature thing."

Nat smiled. "I know they'll always come back to me." Nat turned with Kandace and walked back to the house, to their kids, their family, their life.

<<<The End>>>

THANK YOU!

Thank you for being one of my beautiful, amazing readers! I can't do what I do without you! If you liked the book, please leave a review! I read them all, looking to improve my craft so I can write more fun stories for you.

Thank you to my beta reader team. My editors Lynda and Talented_Fixer are amazing, and so is my critique partner, Alyssa. Crooked Sixpence created my incredible covers. Any errors left in the manuscript are entirely my own. Please let me know what they are so I can fix them in your online review! Or, you can contact me on social media at Facebook: Facebook.com/lj.hawke, Instagram: Instagram.com/ljhawke, and Twitter: Twitter.com/Hawkelj, and my website: ljhawkeauthor.com.

Books in the Forever Loved series:
Forever Challenged (novella, prequel, male point of view)
Forever Charmed
Forever Claimed
Forever Wild
Forever Challenged

THANK YOU!

Forever Fierce
Forever Untamed

ABOUT THE AUTHOR

L. J. Hawke is an author, university professor, and an avid reader. She writes what she loves to read—paranormal romance, urban fantasy, and science fiction, as well as some nonfiction titles in her fields of expertise. She can be found petting her cats while writing, or with a backpack on her back, traveling the world—after calling the cat sitter.

One last thing...

If you enjoyed this book or found it useful, I'd be very grateful if you'd post a short review on Amazon. Your support really does make a difference, and I read all the reviews personally so I can get your feedback and make this book even better.

If you'd like to leave a review then all you need to do is click the review link on this book's page on Amazon.

Thanks again for your support!

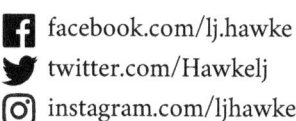

facebook.com/lj.hawke
twitter.com/Hawkelj
instagram.com/ljhawke

www.ingramcontent.com/pod-product-compliance
Lightning Source LLC
Chambersburg PA
CBHW061606170626
46811CB00001B/333